Cause of Death: ???

K.N. SALUSTRO

ISBN-13: 978-1-7370670-1-6

Also by K.N. Salustro

The Star Hunters:
Chasing Shadows
Unbroken Light
Light Runner

The Arkin Races: A Star Hunters Novella

DEDICATION

This one was written for fun,
but if you need it,
it can be for you.

Acknowledgements

Writing a book takes more than just an idea for a plot and some words to shove into your characters' mouths. It takes time, and dedication, and people who are willing to give both of those things. That's certainly what I got from my beta readers, who I need to thank until the end of time for their input. So thank you, Charlie T., for the full read and all the excited Facebook messages that made me smile. Thank you, Shira, for early chapter reads and thoughts, which you heroically took on while managing a hectic family life. Thank you, Ariella Axelbank, for going above and beyond anything I could have hoped for, and for helping me make this book the best it could be. And thank you, final beta reader who did not wish to be named, but who provided invaluable feedback and character input on the first ever draft.

The thanks do not stop there, of course. I have to thank Ben, who has been with me through so many ups and downs, and who tolerated me putting SlickyNote plot points up on the wall while I was brainstorming this book. And for not getting annoyed when those notes kept falling down. And for helping me chase down the cat whenever she tried to steal one of those fallen notes. And for putting up with all those other really annoying things that I am certain I did while writing this book. Life is wonderful while you're in the world. (I'm dead certain you'll tease me for that reference, but I'll let you have the moment.)

Thank you also to my family for always being supportive and encouraging. We may be a little farther apart now, but I love you all dearly and will always be grateful for you.

Finally, thank YOU. This was a fun one to write, and I hope you have fun reading it. Maybe not too much fun, though. We are dealing with Death, after all…

Contents

Part Three: Bargaining

Part Four: Depression

Part Five: Acceptance

- Part One -

Denial

This agreement, made between the parties of Life and Death in exchange for creation of and dominion over their joint project of "mortality" and the "mortal world", binds these parties and all other Forces who would seek to profit from said project to the following rules...
-- excerpt from the Contract of Mortality

- 1 -

The morning my entire world broke, I was slumped over my desk in my windowless bedroom. My legs were thrown haphazardly over the side of my chair, my face was buried in my arms against the surface of the desk, my spine was twisted at an uncomfortable angle to accommodate both of these things, and I was too exhausted to care.

My room was small and dark, with my sturdy wooden desk and chair and the hard, narrow bed in the corner as the only furniture. The walls were bare, no trinkets or clutter resided anywhere, not even a rug on the hardwood floor. I liked it that way. Nothing to distract me whenever I went to work, and nothing to bother me whenever I needed a respite.

Of course, that stolen moment was the first time in a long, long time that I'd actually been able to rest. So long, in fact, I found my empty room (usually so comforting in its austerity) crushing down around me. What had once been my retreat now felt more like my prison, and even though I knew I could stand up and walk out of the room at any time, the very thought of moving exhausted me all over again. I'd been working for days without stopping, and the air in my room was stale and stifling, but I still could not bring myself to so much as twitch. I think I was afraid that I would break that moment of tranquility, rare and fleeting as they were.

Perhaps I was being a tad dramatic, and I will admit that I remember thinking to myself that I would have given six of my ribs just to keep the silence and the solitude going for a little while longer. I just wanted a few minutes more before I had to return to work, or emerge to clean up some disaster my roommates had managed to create, or some combination thereof.

Then the smell of a freshly brewed pot of coffee seeped under my door.

I did not get out of my chair so much as I was suddenly on my feet, bones creaking with stiffness. I relished the rich scent coming from the other side of the bedroom door as I stretched and cracked my various joints, all fears of a disaster forgotten when faced with the promise of the elixir of the mortals. They had gotten nearly everything wrong over the past few millennia, but coffee... Coffee was so right.

I drifted out of my blissfully dark room into the agonizing brightness of the sunlit hallway. I threw an arm across my face to block the light and let my feet guide me past my roommates' larger and overly lit bedrooms, past the front door, past the living room, past the bathroom we had no use for, and into the kitchen.

"Morning, Death," Destiny's voice greeted me from

the general direction of the table.

I grumbled something resembling a response and dropped my shielding arm from my face. It took a long time for my senses to adjust to the sunlight pouring in through the east-facing window over the sink, but my feet knew the way and by the time I could see again, I was already fishing a mug (one of the big ones) out of the dishwasher.

"Just so you know," Destiny began, but I cut her off with a raised finger.

"What did we say about fate readings before coffee?" I asked as I went for the kitchen counter. The coffee maker was nestled contentedly between a gleaming toaster and the tidy library of brightly colored cereal boxes that were the main source of my female roommate's sustenance. The pot was full of steam and perfect black coffee. The liquid sloshed beautifully as I lifted the pot, a lovely ring of bubbles dancing across its surface.

"It has to do with the coffee," Destiny said.

That made me pause. "What is it?"

"If you pour a cup before nine, you'll break the mug."

"What time is it now?"

"About eight-thirty."

I considered this carefully. "How much is in the mug when it breaks?"

"About half a cup."

"Is that because I will have already consumed the rest of the coffee?"

"Well, yeah, plus another full cup before that, but—"

I poured the hot coffee and took a long, loud sip.

I felt Destiny's disapproving stare on my back as I

drank. She never liked it when I ignored her prophesies, but given that the mortals could defy her just by flexing their free will, it was laughable to think that she should have any control over *my* actions, never mind that she was usually right. I had learned a long time ago that it was best to enjoy the moment and worry about the consequences when (and if) they came.

Also, half an hour was far too long to wait for coffee after I'd already smelled it.

Destiny decided that this was not an acceptable excuse this time, and she hit me with the one argument she knew she could win: "You forgot to pay rent again."

I did not turn around, but I let my presence fill the room, darkening the sun and vibrating through the air until I could feel the threads of existence that stretched out from every being in the area, from the spiders in the walls to the mice in the basement and the mortals that occupied the other apartments in our brownstone walkup and the neighboring buildings beyond. I separated out the thread that came from Destiny, the endless loop that marked her as an undying Force. I plucked at her thread and let her feel its fragility when it was in my grasp, and made her understand that I could snap it at my whim. My voice was timeless and deep as the void when I spoke again. "I am the eldest. I was there when the universe was born, and I will be there when it burns itself out. I am inescapable. I am absolute. I am the end."

There was a long silence as I released her thread and retracted back into myself, returning to my position at the window with my back to my roommate and hot coffee slipping past my teeth.

"You still have to pay rent," Destiny finally said.

"It isn't due until the end of the day," I muttered into my mug.

"I want to pay the landlord before noon."

I began to seriously contemplate the consequences of ending Destiny's existence early and the impact that would have on the mortal world, but decided that I simply had not had enough coffee yet. I was about three-fourths of a mug deep by then, so I still had a little more to enjoy before the predicted shattering came, if it came at all.

I refilled the mug to the brim and moved to join Destiny at the table.

She was an interesting Force, choosing to spend most of her time wrapped in her favorite illusions instead of her natural form. When not using a glamour to masquerade as a human, she was little more than wisps of colors shifting and flirting with the idea of solidity. Disguised as a mortal, she was an athletically built young woman with brown skin, thick black hair that she wore in microbraids, deep brown eyes, and a jawline that could have cut the world in half. She wore glasses that she did not need, mostly as a way to explain why her glamour's eyes did not always track motion. The lie was that she was incredibly nearsighted, and not even her glasses let her see everything. The truth was that she simply did not use her eyes to see, and often forgot to move them. The mortals she dealt with—including our landlord—easily swallowed the lie.

Whether she was wrapped in an illusion or not, Destiny also had a bottomless appetite for sugar, a quirk that was at its least endearing when a mortal had defied the fate she had so painstakingly laid out for them. I might have found the capacity to feel bad for her whenever her hard work went to waste, were it not for the inevitable rage tears followed by rapid consumption of pints of ice cream and containers of fudge frosting, always resulting in a mess scattered across the apartment that I had to clean up.

Still, as far as roommates and colleagues went, I could have done worse. Destiny paid her share of rent on time and without fail (often supplementing my contributions when I forgot to have my reapers scrounge up loose cash from reaping sites), served as an excellent source of creative inspiration when the time for a mass extinction came, and was a skilled baker. We had also reached the understanding that I would tolerate her meltdowns as long as she kept the coffee pot full and a steady stock of ninety-percent cacao chocolate bars in the pantry for me.

No, Destiny was not a bad roommate. Just annoying, sometimes.

I saluted her with my mug as I sat at the table. She wrinkled her nose at me and went back to devouring her bowl of neon breakfast cereal.

"I still think you should wear a glamour when you're not in your room," she informed me, clearly still peeved over my decision to ignore her fate read.

I held up my hand and admired the way the bones caught the morning sunlight. "And stifle this natural beauty?"

Destiny shot an exasperated sigh across the table. "At least wear something other than the robes. You make me feel like I'm an extra in a bad horror movie in my own kitchen."

"*Our* kitchen," I corrected, "and I do wear these robes for a reason. As you may recall, the mortals and even some of our fellow Forces tend to be prone to terror whenever they see the swirling void that is my core."

"You could cast a glamour to hide that."

"Glamours *itch*."

Destiny huffed an exasperated sigh. "You're determined to never see the landlord except on Halloween, aren't you?"

"I feel our annual, two-minute conversation on the repetitiveness of my so-called costume and the various historical inaccuracies of his have been honed to perfection."

Destiny gave up the argument and went back to her cereal.

I returned to my coffee, content with the silence. I took more time with my second mug, out of both enjoyment and a desire to procrastinate before shuffling back to my room and calling my reapers in. As I drank, I idly wondered what would be the trigger that could possibly cause me to drop the mug. Would I be holding it? Would it be sitting on the edge of my desk when I summoned my reapers and began the tedious task of distilling the taken souls? Would one of the reapers knock the mug off the desk in their eagerness to get to me first?

So many possibilities. So many ways to tease Destiny about her mundane little prophecy.

But I was not feeling cruel, and decided to let the

moment pass. After all, it wasn't every day that we got to enjoy a quiet morning. Which did beg a certain question.

"Where is Life?" I asked.

"Still in his room," Destiny said. She took a sip of coffee so overloaded with cream and sugar it was almost white. Actually, she may have just been drinking cream and sugar at that point; to have included coffee in that concoction would have been a crime against creation. "Last night, he said he was getting close to finishing something big, and then he locked himself in. Haven't seen him since."

I groaned.

Lately, and in spite of my protests, Life had been throwing himself into creation, spitting out creature after creature in a desperate attempt to have something he could completely call his own. By the language of the Contract, he was free to create, and to ask him not to would have been asking him to let his power go stagnant. I still sometimes asked him to do just that, if I'd had a particularly rough day. We usually fought then, but we always managed to find our way back to each other. Every time, he would promise me that he would stop as soon as he had succeeded. And yet, the only thing he was creating with any steady degree of success was more work for me.

He also technically *had* succeeded a while ago, producing an animal that did not need to know me. It was an impressive feat, I had to admit, but Life claimed that jellyfish were not the immortal victory he was looking for, and in a moment of weakness, I could not help but agree with him. That had been a mistake. A big one. Motivated by the success and inadequacy of the jellyfish, Life threw himself into creating with a vigor that I both envied and feared.

I did not like those strange, aquatic bag creatures as it was, but at least they were stable. Far worse were all of Life's failures, which *I* had to clean up, as though I did not already have enough to do as it was. I'd hoped my partner would eventually understand that his constant need to create was leaving me burned out and with little room to do much of anything on my own time. So far, he hadn't.

Hence why only fresh coffee had been able to draw me out of my solitude.

"I wish he would stop the solo projects," I admitted out loud.

"I don't like them either," Destiny said. This startled me. I watched her swirl her cereal around with her spoon for a moment before she added, "They're usually really creepy."

I hid my smile behind my mug.

Life tried in earnest to make his creations beautiful. He understood and appreciated the perfection of delicate colors and bold patterns alike, and knew how to balance symmetry with nonuniformity. And yet, he always forgot some key feature. Like a functioning brain, or lungs, or—in one very tragic case—a skeletal structure. That poor thing had been a screaming puddle of feathers and organs on the floor by the time Life had dragged Destiny and me back to his room to see it. Destiny had not found that particular attempt anywhere nearly as funny as I had.

"You know why I think he does it?" Destiny asked,

pulling me out of my reverie.

Admittedly, I cared not for the theories behind why Life was piling on to my workload, but I was open to another excuse to linger over coffee before getting back to work. "Enlighten me," I said.

"I think he's trying to counterbalance your creation."

That managed to catch my interest. "Do you mean my reapers?"

"Exactly," Destiny said. "You made something on the mortal world born of you and you alone. I think that scares him."

I motioned for her to go on.

"I think Life is looking for their counterbalance," she explained. "You two built the entire mortal world around the promise of balance, but with you finishing the reapers, I think he feels threatened."

"He made that one species of jellyfish," I pointed out, rather lamely.

Destiny gave me a small, patient smile. "Yes, but you modified them so that they could be eaten and therefore die."

"I had to ensure that they could exist on the mortal world without violating the Contract," I said.

Truth be told, I should have pushed for more changes to that deathless creature than I had. That particular species of bag fish could still threaten the Contract if the right stars aligned. I let that be, however, and instead pointed out that my reapers did not exist in every sense of the word. They could interact with souls, certainly, but beyond harvesting their assigned targets, they were incapable of impacting the mortal world. They were surrogates for me, created so that I would not have to divide my attention across every dying being on Earth. Exhausted and diminished as their making left me, my migraines and moods had improved exponentially ever since I'd sent the first wave of reapers out.

I had also been very careful with them, ensuring that the reapers had no power of their own beyond what I bestowed upon them. I gave each of the reapers a small piece of myself, lessening my own power in exchange for a chance to rest, however brief that ultimately turned out to be. With Destiny's help and Justice's blessing, I had also run exhaustive tests and calculations to ensure that the Contract would remain intact long before I created my first reaper. I knew all too well what the consequences of a Contract violation were.

We all did. It was the agreement we made in exchange for a chance to benefit from the mortal world; a chance to flex our influence and grow our power without tearing apart our home realm Eternity. We had beneficial impacts on the mortal world more often than not, and in return, the mortal world gave us room to grow, and the chance to better understand ourselves. To violate the Contract was to invite capital punishment, and even I had cause to fear that.

When I reminded Destiny of this, she agreed. "But I do think that Life feels like he needs to keep up with you," she said.

"Keep up with *me*?" I said. "Did you see how many souls he put out last week alone? *I* can barely keep up with *him*."

Destiny gave me another soft smile. "He says the

11

same thing about you. And he's afraid of being left behind. It's just… in his nature, I think."

My mug of coffee was down to a little more than half-full at that point. I swirled it absently, wondering what Life's next attempt would look like. I think that Destiny and I both knew that if Life succeeded in creating a truly deathless creature, I would either need to find a way to destroy it, or banish it from the mortal world.

The decision would hinge on how pretty it was; something beautiful could potentially find a permanent home in Eternity. Everything else would meet the sharp end of my scythe. Given Life's penchant for aesthetics, chances of an endless existence among the Forces were high. Of course, given his extensive record of failures, it was very unlikely we were anywhere near that possibility.

I had the sudden thought that perhaps Life could use a vacation along with me. It had been a while since we'd had time together without work getting in the way, and if this next attempt was a failure, a trip away from the mortal world could have done us both good.

My thoughts slipped back to Life's past creations, and I absently tried to imagine this new species. I had hopes for something sleek and muted in color, but I would not have minded a dark iridescence to it. A living embodiment of black opal, perhaps. Life had been drawing inspiration from gemstones lately, and if he could remember to get the details right, he had the potential to create a beautiful creature in—

"I'VE DONE IT!"

—deed.

I jumped in my seat, and felt the mug start to slip through my fingers. With a lurch and a slosh of coffee over the edge, I managed to keep my grip on the handle as my partner came sailing into the room. A few precious drops of coffee fell to the floor, but the mug and the majority of the still-steaming drink were saved. I gave Destiny a smug look as I carefully set the mug on the table, well away from the edge.

Destiny glared into her cereal and tried to sneak a look at the clock on the wall without me noticing.

"I have finally, absolutely, unquestioningly *done* it!" Life proclaimed, practically dancing across the kitchen. He paused long enough to plant a kiss on my forehead before spinning away and pumping his fists in the air.

In spite of my exhaustion and certainty that this would be more work for me, I smiled as I rose from the table and moved to grab the paper towels. I always liked seeing Life happy, even if it signaled trouble for me.

"So-called evolution can kiss my ass," Life sang, "I've finally created the *perfect* species!"

"What have you unleashed upon the lowly mortals this time?" I asked as I bent to clean up the spill, my victory over Destiny's prophecy taking on a bittersweet note. Spilled coffee was still spilled coffee, after all.

Life began to tell us of his decision to work small this time (probably for the best), and much as he loved to add them, leave off any unnecessary ornaments (absolutely for the best). He'd created a bipedal creature, fluffy with shining silver fur and a head that could rotate one-hundred-and-eighty degrees on a well-protected neck. It was nocturnal, used small primate-like hands to gather food, and ran from place to place on strong, silent legs.

He described it in such loving detail, even I was partially enamored with it by the time he was done.

There was just one problem.

While he'd been speaking, I had been ticking off every feature he described against my mental checklist. After he was done, I looked up at him, at his bright, shining eyes and his perfect green skin that spoke of spring. It was a testament to his vanity (and my blatant admiration) that humans looked like him, although they were much stubbier than Life, and cut rougher in their features. They also had noses—ugly, bulging things—whereas Life boasted a smooth, perfect face. So proud, he was, so beautiful, so prolific, and so utterly stupid.

"Life, my darling," I said, "did you remember to give it the ability to *breathe*?"

He opened his mouth, but no sound came out. The smile drained from his face, and his eyes lost focus as he thought back on his precious project. That was answer enough.

"I'll take care of it," I told him. Just as I always did.

"I *had* it this time," Life moaned as he slid into the seat I had vacated.

I grabbed my mug from the table and leaned against the wall, watching my partner. I had the feeling that Destiny was right about him, which rankled me. Life and I had created mortality together, and that was quite possibly the greatest achievement either one of us were truly capable of. We certainly could not have done it without each other. I had not meant for my reapers to undercut that. They were not alive—nothing made of me alone could be—and that often felt like a shortcoming compared to the things that Life could do by himself. Or would be able to do, if he'd only remember the key details.

It was not his fault, really. It simply was not in his nature to consider all the things that could destroy something.

But that was more than an inconvenience for me, since I was the one who had to clean up his messes, too.

At least Life had a sense of humor, and once he'd worked through his grief, he let Destiny tease him about this latest overlooked detail in a long, catastrophic series of overlooked details. Life made a remark about being glad that I was always there to fix his mistakes. My response was a strained smile.

Destiny caught my expression. "Poor Death really needs their vacation soon," she said.

My smile was more genuine this time. "More than you know."

Life looked over his strong shoulder at me. "Are you still set on taking one?" he asked.

"Oh, absolutely. I thought I'd mentioned that before?"

"Several times," he said.

"Yesterday alone," Destiny added.

I drained my coffee mug and then refilled it to the brim, making sure Destiny saw my every move.

"I was sure you'd break it," she grumbled.

I watched her over the rim of the mug as I slurped another gulp.

"Would you leave?" Life asked.

I broke off my petty battle with Destiny to look at him. "What?"

"The mortal world," he said, tracing a knot in the woodgrain of the table. "Would you leave it, if you took a break?"

I had been so busy that I had not seriously considered what I would do with a vacation once I got it, but I knew the answer to that question. "Yes," I told him. "It would be nice to see something other than the mortals and the inside of this apartment for a change."

"If you wore a glamour," Destiny grumbled, "you could go outside. We live near a lovely park, and the night life a few blocks over is exciting enough that the mortals might not even notice your creepiness."

I took another loud sip of coffee.

"How long do you think you'd stay away?" Life asked. He kept his voice casual, but I knew what he was asking.

I reached over and squeezed his shoulder. "Not too long," I said. I remembered my earlier thought of inviting him along with me, but I still owed him for the unbreathing mess he'd left for me in his room, and his earlier teasing. "Unless I spontaneously develop a libido and run off with Lust, of course."

Destiny snorted, sending a fine spray of milk and half-chewed cereal across the table. I tossed her the paper towels.

Life caught my hand and lightly ran his thumb across my knuckles, smiling at my joke, but there was a tinge of sadness to it. I was too familiar with his moods to think that he was truly upset, but he seemed to be missing me already, and I had not even left the

16

room. I wrapped my arms around his shoulders and wondered if he would come with me, if I offered to take him off the mortal world. Part of me knew that he would not; I'd been able to make my reapers, but Life was too ingrained in the mortal world to be away for long. That realization made me hug him tighter, and he leaned into my embrace.

Destiny abruptly gave a pointed cough, clearly aiming to distract Life and me from each other. "How close are your reapers to being independent?" she asked.

"Very," I said, settling back against the wall with my coffee again. "They have been out on their own for a while now, and I just sent off what I hope is the last wave. I'm giving them a little time to test their wings and see how they do before I introduce them to the soul distilling process, but they've been doing perfectly so far. This time next year should see me packing up my scythe and bidding you a fond farewell."

"You don't want to leave your oversized farming tool with me?" Destiny asked.

"What do the mortals say?" I traced the rim of my mug. "I trust you as far as I can throw you?"

"I'm an incorporeal cloud," Destiny said. "You couldn't throw me at all."

"That would be my point, yes."

Destiny and Life were both laughing now, and I was smiling in the sunlight. Everything felt right. And then something slipped out-of-kilter, and the world seemed to stop.

I knew that it hadn't. Time was still running the way it was supposed to, and Life was grinning sheepishly at a fresh barb from Destiny, but there was something very, very wrong in the universe now.

Almost like…

A nasty feeling wrapped itself around my spine, and a shiver ran through me. Life froze in bewildered horror a moment later, and then Destiny was on her feet, trembling. They both turned to look at me as the bad feeling crept up my back and through my skull. I felt it leave me as quickly as it came, but it sapped away a good chunk of what little energy that morning had given me, and left an aching pain in its place. I recognized the warning, but the bad feeling wasn't done with us yet. It coated the room like a thick fog, growing denser as something approached.

It finally coalesced at the kitchen window, and I turned to see one of my reapers perched on the sill. The reaper knocked its hoof against the glass, and rustled its leathery wings. I could see light seeping through the thin skin of its body, right where it would have stored a swallowed soul. The reaper would not look at me.

All three of us had been given a warning, then one of my reapers had come to me unsummoned, loaded with a soul, and ashamed of itself. This could only mean one thing: the Contract had been breached.

The coffee splattered my robes when my mug shattered on the floor.

… A soul may not be severed from its original host unless done through Death's power.
-- excerpt from the Contract of Mortality, Rule 2

- 2 -

When I first had the idea for the reapers, I knew what I would need to sacrifice in exchange for help on the mortal world. I knew that each new reaper would require a piece of myself. A small piece, certainly, but when multiplied out over hundreds upon thousands, another Force might have balked at the idea. Not me. I willingly traded away my power bit by bit, knowing that each fragment chipped away at the tethers that kept me here, that kept me from enjoying even a moment of existence on the mortal world. In spite of the rigors of bringing each new one into existence, Life never faltered, never stopped making souls. He thrived. I could not keep up. I needed help.

My earliest reapers had barely been able to stumble around the room on toothpick legs too weak to support their own weight. Over time and countless mistakes, I slowly improved them to the point where they could soar on silent wings, harvest expiring souls, and return them to me in a steady, easy rhythm. There may have been a few hitches early in the process, including one or two reapers that had gotten confused on their way to their assigned reaping site and joined flocks of migrating geese instead, but I had smoothed over every problem, picking at each flaw until I untangled it and knew how to keep it from ever happening again. Not once, however, had a reaper ever come close to violating the Contract. They simply were not strong enough for that.

Which was why I found myself sitting with my elbows on the kitchen table, fingers laced in front of my face, and my gaze locked in a hard scowl on the reaper before me. It fidgeted as it waited for me to figure out what to do.

Life and Destiny hovered over my shoulders, also looking at the reaper. It whickered self-consciously under the combined weight of three Forces staring at it.

None of us had uttered a word for well over five minutes.

The equine reaper was no bigger than Destiny's cereal bowl, and easily would have fit in my hands. I'd learned early on that they did not need to be any larger to be able to harvest the souls in my stead. That was why I had been able to make so many of them over the years. Strange, then, that a Contract breach had only come now, from just one reaper.

The reaper tossed its head and whickered again, fear and impatience winning out over its discomfort under our gazes.

"All right," I finally said. I extended my hand to the reaper. "Give it here."

The reaper stamped its foot, and turned to present its side to me. With a shudder, its whip-like tail flicked around, the bone blade on the tip lashing against its side and tearing through the thin hide. I heard Destiny give a strangled cry as the reaper's harvest cavity opened, and the soul inside came tumbling out. It was heavy and solid when it landed in my hand.

How curious.

The reaper shook itself as its flesh began to knit back together, and I heard Destiny whimper again as I brought the soul in for closer examination. "They don't feel pain," I informed her absently as I began to study what the reaper had brought me. The soul immediately drew every fragment of my attention and I did not hear her reply, if she made one.

The soul was a golden sphere thick with life. This was not unusual in and of itself. My reapers often went out to retrieve souls that were set to expire in the so-called prime of a mortal's life, but in every case, no exceptions under *any* circumstances, the tethers binding the soul to the body had thinned to mere threads, simple and clean and ready for my reapers to cut. It was what happened when a mortal's life was at its end, no matter how young or healthy they were.

This soul, however, had thick cords of mortality hanging from it, strong and sturdy and impossible for one of my reapers to sever. At least, they should have been. These mortality cords had been hacked and sawed until they were fraying at the ends.

That I had certainly never seen before.

A sudden hand on my shoulder startled me. I looked up into Life's questioning face and realized he had asked me something.

"I did not catch that, I'm afraid," I said.

"I asked what your reaper brought you," Life said. His gaze returned to the reaper and narrowed with suspicion. "And how it managed to violate the Contract."

The reaper snorted and planted its feet, meeting Life's stare with open defiance.

I sat back in my seat, Life's hand a gentle presence on my shoulder. "I was so careful," I said, more to myself than the room at large. "I did not give them that kind of power."

Part of my earliest experiments with the reapers had tested the limits of the Contract that bound all Forces who sought to influence the mortal world. Written by my own hand with input from Life, and then amended and sealed by Justice himself, the Contract kept any one Force from becoming too powerful on this world and, by extension, back home in Eternity. It also kept the mortal world from becoming a fountain of chaos. Without rules in place and severe consequences for violating them, this world would have spat chaos everywhere, destroying itself and all its bordering realms, including Eternity. Those of us who were old enough to remember the price we'd already paid when we did not understand chaos enough to fear it were reluctant to repeat that mistake.

After it was signed, the Contract took on a power of its own. It maintained itself, only growing stronger and more absolute with each new Force that added their signature in exchange for the chance to build their strength and influence. Those who reached too far or tried to break set limits were given stern warnings to undo the damage, or face capital punishment.

I had written that clause myself. I knew exactly what that meant. I simply had never expected to be subject to it. The unpleasant twinge in my spine told me that had been a foolish assumption.

"It couldn't have done this," I muttered, glancing from the soul in my hand to the reaper and back again. I lifted one of the thick mortality cords, rolling it between my fingers and frowning at the ragged tip. Something did not match up.

Before I could follow this line of thinking, Destiny asked, "Haven't you had reapers come back to you empty before?" She crouched down, bringing her gaze level with the reaper. "Maybe this is just another quirk like that?"

"Empty reapers don't breach the Contract," I said flatly. "The free will clause ensures that."

Part of the stipulations that limited me, Life, and all the other Forces dictated that the mortals must have free will. They are subject to our influence, but they can defy us if they truly wish. Most of us. The Contract states that Life and I are absolute on the mortal world, but even then, when it's appropriate, the mortals must have the chance to evade me, just as Life needs to give them the freedom to destroy each other if they so choose. No Force particularly likes the free will clause, but it does allow some room for error on our part. I could not imagine how burnt out I would have been if I'd needed to harvest every soul in existence at exactly the right moment for all of human history.

But this…

"I've had mortals avoid me before," I said. "If they

succeed, the reaper cannot cut their soul away, and comes back empty." I raised the soul and raked my fingers through the thick mortality cords so that Life and Destiny could see the fraying ends. "*This*, however, has never happened before. A mortal who escapes me does not have their tethers cut, and it follows that my reaper does not come back with that soul." I leaned toward my reaper again, finally realizing just what had gone wrong enough to breach the Contract. The reaper flattened its ears and whickered. "This one—" I poked the reaper in the chest, "—came back with the *wrong* soul."

There was an uneasy silence in the wake of my words. Then the reaper gave a pathetic whimper and stamped its hoof on the kitchen table.

"Do *not* scuff the furniture," I growled.

The reaper quieted but kept fidgeting.

"What do you mean, 'the wrong soul'?" Destiny asked.

"Exactly that," I said. I held the soul up again and shook it so that the hacked-off ends danced in the air. "A soul so bonded to its mortal vessel never should have been cut by a reaper." I turned my head to peer at the ends of the cords as another thought occurred to me. "Taking this would have been a struggle. Probably painful for both parties, not just the mortal."

Life's hand tightened on my shoulder. "That's horrible," he breathed. "Death, what's to stop your reapers from taking even *more* souls before their time?"

I turned my attention back to the reaper on the table, which cowered under my gaze. "A reaper should not have been able to do this," I said, and I knew it was true.

I'd purposefully made them too weak to cut through anything stronger than the end of mortality. Even working together, a swarm of reapers would not have been able to cut a soul free before its time.

"Well, that thing clearly did it anyway!" Life snapped. "This is *dangerous*, Death! You can't let these creatures do this to the mortals! What would happen to the Contract? What would happen to *you*?"

I looked between the bone scythe on the end of the reaper's tail and the ragged ends of the mortality cords trailing off the soul. "It couldn't have done this," I repeated.

"Death—"

"Hold this," I said, and thrust the soul into Life's hands.

He yelped and dropped it.

There was a frantic scramble as I shot out of my chair and tried to grab the soul, got my fingers tangled with Life's, and then managed to catch one of the mortality cords before the soul hit the ground. Life and I stared at each other for a long moment after that, him breathing hard and me with my mouth hanging open.

A lost soul loose on the mortal world would have caused no end of chaos. We *both* knew that. And we both knew that was why I was so important. If there had not been anyone to catch the souls as they snapped free of their mortal bodies, they would have decayed into raw chaos and swallowed the universe.

"I couldn't help it," Life said, horrified at what he had almost done. "I… felt its pain."

I took a firmer grip on the soul and sat back down. It pulsed lightly in my hand, but that was all. "Its pain?"

I asked.

"I've never felt that before," he said, dropping his eyes to the soul in my hands. "The severing, it… it must have been agony." A deeply unsettled look came into his eyes. "I didn't know it would feel like that."

"Haven't either of you ever dealt with this before?" Destiny asked. "I mean, Life is the one who created the souls, and Death bound them to the bodies." She walked around the table until she was facing us. She planted her hands on either side of the reaper as she challenged our attention to detail. "I thought you two understood everything about mortality."

"This," I said, waving the soul so that the mortality cords whipped at her, "was never supposed to happen. There were so many rules in place that should have stopped this." I jabbed a finger at the terrified reaper again. "And *you* should never have been able to do this."

"Yes, we heard you the first three times," Destiny snapped. "But clearly something *did* happen, or we wouldn't be dealing with a Contract breach, would we? So what was it, then?"

I frowned at the reaper for a moment before turning back to Life and offering him the soul. "Do you think you can hold on to this?"

He winced. "Not for long."

"I don't need long."

Reluctantly, Life reached out and touched the soul. He grit his teeth against the ripple of pain that ran through him, and lifted the soul out of my hand.

"I'll be quick," I promised.

The reaper came when I called, as it was bound to do, but it crept along almost on its belly from pure fear.

It placed itself in profile to me, presenting itself for inspection. Its small, equine body shivered where I touched it, black hide contracting under my fingers. I examined its chest and gently felt around the cavity where it stored its harvested souls, then moved on to the reaper's whip-like tail, testing its flexibility before focusing on the scythe at the tip. The bone blade was sharp and strong. No chips or signs of wear.

I frowned again and glanced back at the soul in Life's hands. The frayed mortality cords spilled over his fingers, shaking as Life trembled with pain.

I turned back to the reaper and concluded that, even if this one really had lashed out at the wrong target, there should have been some sign that it had struggled to cut those cords. A dulling of the bone scythe, perhaps. Knicks and ridges where the cords had resisted. A loosening of the scythe from such hard use.

But there was nothing.

I turned the reaper to face me and pried open its jaws so I could peer down its throat. Past the flat teeth, I saw no blockages or signs of distress that might have caused the reaper to act out. I stared into its red eyes and checked each of its pointed ears. I checked its wings and its legs, and searched its hooves for cracks. I even ran my fingers through its thin mane to see if there was something the wrong with that.

Nothing.

As I had intended, the reaper was flawless, functional, and fearsome.

I took the soul back from Life, who staggered with relief before sinking into the chair opposite me. "It wasn't the reaper," I said.

"Then what happened?" Destiny demanded.

"I don't know," I admitted.

Life shook his head. "It had to have been the reaper. Nothing else could have done this."

"I could have," I murmured, "but we all know I would *never*. This is not right."

"So what do we do about it?" Destiny asked.

Life sighed and fixed his gaze on me. "You have to call back the reapers. They can't be out there anymore."

"It *was not* the reaper."

There was a small pause before Life leaned across the table and touched my arm. "I know you worked hard on them, Death," he said gently, "but if they're violating the Contract, you can't—"

I shot to my feet. "For the last time, it was not a reaper!"

Life did not move. He barely had to tilt his chin to look up at me, I had given up so much of myself to make the reapers. His green eyes were dark with sympathy. "Death, I know what it's like to put so much into a creation only for it to fail. I know you know that, because you've seen all of mine. And I know you know that it's going to be okay. You can try again. Maybe I can help you this time, and—"

"We are not doing anything!" I snapped. I brandished the severed soul, sending the mortality cords dancing. "My reapers do not have this flaw!"

Life sat back in his seat and frowned at me. "What do you propose we do, then?"

"I don't know!"

"You'd better figure something out," Destiny cut in, "before things gets worse."

Life and I both turned to look at her, and I realized that Destiny had abruptly dropped her mortal glamour. She swirled before us, an agitated whorl of color shot through with a red vein of anxiety.

"What's happening?" I asked.

"Chaos ripples," Destiny said, her voice taking on an echoing, incorporeal quality now that her glamour was gone. "I have to contain them." She shot across the room in a graceful arc and disappeared down the hallway.

I sank back into my seat.

A Contract breach. Chaos ripples. Wasted coffee. What a terrible morning.

"There is something we could do," Life said.

The gentle tone of his voice instantly made me wary. I cut a suspicious glare at him and waited for him to continue.

"Justice does reign over these issues. We could summon him to—"

"No."

"I didn't even say—"

"No."

"But he's supposed to—"

"NO."

Life threw up his hands. "Death, you have to face facts here. The Contract was breached, chaos has started to form, and your reaper showed up with the wrong soul. No matter what you say, it's very clear what happened, but if you won't call the reapers off yourself, we have to bring in Justice and let him do it."

I shook my head so hard, my jaw rattled. "I know my reapers. They didn't do anything wrong."

Life huffed a sigh that was somewhere between pity and disgust. "Death—"

"Just… just let me try to figure out what happened. Please."

My partner frowned. "I don't think we have time for that, Death."

"Destiny can contain the chaos for a little bit," I said, trying to work out my own logic even as I fought to convince Life. "I'll get to the bottom of this." I stood up, only to hesitate. Part of me knew beyond any doubt that I was right, that my reapers were innocent. Another part of me, smaller but still present, had to admit that Life had a point; if my reaper somehow, some way had managed to take a soul before its time…

"I'll destroy them," I said. "If it's true that the reaper really did this, or if I can't find out what really happened before Destiny can't control the chaos anymore, I will destroy the reapers myself."

"Really," Life said blandly, but he did not fully mask the suspicion in his voice. "Just like that?"

"Yes," I said.

Life held my gaze for a long moment before nodding his acceptance of my terms.

Which meant that I needed to come up with a plan to prove my reapers' innocence, and fix whatever had caused this mess. And before I did that, I needed to do something with the severed soul in my hand.

I made to offer Life the soul again. "Can you hold on to this for…?" I trailed off when he blanched. "Right. And Destiny can't touch souls, so if I want to keep this safe for a bit…" I turned back to the reaper on the kitchen table, which shrank away. "You are not at fault,"

I told it, pointedly avoiding Life's gaze while I spoke. "You will not be punished."

The reaper sprang up and ran in a tight circle around the table, baying happily.

"Be quiet and get over here," I growled.

It trotted back to me eagerly. I gave it an affectionate scratch under the chin before holding out the soul. The reaper snapped it up and swallowed it whole.

Life gave an agonized cry and bolted to his feet. "Did you just *feed* the soul to *your reaper*?"

I gave him a sidelong look. "You saw where it was keeping the soul. How exactly do you think the reaper got it in there in the first place?"

"They *eat* them?"

"I can assure you, no digestion is involved."

Life fell back into his seat and stared in open horror at the reaper, which now glowed and looked far too content for the circumstances.

I gave the reaper a final scratch and told it to stay in the apartment until I said it could leave. It whickered in acquiescence and settled on to the table to wait, folding its legs neatly under itself. I left Life gawking at the reaper in the kitchen.

I hurried down the hallway, pausing briefly at Destiny's room to poke my head inside and see how she was doing.

She had recast her human glamour and was hammering furiously at her keyboard. A set of three massive computer screens glowed in front of her, displaying maps and complex readouts that shifted as she input commands. I was struck for a moment by how familiar the sight was. Many, many times I had seen Destiny just like this, surrounded by towers of notebooks with fate craftings scribbled across the pages, her bedroom walls crowded with whiteboards marked up with symbols that only she understood and clocks and calendars tracking every measure of time the mortals had come up with, along with a few they had yet to recognize.

I never thought I would long for a normal morning that would have seen me trudging back to my room to get back to work. A crack on the mortal world was not how I had intended to take the break that I so desperately needed.

"How are things looking?" I asked from the doorway.

"Not good," Destiny said without turning around. "There's a lot of fresh chaos cropping up, and it's spreading faster than I anticipated."

"Don't we already know the source?"

"Actually, no," she said. "That soul your reaper brought threw out a little chaos, but I killed that bit easily. It's this other stuff that's the problem."

That brought me inside her room, right up to her computer screens. "There's another source?"

Destiny nodded grimly. "A bigger one."

"Where is it?"

"I'm looking," she said, "but it may be too late for that. There's too many ripples. Can't find the source and contain the spread at the same time."

I tensed. "How bad is this?"

"We don't need a Ride," Destiny said, then paused for a fraction of a second. "Not yet."

I was surprised that Destiny was even considering

the possibility of an Apocalypse Ride, but that told me how much trouble we were in. This was more than a wrong soul being taken; it went much, much deeper than that. We needed to figure out how deep, and how to stop the bleeding. The last time we'd seen an uncontainable amount of chaos overrun the mortal world, we had ended up with irreparable damage back home and an ice age on Earth that had nearly destroyed our grand experiment before it even got off the ground.

And Destiny was telling me that she was already having trouble containing this new wave of chaos. We really did not have a lot of time.

"I'll be back," I told her as I stepped away.

"Where are you going?" she called after me.

"The reaping site," I said. "There must be an answer there."

*The threat of an overspill of chaos from the mortal world into
Eternity shall justify any necessary countermeasures...*
-- excerpt from the Contract of Mortality, Addendum 2
authored by Death, Life, and Destiny, countersigned by
Justice

- 3 -

If that morning's events truly had been as simple as one of my reapers going rogue and taking the wrong soul, of course I would have acted on the only acceptable response: I would have destroyed the defective reaper, tracked down the soul that was supposed to have been taken, reaped it myself, and then followed the stench of wrongness all the way to the vacant body the defective reaper had left behind. I do not know if I could have returned the wrongly taken soul to its body, but I would have tried. Then I most likely would have recalled all of the other reapers and destroyed them, if that was what it took to maintain stability. Just as I had promised Life.

Nothing about that morning was simple, however, as I would soon come to understand.

But long before I learned just how complicated everything was, I learned that there was no trail to follow. I did not know if that was because of the increased chaos levels in the area, or if this was such a bizarre mistake that I did not understand how to trace the wrongly taken soul back to its original host. I had expected to pick up on at least a scrap of a clue, but there was nothing.

Before I left for the reaping site, I consulted my catalogue, skimming through the endless lists of ready-to-be-harvested souls, until I found the expired mortal that this particular reaper had been assigned to track. I frowned as I read through the information. The mortal in question had been quite old by human standards, but still kicking at a steady pace. He was supposed to have died from a heart attack earlier that morning, a fast and relatively painless end, all things considered. Perhaps he had somehow not suffered the cardiac event, and the reaper had tried to go through with harvesting the soul anyway.

That did not explain the speed and strength of the chaos ripples, however. I'd seen what Destiny was dealing with. This was so much more chaos than one confused reaper could make.

Moreover, the mortal's expected place of demise did not match the location I had gleaned from the reaper, which was still residing in the kitchen where it lapped up the last of the sugary milk left over from Destiny's abandoned breakfast. I hurried back to Destiny's room and showed her the discrepancy. Between battles with the chaos ripples, she pulled up an online map of the two locations for me, too busy keeping the world together to scoff at my techno-illiteracy.

I studied the map with growing unease. Instead of the posh, elegant home the mortal had lived and was supposed to have died in, the reaping had taken place three cities over, in a sad little apartment in a neighborhood even I did not want to go to after dark.

Entertaining as it was for my roommates whenever someone tried to mug me, it usually did not end well for any parties involved. Thankfully, it was now mid-morning on a sunny day, and I thought it unlikely that I would run into much trouble.

I still took precautions, however.

I did not bother with a human glamour, opting instead for the form of a common crow. At the height of my power, I could whip myself across space and time as I saw fit, but I had been sacrificing that ability to the reapers over the millennia and was now bound by the laws of distance. I went as fast as I could, surging through the skies on the back of a sturdy wind, but it still took me precious time to get to the apartment. Far more than I would have liked, but it could not be helped.

On the way there, I saw firsthand what the chaos ripples were doing to the mortal world. They were small, subtle things, nothing that would have alarmed the humans, but to me, they were like violent alarms shrieking in my face.

I saw animals twitching and moving in slow, confused circles, trees with fresh leaves turning brown despite the spring season, a river trembling and beginning to flow along a new course.

Humans had always proven a little more resilient to chaos than nature, or at least more oblivious to it. Those that I passed as I flew overhead were going about their days, hardly any of them noticing when another human started making animal sounds in place of normal conversation, or began nibbling on their own shirts. Minor things that they either ignored, or took to be some strange little quirk and nothing more.

I knew that would not last long.

Especially since, by the time I got to the reaping site, the police were already there. There were two of them, one inside and the other down by the squad car keeping radio contact with the dispatcher. The chaos levels had made the officers bold, and they had cut off sightlines to each other, leaving a full building made of stone and glass and mistrustful neighbors between them. The one outside had also taken off his pants and thrown them over a telephone wire. Evidently, the chaos was a little stronger at the reaping site.

I came in to land on the second-story railing of a fire escape winding up the side of a brick building that was well past its prime. A small window was open in front of me, likely in an attempt to coax an early autumn breeze inside and drive out the last of the summer heat. I hopped from the railing to the sill and peered inside.

As I expected, I saw the other cop standing just outside the apartment door, which was open and crisscrossed with yellow police tape. He, thankfully, was still fully clothed, although it looked like he was trying to hand a taser over to one of the many neighbors that had clustered around him. I heard them asking questions about what had happened and if someone named Michael was all right before adding an insistent meow at the end of their question. The cop told them that the apartment was off limits and tried to pass his taser to a sixty-eight-year-old woman.

I cawed softly to test the perception levels of the humans. None of them looked my way, so I turned my attention to the apartment itself.

Unsurprisingly, the apartment was small. The living area was just large enough to contain a threadbare couch and a plastic table. An old rug covered the floor, which was bare wood everywhere else. There was a cramped kitchen off to my left, along with a tiny bedroom that held a narrow bed and an open rack of clothing, and to my right was a bathroom that would have required inhuman amounts of flexibility to use with any degree of success. Aside from the body that lay sprawled between the kitchen and the living room, the apartment was immaculately clean.

Actually, the body was quite clean, too. It was dressed in rich, tailored clothing consisting of dark gray slacks and a matching suit jacket. The collared shirt underneath was a blue so pale, it was almost white. This matched the color of the fine hair on the head, which might have contrasted a ruddy skin tone at some point, but the weathered, wrinkled skin had already begun to fade as the last of the blood stilled and rigor mortis began to take its preliminary grip on the muscles. Gray-blue eyes stared out from the lifeless face, and the mouth was partly open, either from the force of the left cheek hitting the floor, or shock.

I could not tell which, but that was the least pressing question on my mind at that point.

The mortal's face matched the image I had pulled from my catalogue, and the death I read inside the corpse was the one it had been slated to experience. Without a doubt, this was the correct body, and the reaper had done its job and taken the soul during the heart attack, just as it was supposed to.

How, then, had the reaper ended up with the wrong

soul?

I spent a moment making certain that there were no other mortals in the apartment (at least, not any human ones—I trusted the insects in the walls to mind their own business as I explored the site) and the ones outside were not paying me any mind. I jumped inside, positioned myself behind the kitchen counter, and returned to my normal form with a twist of shadow and a soft rush of air.

Steering clear of the open apartment door, I slipped from room to room, trying to piece together what had happened, absorbing the details of the mortal who had lived there: strands of black, curling hair in the shower drain, clearly not from the grayed body on the floor; photos taped to the bedroom walls, many showing a brown-skinned young man smiling with a few different groups of people around him; clothing in the bedroom that looked a bit smaller and considerably less expensive than what the body in the other room wore; the calendar in the kitchen with work shifts written out for each week and a date earlier in the month labeled *DAD'S FUNERAL*.

I would need to check my catalogue to confirm, but I had the impression that the mortal on the floor had buried his father several decades ago, not two weeks ago.

"Right," I muttered. I threw a glance over my shoulder at the body before turning back to the calendar. "This certainly was not your home."

So where *was* the man who lived here?

The question left me scratching my skull.

I returned to the body and crouched down next to

it, keeping the kitchen counter between me and the officer in the doorway. It sounded like he had successfully handed off the taser and was now offering his badge to the meowing neighbor.

Safe for the moment, I turned my attention to the corpse. The sightless eyes stared up at me as I placed my hand against the corpse's back, as close as I could to the dead heart without disturbing the scene. Slowly, I drew my hand up, feeling the sticky threads of mortality suck at my bones. They were golden and thin, exactly as they should have been... save for the sludgy, poisonous-looking tips that were trying to burrow into my bones.

That was disconcerting.

I quickly shook my hand free, scattering the threads. They drifted back into the body, vanishing from sight without a sound. I looked at my hand, almost expecting to see minute gouges where the threads had tried to dig into me, but I had proven too strong for them. I still felt a chill as understanding settled over me.

"Soul jump," I whispered.

That was the only explanation that made sense. Someone had switched the souls of two mortals, forcing the wrong one into the body my reaper had been tracking. From the look of the chaos-tipped mortality threads of the gray body, they had not been kind about it.

But why? And how? And *where* was the other body and soul?

I had no answers for my own questions, but I did know for certain that my reapers were innocent here, and I had a sense of what I needed to look for next.

I took one of the photos off the wall, one with a clear view of the smiling young man in it. I grabbed a piece of unopened mail from the kitchen counter, and seared the young man's face and name into my mind. Concentrating hard, I held the photo and the unopened envelope, filling my senses with the traces the young man had left behind. I pulled my power close as I drew in every detail that I could, then thrust outward, scattering my consciousness across the city. I flitted from body to body, searching, until I picked up the trail of poison that would lead me to the missing body and soul. I began to follow it, feeling the influence of the mortal vessel as I went, all the places he had gone and the people his existence had touched. I followed him as far as I could, until I slammed into a solid wall of chaos.

The chaos pressed down around me with a freezing, bone-cracking weight, trying to devour me. I felt it gnawing on my bones as I fought to pull myself back. I had never seen this much concentrated chaos, not even in the days of the void when I had been alone before the birth of everything. For a panicked moment, I thought that I was lost. Then I realized that there was something odd about this chaos, even as it struggled to destroy me. Instead of the frozen, tasteless oblivion that normal chaos felt like, this was interwoven with the scent of something rotten, and laced with trace amounts of power instead of raw wildness. It was all wrong.

That was enough to center me, and remind me that I could escape. I knew I could not be too far into the chaos yet, and I thrust behind me, reaching for the freedom I trusted to be there. I broke through to the warmth of chaos-free air. I quickly pulled as many shadows to myself as I could, wrapped myself in their warm, safe embrace, and left their shell behind as I slipped out of the chaos.

I fell back on to the floor of the apartment. If I had lungs, I would have been gasping with raw shock. I had no lungs, so I remained still, trying to re-center myself and remember who I was, which rules shaped my power and the order of my existence.

"What was that?" a voice asked from the hallway.

I tried to re-center faster.

"Stay back," I heard someone bark, and then the police tape rustled and footsteps sounded on the floor.

I somehow managed to get ahold of enough of my power to shift forms again, folding in upon myself and shaking feathers out where my robe used to be. I shrank back down to crow-size and spread my wings, only to realize that my feet were still skeletal, and my head was exposed bone.

I hopped under the living room table just as the cop walked in, closely followed by the senior citizen who had been gifted the officer's taser. She held it at the ready as she shuffled forward, peering suspiciously over a thick pair of wire-rimmed glasses.

I watched both humans as I fought to finish my transformation, waiting for an opportunity to slip out unseen. Unfortunately, the old woman was proving to be the best back up the police ever could have hoped for. She positioned herself with her back to the wall and kept a clear, steady gaze on the space around her while the cop wandered past my hiding place and stuck his head in the bedroom.

Then it dawned on me that, even with chaos ripples having odd effects on everyone in the area, the old woman was still wearing heavy glasses, and she was making a point of not looking through them. I took a tentative hop out from beneath the table. She turned her head in my direction, looked right at me, and then looked away again.

I made a break for it, and heard someone yelp in surprise as I rushed out the window, leaving a stray feather behind and throwing in a few panicked caws for effect.

As I flew home, slowly completing my transformation and proving that I had not left my sanity back in that apartment, my thoughts returned to the strangeness of the chaos I had encountered. It had been oddly aggressive, latching on to me with a sense of purpose that pure chaos never had. And there had been the traces of power, and that rotted scent. Or corrupted, maybe, was the better word. Whatever it was, this was not pure chaos. There were threads of something else running through it. Something familiar.

Something from back home, in Eternity.

With a groan, I flapped harder and pushed myself to get back to Life and Destiny as quickly as I could. I was not pleased with what I had found at the reaping site. It was both far more and far less than I had hoped for, but I had learned two solid facts: one, my reapers were clear, and two, a Force had messed with the mortal world.

Example countermeasures against a potential chaos overspill include but are not limited to: [...] neglection of duties insofar as additional chaos is not generated and said duties are resumed as soon as the chaos has been contained...
-- excerpt from the Contract of Mortality, Addendum 2 authored by Death, Life, and Destiny, countersigned by Justice

- 4 -

When I returned from the reaping site, I found Life in Destiny's room, hunched miserably on her bed while Destiny attacked her modified computer keyboard with enough zeal to rival War on a fresh campaign. One glance at her monitors told me that she was losing the battle to control the chaos. I knew that she would keep losing if she continued to use the normal containment methods against this series of chaos swells. I told her as much.

"And what makes this particular swirl of nightmare fuel so special?" she snapped in response.

"There are threads of power and corruption running through it," I said, making a serious effort to keep my voice calm. "Someone from home did this."

Destiny did not pause in her typing, but she did turn to stare at me. Life lifted his head and did the same as I briefly recounted my discoveries at the reaping site, leaving out the part where I almost let an elderly mortal and a chaos-muddled cop corner me under a table. I

44

told Life and Destiny about finding the old man's body in the young man's apartment, and that their souls had been switched. As far as I was aware, the old man's soul was still running around in the younger man's body, and when I had tried to trace that abducted body, I'd hit a wall of tainted chaos.

"And you're sure that someone from home did this?" Life asked once I'd finished.

I nodded.

"But can any of them even perform a soul jump?" Destiny asked. "I didn't think any of the other Forces had enough influence here to defy you and Life like this."

"Well, they shouldn't," I admitted, "but there is a… loophole in the language of the Contract."

Destiny spared me another glance, possibly for dramatic effect, but her gaze was hard and focused as she looked at me. "What kind of loophole?"

"The team-up-and-by-your-powers-combined-wreak-havoc-on-the-mortal-world-behind-our-backs kind of loophole," Life put in.

"You're kidding," Destiny said, but without any real hope in her voice.

"Justice ensured that balance would be maintained," I said dryly. "Meaning, while I can limit the others, I cannot control them completely." I grudgingly added, "If only we'd taken as much care with Rule Six as the rest of the twice-cursed thing."

"Hindsight is all-knowing," Life muttered.

Destiny continued thrashing her keyboard. "Has this ever happened before?"

"First soul jump," I said.

"No, I mean the other Forces finding ways to exploit the loophole. Has anyone done *that* before?"

I grimaced. "Unfortunately, yes."

"When?"

"There was that time the twins threw a comet at this planet because they were bored, but the best example is probably the Trojan War. If you haven't already heard the story, I'm sure War would love to chew your ear off about it for a decade or two."

There was a whicker from Destiny's lap in response to that. I peered over her shoulder and found my reaper staring up at me, looking inappropriately content for the situation.

"Did you know you have a herald of doom on your lap?" I asked Destiny.

"I am very aware of that."

"And you're okay with it?"

"Back off, loophole-enabler. It's cute."

"My reapers are *not* cute."

"This one is."

The reaper whickered smugly.

I cut an irritated glare at the reaper, but as long as it was still safeguarding the severed soul, I could not banish it out of spite. It seemed all too aware of that.

A deliberate cough from Life drew my attention to him. For a moment, I was taken aback by how miserable he looked. Hopeless, almost. I went to the bed and sat beside him, taking one of his hands in my own. He smiled weakly but did not look at me.

"Are you all right?" I asked.

He frowned at the floor. "I never imagined something like this," he murmured.

I inched closer to him until our shoulders touched. "Neither did I, and it's my job to think of all the ways the world could end."

He jerked sharply away from me. "It's not ending," he said. "Is it? Surely you don't need to call a Ride over this?"

"I don't want to if I don't have to," I answered, throwing a meaningful glance at Destiny.

She felt my scrutiny touch her shoulder and said without turning around, "I'm still holding the chaos back, but you're right. This particular blend of horribleness is fighting back hard."

Life's hand tensed beneath mine. "There has to be a way to fix this," he said quietly.

"I think I may know how to start," I said.

Life's attention swung back to me. "The reapers…?"

"Are innocent," I finished, my tone brokering no room for argument. *I* knew that the reapers were innocent, but I had not really found solid proof of their lack of involvement in the soul switch. Nothing that I could point to, at least, in order to convince someone like Life or Destiny. Or Justice. I did not want Life to press me on the matter.

"So, then, Justice…?" he started.

"Doesn't need to be called yet," I said, perhaps a little too quickly. But I did not want Justice passing judgement, not when I had a head start on figuring out who had framed my reapers for a soul jump. I had my own punishment in mind for the fool who had caused me this much trouble.

"What are you going to do, then?" Life asked. His eyes were dark with confusion and doubt, which made me bristle a little. "I thought you said you didn't know who did this?"

"I did not get a good read on whoever threw their influence into this," I admitted, "but I know it was someone from home, and I know I can find them."

Life's hand twitched in my grasp. "Are you certain of that?"

Right then, I would have promised my partner almost anything if it would have made him smile again. For the moment, all I had to offer was a determined nod. "I have some suspects in mind. I'll get the truth out of all of them soon enough."

Life's fingers closed around mine, and he shut his eyes tight. I leaned toward him, letting our foreheads brush.

A loud swear from Destiny ruined the moment.

I gave Life's hand one final squeeze before returning to Destiny's side. "How much time do we have until the chaos is beyond control?"

"If you want to keep the mortal world intact," she huffed, "less than one day."

I did not try to hide my surprise. "The chaos is spreading that quickly?"

"Thanks to me, no, but that is how long we have before we hit the critical point where I can't contain it anymore. It's already caused some minor damage. No deaths, but some injuries and a building collapse. I'm keeping it isolated for now, but it's only going to get exponentially stronger with each passing hour. If we can't cut the source before the breaking point—"

"Believe me," I growled, "none of us want a repeat of what happened the last time the mortal world spilled into our realm."

"Then *go*," Destiny snarled. "I can only bury so much of this under random accidents and coincidences before the mortals start suspecting divine intervention or aliens or something."

As I headed for the door, Life intercepted me. "Death, wait."

"We *just* established there is very little time to work with here!" Destiny snapped over her shoulder.

Life shot a venomous look at her back. I cupped his cheek and turned his attention back to me.

"I won't be gone long," I promised. "I know what to do."

"What *are* you going to do?"

I twisted my teeth into a smile. "I'm going to take that vacation a little sooner than I expected." My robes swirled around me as I left Destiny's room. "I just wish it wasn't going to be a working vacation."

As long as the mortal world continues to exist, all Forces who interact with the mortal world in any capacity must make conscious effort to uphold the rules outlined in this document. Failure to do so will be considered a breach of contract, and result in consequences against the guilty party tailored to fit the form and severity of the breach.
-- excerpt from the Contract of Mortality

- 5 -

It had been a long time since I'd wanted my scythe. Long before I'd made my first reapers, I had outgrown my need for the tool, but I had held on to it out of a combination of sentiment and precaution. Throwing Death's scythe out on the mortal world for any human to just pick up was beyond stupid, overshadowed only by the possibility of another Force managing to get ahold of it and wreaking havoc back in Eternity before I could stop them.

Also, walking around with a giant blade on a pole was a decent way of intimidating other Forces. Given that I had been steadily bleeding off power on the mortal world, I knew that I would need all the help I could get to keep the respect of those back home.

I found my scythe exactly where I had left it: deep in the back of my closet behind stacks of vintage board games Life had collected over the last few decades, and the numerous holiday decorations Destiny had somehow convinced me that we needed if we were going to exist among the mortals. I was not exactly sure how *my* closet had ended up as the communal storage unit, but at least the clutter hid my sole possession from prying eyes on the off-chance we ever needed to call upon our landlord for something.

I dove into the closet, knocking over board games and sending tinsel and plastic animals wearing various holiday hats flying as I wrestled the pieces of my scythe free. My scythe knew me, and it knew when I did not need it. So it often let itself fall apart when I wasn't looking, whether out of spite or dejection I have never been able to figure out. Either way, having to reassemble the tool while I was in a hurry was far from convenient.

My scythe was made from materials that could only be found on Eternity: raw chaos sealed safely away in a binding of ritual habit and mantra, to create the handle and ornamentations; and a blade carved from steadfast order that would never wear or break. I managed to dig out all of the pieces save for one small point that was supposed to adorn the top of the scythe, but it was a purely decorative piece that the tool could function without. I still made a note to find it as soon as I got back and I had the time to look for it; a scrap of chaos (even a contained scrap) lost on the mortal world would never be anything but trouble later. I knew that it could wait, however, and pushed it out of my mind once I had all the other pieces laid out on my floor. I snapped everything into place and fed the scythe a thread of my power, tying it all together and ensuring that the tool would not fall apart on me while I needed it. My scythe hummed contentedly in response.

When I picked it up, the handle fit like a memory in my hand.

Fully assembled save for that one little decoration at the top, my scythe was over a full head taller than I was. I had to reach up to wipe the last of the dust off the thick, double-edged blade. Curling filigree decorated the place where the blade met the handle, tracing out an intricate spiral of black against the bone white sharpness. Any other day, I might have paused to admire the tool. I always seemed to forget just how beautiful it really was.

Stunning and deadly though it may be, my scythe has always been more of an intimidation tactic than an actual tool. Before the reapers, I could take souls from mortals simply by touching them. I did not know if I could still do that after giving so much of myself to the reapers, but Life, Destiny and I had all agreed that it was better not to find out (which made for interesting interactions whenever it was my turn to deliver the check to the landlord, and is probably why Destiny never asked me to pick up groceries). In my defense, healthy souls with time to burn were supposed to be much harder to sever from their bodies than what I could do with my mere fingertips.

I just did not know if that particular safeguard extended to souls inhabiting the wrong bodies.

In case that really was enough to protect the rogue soul from my touch, I wanted to be certain that I could cut the soul free, should I happen to come across the little chaos fountain over the course of my investigation.

I also wanted to be sure that I could properly

intimidate the Force who had dared to go against me, and the order that Life and I had so carefully built together. Death coming after them armed with a giant farming tool that could cut through anything (yes, *any*thing) would send a clear enough signal that they had better be ready for a bad time.

Thus armed, I turned to begin, only to find Life standing in my doorway, watching me.

"What's wr—"

"Don't go," Life said.

I lowered my arms and gently rested the butt of my scythe on the floor. "I am the best one to find out what happened, and do it quickly. I have to go home and learn who did this, and why."

Life shook his head and took a step into my room. "If you stay, we can find a way to fix this." He held out his arms to me. "We're good together. We could make this better, you and I. Just please stay."

I hesitated, struck by how lovely Life was in that raw moment. It killed me to have to say no. "We just have to be apart for a little while," I said. "Destiny needs your help with the chaos here, and I need to find the ones who did this and see if there's any way we can set things right, not just make them better."

Life started to smile, but it was strained. He looked like he wanted to say more.

I kept going before he had the chance. "Even if we could find a way to cut the problem here," I said, "there would still be the Forces out there who made this happen." I almost moved toward him, but I knew that if I did, I would not want to move away again. I did not have that kind of time to lose. "I will find them," I promised instead, "and I will make them pay."

I raised my scythe then, and slammed the butt down on the floor. There was a thunderclap of power, and the world cracked around me. As the shards fell away, I saw Life staring at me, his pain fractured into a hundred different pieces. Then he was gone, along with my small, cozy bedroom. A chasm yawned in front of me, dark and sucking. There was no wind, but I felt drawn to the edge, as though something invisible dared me to jump.

I dared, and stepped off the mortal world.

- Part Two -

Anger

Any Force may use the mortal plane to grow and strengthen
himself/herself/themselves by exerting his/her/their influence
and building his/her/their power. A Force's efforts to do so may
not violate any of the previous Rules, but may contradict and
override the influence of other Forces (excepting that of Life
and Death).

-- excerpt from the Contract of Mortality, Rule 6

- 6 -

hen I landed, a wave of vertigo crashed over me. I had not had a rough landing. Far from it, in fact; in spite of how long I had been away, Eternity knew me well, and it had received me willingly. I simply seemed to have overestimated my ability to tolerate jumping off a ledge into the abyss between two realms, only to abruptly find myself standing on solid ground when I should have been freefalling into infinity. It was through a combination of sheer willpower, a stubborn refusal to waste perfectly good coffee, and a firm reminder to the laws of the universe that I did not have a stomach that I managed to keep the nausea under control.

When I felt that I was no longer in danger of losing my beloved coffee, I shook the last of the dizziness off and looked around. I found myself standing on a path built from white stones that gleamed like clean bones in the undying night. In the distance, there were dark mountains carving out blots of nothingness against a sky spotted with immortal stars. There was no whisper of wind, no scent on the sterile air, nothing but the total stillness of a realm holding its breath out of fear or anticipation. Or maybe it had never needed to draw breath at all.

I was home.

It was just as boring to look at as it had always been.

In my youth, shortly after learning how not to be torn apart by the void, I had entertained myself by painting what became Eternity's sky with constellations, often changing them to suit my fancy. Some of those shapes I brought with me to the mortal world. Many, many others I had wiped away and never thought of again. As other Forces came into being and we all learned more about ourselves and each other, I found other things to distract me, and I let the stars be.

Looking at those stars after going so long out from underneath them, I was reminded once again that the mortal world would eventually end, when it could sustain us no longer and we were required to turn our attention elsewhere. Someday, I would call up the Riders. Then Life, Destiny and I would return here, and either plot our next great scheme, or go our separate ways as we each sought out something new.

Such was the nature of our kind. As the oldest, I knew that better than any of the others. Being the eldest granted me certain responsibilities and privileges, in exchange for steadfast respect from those Forces who valued age above all else. For the exceptions (most notably War), my early eons alone with raw chaos had also taught me strength. Even diminished by my creation of the reapers, my power would hold equal with the strongest Forces, if not better. At least, I hoped it would. Even if it didn't, my age and my experience would continue to grant me the privilege of teaching the other Forces harsh lessons whenever they stepped out of line, and I was not in a forgiving mood as I gathered my bearings.

I picked out the anchor stars above me and oriented myself in Eternity. To my left, the path thickened and ran straight into the heart of the nesting grounds of the self-styled Blessings and Virtues, with a few rogue Forces mixed in that did not meet the lofty requirements to fully identify with that group, but also did not feel quite at home on the other end of the spectrum. I did not know how these in-between Forces tolerated those pompous nitwits, but as long as they were comfortable and not lashing out at anyone in particular, I could let them be.

And in spite of the terrible thing the Virtues had once done (something I still had not forgiven them for), I did not have any suspects down that path.

While the idea of visiting the Virtues in order to dole out my own kind of long-overdue justice was tempting, I knew such actions would attract the actual Justice's attention faster than I could run, and I was still aiming to avoid him. So, I made myself turn right, and head for the domains of the biggest troublemakers I knew.

They had separated out into two clans a long time ago, back when I still ran with them and had not yet met Life. Thankfully, my primary suspects were not Apocalypse Riders, unbelievable as that seemed given the looming threat of total destruction of the mortal world and Eternity both. I would have needed a far greater amount of naïveté to completely ignore the chance that at least one of the Riders was somehow involved in the soul jump, but I had not sensed any of their presences in the chaos I had run into back on the mortal world. The undercurrent had been far too muddy and subtle for a Rider.

A Sin, however, was another matter entirely. I mulled this over as I trudged along, minding where I put my feet as holes began to appear in the path, which was thinning and deteriorating as it wound its way along. I muttered a curse on the Virtues as I went, for they were who I had to thank for the integrity (or lack thereof) of the path up here, but I forced my thoughts to focus back on the Sins for the time being.

I knew that I could safely eliminate Lust and Sloth from my list of suspects. Lust's signature was difficult to miss, and the idea of Sloth going through this much effort would have been laughable under better circumstances.

Wrath, too, was off the list. Her temper was the stuff of legends—sometimes on what could be considered a biblical scale, depending on which mortal was on the receiving end—but something as intricate as a soul jump performed on the mortal world while Life, Destiny, and I were all present surely demanded more preparation than a short fuse and volatile anger could provide. Wrath had been known to burn cold and hold a grudge every now and then, but her ability to bide her time was limited, and this soul jump reeked of careful planning and organization. Whoever had orchestrated it had known how to stay hidden, when to strike, and how to escape. Three things that had never been taken seriously by Wrath.

I couldn't imagine Gluttony or Pride going through those steps, either. Gluttony tended to seek out more immediate rewards, and Pride wasn't smart enough to come up with something like this, plain and simple.

As for Envy and Avarice...

They were my primary suspects, and this would have been far from the first time they had teamed up to wreak havoc on the mortal world. Between their ambition for greater control over... well, anything, really, and their jealousy over—again—anything, it was easy to imagine them plotting and executing this grand scheme. With their minds combined, they might have even been clever enough to come up with the entire plan on their own. Just not clever enough to hide their tracks.

By the time I had come to this conclusion, I was still walking, and growing more and more impatient with each step. The last time I had visited the Sins, I had gotten there fairly quickly, from what I could recall. I also had not needed to trudge up a hill that was only getting steeper the farther I went.

Of course, my legs had been much longer. And I did have my horse at the time.

Neither of these facts soothed my mood. I ducked my head against the incline and muttered through several creative methods to end the universe as I plowed on.

My mood was not improved when, quite unexpectedly, I collided with the Sins' front door. Rubbing my skull and snarling even more ways to destroy everything, I looked around to see that I had been so distracted by the upward climb, I had walked straight through the Sins' territory and charged headlong into their home. Literally.

The Sins' den was carved into a wall of rock the gray color of diluted chaos trapped inside stone. The door was a dark slab of treated wood taken from Eternity's own forest, sealing the only way in or out with a barrier that would never rot or burn, as long as it stayed away from raw chaos. Energy rippled out from the stone around the door, giving the rock wall a faint, pulsating glow.

Even with their potential (or rather, likely) involvement with the soul jump and the Contract violation on the mortal world, I would have been pleased to finally see the Sins again. I liked them, to a degree, and they respected me for the most part. Unfortunately for them, I was in no mood for their usual antics thanks to the uphill walk and my collision with their front door. I was even more put out by the distinct lack of courtesy following this announcement of my presence; someone smacking their skull into a door should have sounded at least a little like a knock, and yet, no one had come to answer.

Grumbling about the Sins' lack of good manners, I pounded on the everwood door, giving each strike time to resonate before slamming my fist against the heavy wood again. I began to straighten my hood as I waited for a response. I paused when I heard the sound of a scuffle inside, followed by muffled but frantic voices.

It seemed that finding the guilty party here was going to be all too easy. I almost felt sorry for the Sins.

Not enough to let them off easy, of course, but enough to be a little embarrassed on their behalf.

When my knock was finally answered, the door opened barely wide enough to show a sliver of a face. I froze in shock when I realized that the face was mortal. It belonged to a pale man with dark, shining hair hanging to his broad shoulders. His hair swung freely as he came up short, revealing violent streaks of purple dye. His brown eyes went wide in shock as they registered me, and then against all of my expectations, a gleaming white smile spread across his face.

"Death!" the man cried joyously. "Thank creation you're here!"

I recovered just enough from my horror to recognize Pride's voice, which I would have known anywhere, regardless of whether he had shifted even further mortal or became a hulking lion-bear of a beast. But before I could say anything, the Sin grabbed me by the front of my robes and yanked me inside.

Suitable consequences for a breach of contract include but are not limited to: Pain. A breach of contract may result in pain, ranging from mild to severe, for as long as the Force is exerting his/her/their influence on the mortal world.
-- excerpt from the Contract of Mortality

- 7 -

Unused to being handled in such a way (or handled at all, really), I flew over the threshold and nearly faceplanted on the floor. The fact that said floor was covered in discarded metallic cylinders did nothing to steady my balance, and it was only through an undignified series of arm swings and leg kicks that I ended up perched on my toes and bent nearly double, most of my weight supported by my ever-reliable scythe.

"Oh, sorry! I expected you to be heavier," Pride said as he sauntered up to join me. He frowned. "Have you gotten smaller?"

I gave him an unpleasant look before straightening up and trying to restore my dignity through careful robe maintenance. I may have siphoned off my own power to create the reapers, but I wasn't the only one who had changed. Pride had looked very different the last time I'd seen him, all heavy muscle covered in gleaming black fur striped with purple. He had walked on four legs and sported a magnificent crest of fur that he had loved grooming and showing off. Now, it was like seeing him naked and deformed. I opened my mouth to tell him as much, but froze when I finally began to take in my surroundings.

The last time I had visited the Sins, their domain had consisted of a shallow network of caves branching off from a central cavern. Each cave had been formed to suit an individual Sins' tastes, all horribly gaudy and difficult to tolerate. In fact, I still had trouble looking at bright colors thanks to my ill-advised visit to Avarice's nest. I had never seen so many glittering crystals or metallic veins in such a large concentrate before, nor have I seen one since.

This, though... this was a human-styled mess.

More specifically, it was the mess one might find the morning after a college fraternity party gone wrong. Or perhaps gone right, depending on who was describing the party.

Instead of the network of caves, I found myself in a large living space complete with cheap couches and cushioned chairs, an inert body draped facedown across one of the couches, rugs that had once been decent but were now stained with beer and what I hoped was red wine, a graveyard of liquor bottles inside a bookcase, and what I had initially thought of as metallic cylinders were, in fact, empty beer cans thrown carelessly across the floor. An open kitchen piled high with takeout boxes was connected to the living space, and when I located the squat refrigerator, I saw Gluttony—now, quite possibly, the most animalistic of the Sins—staring back at me over its open door. He raised a thin, claw-like hand in greeting, then went back to pouring cold noodles down his throat. To my right, there was a wooden staircase that led up to a second floor and what I assumed were the bedrooms.

I looked over my shoulder at Pride with open horror. "I had no idea the mortal world had already begun to interfere this severely with our realm."

Pride frowned again, this time in confusion. "What do you mean?"

I gestured to the changed room, including Pride himself in the sweep. "Clearly, there was overspill we didn't know about, and it tainted your home until it became a cheap parody of the aftermath of human indulgence! I had no idea it would be so bad!"

Pride turned an interesting shade of mauve at that point, and that's about when I realized that the fraternity house motif had been incorporated quite on purpose, and there had not been any overspill from the mortal world just yet.

While relieved to know that we had not missed something as crucial as a leak between realms, I might have preferred an overspill to the rant Pride launched into about how expertly executed the Sins' new home was, and how perfectly the setting reflected each of their natures. As he indulged in his own bombast, I realized that Pride was dressed in a long, rippling white and purple robe, highly reminiscent of either a Roman emperor or a college junior on his way to a toga party. I could not determine which.

"Please, Death," a voice from the living room's couch grumbled as Pride continued to rant, "this is his favorite look yet."

I turned to see that Sloth had rolled over on to her

65

side and was now watching me with half-lidded eyes the color of ice. Sloth's eyes were the most intense thing about her, and would have been terrifying on another Force. On Sloth, they were offset by… well, her everything else. She was nothing but fluffy gray-blue fur all over, a vivid contrast from Pride's new human form. I was glad that Sloth had not shifted much from how I remembered her, instead continuing to exist as a halo of soft, tangled curls with a blunt snout and sleepy eyes peeking out from her thick mane. It was difficult to think of her as anything but a breathing, rarely moving mound of fur. She was, however, wearing human-styled pajamas with clouds on them, which hung oddly off her distinctly inhuman form and pulled her curling fur into strange shapes and puffs.

I was distinctly reminded of the sweatered Pomeranian I had once seen on the mortal world, and had never really managed to forget about.

Sloth yawned and continued in a soft drawl, "You should've been here when he made us do Spirit Week."

I looked around the Sins' home again, shocked that it could have possibly looked worse than this. I picked my way through the empty beer cans until I was standing over Sloth, Pride still ranting behind me. I did not bother trying to look intimidating; I knew my audience. "If it wasn't to fix all of this—" I nudged a can with the butt of my scythe, "—then why, exactly, was Pride so excited to see me?"

Sloth blinked up at me and offered a lazy smile that revealed blunted teeth. "You'll find out if you stick around," she said before rolling over again, bringing our brief conversation to a close.

Footsteps thudded on the stairs then, and I turned to see a deflated Wrath and a tearful Envy descending from the upper floor, Envy sniffling about something not being fair and Wrath muttering darkly about hating someone so much, she did not even want to put her hands on him to throw him out.

Overall, these were fairly common appearances for these two particular Sins, although I could not recall ever seeing Wrath quite so dejected.

Normally a wall of fire trailed by smoke the color of burning embers, Wrath cut an imposing figure, even among those of us who placed no value on such superficial manifestations. At that moment, however, Wrath had faded to a lackluster gray and dropped ash from her body as she moved, which disintegrated into nothing before it could hit the floor. There was a flicker of fire in her chest, a sign that she had not completely lost sight of her true nature, but something had upset her to the point that her anger had dulled to a single ember, leaving her cold.

And Envy—twisting, flowering, energetic Envy—had wrapped her vines around herself. They sprouted from her shoulders, filling the spaces where arms would have gone on a human, and falling back from her wood-bark scalp in a wave of deep green. Normally, her vines were greedy, rolling and groping over everything they could reach. Now, they were plastered tight against Envy's dark brown body, caressing her gently as she muttered to no one in particular. Tears streamed down her face, thick and vivid with raw anguish.

"What in the name of destruction is going on here?"

I demanded.

Wrath and Envy snapped their gazes around at the sound of my voice, and it was like I had given them permission to wreak havoc on the mortal world. Red flame exploded in Wrath's chest, breathing new vigor into her body, and Envy gave a small cry and ran towards me, her vines unfurling and reaching for me.

I leveled my scythe at her before she could get any ideas about our level of familiarity.

Envy skidded to a halt, her reaching vines swinging forward to almost touch the blade. She pouted at me before eyeing my scythe appraisingly. I withdrew it before she could try to wrap her vines around the handle. Her pout deepened, but then she surprised me by throwing the expression off and allowing a sly smile to bloom in its place. "So you came to deal with him after all!"

"Harshly. Please do it harshly," Wrath added before snarling, "Pride, shut up."

I only realized that Pride had still been ranting when he stumbled to a sudden halt. "But Death insulted our home!" he whined.

"Who cares?" Wrath demanded, her fire blazing brighter. The falling ash turned to rising sparks that vanished before they became a legitimate fire hazard. "They're here now, and they're going to get rid of him for us."

Pride was suddenly at my elbow. "You do that quickly," he said, staring at me solemnly, "and your insults will be forgiven."

I remember thinking to myself at that moment, *Ah, so it was Avarice after all.*

With the current head count and everyone asking me to deal with "him", clearly Avarice was the guilty Force behind the soul jump. And based on the tears and dejection I had witnessed a few moments ago, I doubted that Envy was involved after all. She and Avarice made a natural team, but it wasn't unheard of for one of them to reach beyond the grasp of the other. If I'm honest, the only part of the entire situation that gave me pause was that the other Sins seemed so willing to give up Avarice to me. I knew how close their group was, and it wasn't like them to turn on one of their own. Still, I was a little relieved to know that the rest of the Sins were on my side. It may have been unexpected, but it was not unwelcome. It certainly simplified things.

"He will be punished," I assured the Sins around me, "but first I need to know how and why he did this."

Wrath burned with bright impatience, making me turn my face away. "You know what he's like," she snarled. She thrust a finger overhead, pointing up to the second floor as she advanced on me. "Now go up there and deal with him before he makes it worse!"

My own anger flared, and suddenly I had my hand around Wrath's throat, holding her in the air. The Sin clawed at my arm, and I could feel the heat of her grip as she scrabbled at my robes. I shook her roughly. My voice was dark when I said, "Do not presume to command me, little spark, or I will snuff you out."

Wrath faded to a quieter red as she choked around my grip, but I saw the submission in her burning eyes.

I dropped her in a heap of smoke and embers on the ground, sending empty beer cans spinning across the room as she landed. One of them shot toward the couch, and then defied all laws of physics by bending through the air and disappearing behind the cushions. It landed with a metallic clatter an instant later, and I heard a familiar, triumphant cackle.

I froze.

"Avarice?" I asked tentatively. "Are you down here?"

"Of course I am!" The Sin of greed poked his head up over the couch and fixed his glittering gaze on me. He was covered in empty cans, having magnetized them to his body.

To this day, I have no idea what Avarice really looks like; he has covered every inch of himself with his obsessions since his inception. The shiny beer cans were no exception. For all anyone knows, Avarice is little more than a whisp of smoke and light that takes possession of heaps of objects and animates them like a monster from a mortal-world horror movie. The new beer-can-monster was firmly a B-movie creature.

"You really think I'd want to be up there with *him*?" Avaraice scoffed, his claimed beer cans folding into a frown across the clump that passed for a head.

Several questions skittered to the forefront of my mind, but Pride jumped in before I could speak.

"Wait a minute," he said, looking at all of the Sins gathered in the living space before focusing on Wrath and Envy. "Did you leave Lust *alone* with him?"

"I'm very confused," I put in. "If Avarice, Pride, and Gluttony are all down here, who's the 'him' up there?"

"The worst Force in existence!" Pride cried as he sprinted for the stairs. He took them two at a time as he raced up to the second floor.

I watched him go, more questions seething against my teeth, but a new thought was slowly taking form in my mind. I could only think of one Force that all the Sins would loathe so intensely that they would actively avoid him, and ask me to destroy him. I looked around the room with mounting dismay. "Surely, you don't mean…?"

"Isn't that why you're here?" Envy asked.

"No," I said, "but if all of you are down here, am I to understand that you really did leave Lust alone with him, and none of you are going to help?"

"Well, Pride just went back up," Envy pointed out, but her voice was small and she did not meet my gaze.

I looked at each of the other Sins in turn. Wrath became very interested in the pattern on the rug; Sloth remained immobile; Avarice sank back down behind the couch; Gluttony watched me from over the edge of the refrigerator, cold noodles hanging down from his sharp snout.

"Not even you?" I asked him.

Gluttony's narrow eyes drifted over my shoulder, to the staircase. He munched thoughtfully on his noodles, and one russet, lupine ear flicked forward as a thud came from upstairs. Then he offered me a shrug of his thin shoulders, slurped up the noodles with a loud smacking sound, opened his jaws wide to let his tongue loll, and dove back into the refrigerator.

"Never ask a Sin to do a Rider's job," I grumbled as I started for the staircase. "At least Pride made an effort."

As my hand came to rest on the bannister, another hand came down on top of it. Wrath's red hand.

"We all tried," she said, but without heat this time. "We just weren't strong enough."

I looked at her for a long moment, saying nothing.

Wrath withdrew her hand. "Please, Death. Stop him."

I nodded and continued up the stairs.

Up on the second floor, I emerged in a short hallway with seven doors, each with their own decorative flare, save for one that was bare and dusty. I assumed it was Sloth's room. I doubted she'd even been inside yet. I made my way down the hall to a door shut tight with a "Do Not Disturb Unless You Want to Watch" sign hanging on the handle. The door itself was decorated with vibrantly colored construction paper hearts and empty condom wrappers.

Pride was pressed against the door, saying something about opening up before he broke the door down.

I heard muffled words drifting through the cracks in the threshold as I walked over. I gently pushed Pride out of the way and tried the handle.

It was locked.

I could not imagine Lust ever locking their door. They were many things, but private was not one of them. So I broke the handle, and slammed the door wide.

Any Force may attempt to exert his/her/their power over any given mortal and influence the mortal's existence, but the mortal must willingly accept this influence.
-- excerpt from the Contract of Mortality, Rule 5

- 8 -

The two Forces in the room jumped as I barreled my way inside. It took me a moment to recognize Lust. Like Pride, Lust had also shifted towards a human appearance, although where Pride's was distinctly masculine, Lust's new look reflected their nonbinary identity. Lust had also kept their favorite coloring, which marked them as distinctly inhuman. I was oddly proud of them for it.

Clad in tight, belted pants and a slash of a shirt that showed off the deep blue skin of their midriff, Lust looked at me with raw relief when they realized that I had broken down their door. They took a quick breath and raked their hand through their midnight hair before hugging themselves tightly across their chest. They hitched their expression back into a sly mask before Pride could poke his head into the room, but their eyes were dark and shining with distress.

Standing well within Lust's personal space and looking at me as though he wanted to rip me apart was Shame, the Force that we all hated on principal and loathed through experience.

Sallow-skinned with black hair, pale eyes, and a tall, lean body dressed in blue jeans and a black t-shirt, Shame looked distinctly human. He had always looked human. The day he appeared in Eternity, the other Forces were certain that a mortal had somehow crossed the division between realms and invaded. They weren't completely wrong; Shame came into being the first time the mortal world overstepped its boundaries and washed its influence over our lands. He was the only manmade Force in existence, having been birthed from the disgrace the human mortals began inflicting upon each other at their inception. All it took was one small chaos breach, and he rode the overspill into our home.

Shame was not like us. He did not embody his own nature so much as he tried to press it upon others. He fed off their discomfort with themselves, off their embarrassment and self-loathing. He ground us into weakness to make himself stronger. And because he was not born of our realm, none of us were immune to Shame's power. Not even me.

That did not, however, mean that I was about to stand by and let him hurt another Force.

Neither was Pride, judging by the way he shoved past me and threw himself at Shame, shouting, "Get away from them!" as he went.

Shame cocked an unimpressed eyebrow at Pride, then came forward to grapple with the Sin. Pride threw a punch that did not land, and Shame shoved him into a set of shelves along the wall. Several trinkets rattled and nearly fell, and Lust made a strangled noise of distress.

I thrust my scythe between Pride and Shame before they could launch at each other again. "Enough," I said. "Both of you, out."

Shame sneered at me and cut his gaze back to Lust. "I'm not finished with that one yet."

Lust huffed in disgust and Pride made the sort of sound I normally heard from Gluttony. I stepped forward before Pride could move, hooking the blade of my scythe into the space between Lust and Shame as I went.

"I say you're done," I told Shame. "Get out."

Shame's eyes roved along the blade of my scythe before returning to me. He tilted his head as he regarded me. "I remember you being bigger," he noted casually.

I stiffened but said nothing.

He smirked, scenting an open wound. "The mortal world must really take a lot out of you, if you're bleeding off power. You look like a shadow of your old self. Do you think you could even keep up with a Sin at this point, let alone your old Riders?" He leaned forward, his grin broadening to show too many teeth while the color of his eyes shifted to red. "I'd love to see you try to—"

I ripped the blade of my scythe across his leg.

Shame yelped and jumped away, clutching at the tear in his jeans along his thigh. His hand came away clean. I had not nicked his skin, just as I had intended.

"Maybe someday I'll test myself against a Sin," I said. "But clearly not today."

Shame gave me a final, scathing stare before shouldering his way past me. He made a point of pushing me off balance, forcing me to catch myself on the wall. I felt a mighty need to carve the smirk off of his face, but another idea occurred to me. A much, much better one that would deal with him far more efficiently.

I followed Shame to the door, watching him closely as he made his way down the hall. I waited until he was level with a yellow-painted door that was heavily bolt-locked before calling out, "Oh, and make sure you put back that thing you took from Avarice's room."

Shame halted and swiveled around at the sound of my voice, his heavy brows drawing together into a deep frown. His confusion cleared, however, when someone screamed, "HE DID *WHAT?*" from downstairs, and then footfalls came charging up the staircase. I caught a flash of a metallic blur tearing across the hallway before Avarice slammed into Shame and tackled him to the ground. Shame snarled various insults as he fell, but Avarice was in his element now, and nothing could penetrate his need to take back what he knew was his.

I drew Pride out of Lust's room and gave him a gentle nudge down the hallway. "Please ensure that Avarice does not destroy Shame before I have the chance to talk to all of you."

Pride watched as his fellow Sin managed to pin Shame's face against the carpet, screaming for his possession to be returned. "You don't need Shame if you want to talk to the Sins," Pride observed quietly.

"When I said 'all of you,' I meant Shame, too."

I let Pride give me a skeptical look before I closed the door.

I turned around just in time to see the first tear slide

down Lust's cheek, and then we were sitting on Lust's bed, them crying and me awkwardly rubbing their shoulder and trying to think of soothing words to heal whatever searing pain Shame had left in his wake.

The best I could come up with: "You held yourself together well."

Lust glared up at me through tear-heavy lashes. A small dribble of snot was leaking out of their nose.

It belatedly occurred to me that I must have sounded sarcastic, and I hastily reassured them that I had not intended to be. "I honestly think you lasted longer against him than any of your fellow Sins did. And you were *alone* with him." A horrible thought thundered across my mind as I remembered the way Shame had leered at Lust. "Did he try to—?"

"No," Lust said shakily. They scrubbed their face with the back of their hand and drew in an uneven breath. "Thankfully, that's one level he won't stoop to." Lust wrapped their arms tightly around their torso and shivered. "But maybe that's because he doesn't need to do anything physical to destroy you." They squeezed their eyes shut and said, "He just gets inside your mind, and he picks you apart piece by piece."

I wrapped my arm more firmly around Lust's shoulders and drew them close, knowing that they would take comfort in the gesture. Sure enough, the Sin leaned against my chest and took a firm grip on my robe.

We stayed like that for a few moments before Lust said, "You know, your ribcage is *really* uncomfortable."

"I would wear padding," I said dryly, "but it tends to ruin the whole 'harbinger of doom' thing I have going on."

Lust laughed and snuggled closer.

"Why were you alone with Shame?" I asked after a moment.

Lust shrugged against me. "I couldn't stand the idea of him getting to the others," they said. "And I thought I was strong enough to keep myself safe. I didn't think he could hurt me."

"Stupid of you to think that," I said.

Lust tensed.

"But very brave and noble of you to try to save the others from that pain," I finished.

The Sin relaxed a little. "Thanks, Death." They sat up and took a steadying breath. "I won't make the same mistake again." They cocked a slow grin at me and shifted their hips, offering me a generous view of their posterior. "Especially since you won't always be around to save this glorious behind."

If I had eyes, I would have rolled them. Instead, I nodded pointedly at the door. "I'm sure Pride would be more than happy to take up that position."

Lust giggled and, to my astonishment, actually blushed.

"Are you two not a couple yet?" Normally, I would not have pried like that, but I knew that Lust would not take offense at the question.

They shrugged and settled back on the mattress. "I don't think he's ready just yet. I know he's interested, but Pride's got this whole—" Lust waved their hand in a slow circle, "—thing about needing to be completely worthy of himself, and me."

"Does that bother you?"

Lust shrugged again. "There's something going on there, but we've talked, and I told him I could be patient while he sorts his stuff out, if he really is interested."

"And?"

"And nothing. He'll be ready when he's ready, and I like him, so I think he's worth waiting for." They looked off and quirked their lips into a smile. "Besides, a little anticipation can be so delicious."

"And that's where you lose me," I said.

Lust laughed.

I stood up and offered my hand. Lust took it and let me pull them to their feet. As I led the way out of their room and down the hallway (which was now blissfully vacant of any other Forces), a question formed in my mind.

"How did Shame get in here, anyway?" I asked as Lust and I reached the stairs.

The Sin shrugged. "I'm not sure. All I know is that he appeared a little before you showed up, and now I would very much like to throw him out." With that, Lust hopped on to the bannister and slid gracefully down to the lower level.

I followed more slowly, thumping my scythe on each step and wondering what the Sins could have possibly done to make themselves vulnerable to Shame. I hoped the key to that would lead me to bigger answers, but I had the nasty suspicion that I would only end up with more questions.

An Apocalypse Ride may be called should Death deem the mortal world to be too unbalanced, unruly, or otherwise dangerous.
-- excerpt from the Contract of Mortality, Addendum 3
authored by Death, countersigned by Justice

- 9 -

When I rejoined Lust and the other Sins downstairs, I found Shame standing against the far wall, cradling his arm and trying to look as though the injury did not bother him. Interestingly, now that he was faced with a room full of adversaries, he fixed his gaze everywhere but on them.

As for the Sins, they were all clustered around the couch Sloth had claimed. Their teeth were bared in a variety of snarls as they all (Sloth included) looked at Shame, from the disgusted slash of Envy's mouth to the literal snarl exposing the sharp fangs of Gluttony. Sloth had shifted enough to let Lust join her on the couch, then had leaned back to rest her head in Lust's lap as she regarded Shame with narrowed eyes and half-curled lips. Lust ran their fingers through Sloth's curly fur, regarding Shame with wary tranquility. Pride stood behind the couch with his hands resting lightly on Lust's shoulders, gently massaging the tension out of Lust's posture. Wrath stood next to Pride, cracking her knuckles in a silent promise of violence if Shame so much as breathed too deeply. Still covered in magnetized beer cans, I could not make out Avarice's expression, but I had the distinct impression that he was pleased with himself. He gripped something in his hands, some trophy he must have taken from Shame, even after discovering that the manmade Force had not actually stolen anything from him. I could not be bothered to feel sorry for Shame.

"Now that you're all in one room," I said, drawing everyone's attention to myself, "would someone care to explain how he—" I gestured at Shame with my scythe, "—got in here?"

The Sins exchanged glances, then looked back at me in silence.

I drummed my fingers on the handle of my scythe. "Anyone at all?"

A few of them shifted and cut their gazes at the others again, but no one spoke.

I focused on each of them in turn, waiting to see who would break first.

None of them did. They all returned my stare evenly.

An exasperated sound scratched its way past my teeth as I rounded on Shame. "What about you?" I asked. "*You* must know how you managed to get in here."

Shame did not move for a few moments, and when he finally did, it was to direct his attention to the Sins as their silence stretched on. I saw the exact moment he decided that he could use my dominance over them to his advantage. He leaned against the wall and offered me a lazy smirk. "Isn't it obvious?" he asked, flexing his injured arm as he tested the depth of the pain. His smile grew as he shook the limb out, already recovered from his fight with Avarice. "They're all far too pathetic to compare with me. Just look at them." He jerked his head at the Sins. "There's nothing they could do to stand against me."

A low growl came from the direction of the Sins' couch.

"Before you make them all prone to terrible acts of violence," I said, "I do believe I asked you *how* you were able to get in, not why."

I watched several barbed comments rise to Shame's lips, but he held them back when he saw me take a firmer grip on my scythe. His dark eyes flicked from me to the Sins and back again, weighing the room's level of defiance against him. He did not like what he saw. With a shrug, he turned his attention back to his arm again, making a show out of flexing and stretching it.

"Any thoughts at all?" I asked, my patience stretching thin.

Shame shook his head and pretended his own limb was the most fascinating thing he had ever seen.

I whipped back around to the Sins, my robes swirling. I leveled my scythe at them, and they all flinched. "One of you is responsible for this mess," I snarled, not quite sure if I referred to Shame or the chaos swirl on the mortal world, but they were starting to blur in my mind. I knew for certain that I had not sensed Shame's power in the tainted chaos, but I had the strong suspicion that his appearance here somehow connected to it, even if I could not see it. "Which one of you had the nerve to go against me?"

A wave of tension washed over the Sins, and I

followed in its wake, advancing on their little group. They all shrank away from me, save for Envy, whose gaze and vines crept towards my scythe. I snapped my attention to her. It seemed I should not have dismissed her earlier, after all, and now was the time to get the truth out of her.

"You," I snarled at the Sin of jealousy, pulling my scythe back and raising it for a swing. "What did you do?"

This time, Envy recoiled as far as she could. Her legs hit the couch behind her and she almost fell, but Wrath reached out and steadied her. Though she trembled, Envy did not try to move away from me again.

"What are you talking about, Death?" Wrath demanded, her fire churning in her chest.

I ignored Wrath, focusing in on Envy. I was determined to break her, if that was what it took to get her confession. "You couldn't keep your greedy little weeds to yourself, could you?" I hissed. I raised my scythe higher, more for dramatic effect than any real intent to use it. At least, that was what I told myself. I still sometimes wonder if that was a lie, especially in light of what happened next.

Looking back, I know it wasn't really Envy's fault, but at the time, with the way she had fallen and I had chased after her, we had ended up with some of her trailing vines underneath me. They twisted their way up my scythe handle, finding purchase as they tugged themselves free. All I felt was the sharp pull on my scythe. I swung the blade down and sliced through the vines.

Envy screamed, and the world seemed to stop for

the second time that day.

I had not really hurt her. Envy's vines were superficial elements she'd adapted a long time ago, and she often lost them to scolding Forces and even her fellow Sins when she reached for their possessions. I once saw Gluttony take three off her head when she tried to steal food out of his mouth. But she had been actively trying to take things. She had been behaving true to her nature, teasing and playing with the others.

She had not been terrified as she tried to get out from under the threat of annihilation.

And I, still thinking I had found the source of the threat to both Eternity and the mortal world alike, prepared to strike again.

Before I could, Wrath ripped around Envy's shoulder, putting herself between my scythe and her fellow Sin. Her fire burned brighter as she stared me down. "You will not cut her down," Wrath said, her voice boiling in the air.

This made me pause.

I was more shocked than anything, as very few Forces have ever stood up to me like that before. Not when I was angry to the point of irrationality and clearly ready to use a very large blade on a whim.

My hesitation was enough for Lust to slip off the couch and gently weave their way between Wrath and me, their hands raised in a soothing surrender. They pressed their fingertips to Wrath's chest, pushing her back before focusing on me.

"Please, Death," Lust said softly, "this isn't like you. You've accused one of us of something terrible, but you haven't told us what it is." They extended their hand to me, and I saw the involuntary shiver run through them. Their next words were whispered. "You wouldn't hurt us like this."

I lowered my scythe, and I looked at the Sins, and I saw how afraid they were. And yet, they all met my gaze, somehow accepting my anger. Even Wrath, who was ready to take the blow I'd threatened Envy with. She did not like it, but she accepted it, and was willing to bear the brunt of it. Envy herself was still behind Wrath, but she had made no move to run. She stared at me with naked terror, and her vines…

Her uncut vines were extended forward, braced against the floor, held taught and at the ready to be sheered by a blade.

Even without knowing what she'd done, even with Wrath's protection, she still offered herself for punishment.

In that moment, I knew that I was wrong. I would not find my culprit among the Sins. And I should have realized that much, much earlier. I could only hope they would not bring this up to Justice and demand retribution. It was unlikely, given that the Sins disliked Justice and his fellow Virtues even more than I did, but they would have been within their right to seek him out.

I reeled my anger back in, taking a few steps away from the Sins to show that I did not mean them harm. (Well, more harm.) "I apologize," I told them quietly, keeping my gaze fixed on Envy. "I have made a mistake."

The Sins let out heavy breaths and relaxed against each other.

Shame snorted from his corner. "Observe the

complete lack of surprise throughout the room."

I turned to see him directing his poisonous smile at me. "Careful," I warned him. "Remember whose presence you are in."

Shame chuckled. "Oh, I know all too well," he crooned. "The oldest Force in existence, clearly going senile in their old age."

His smirk widened as I slowly stalked toward him, my mouth open to retort. He abruptly switched his attention back to the Sins before I could say anything.

"And let's not forget what the others are like, shall we?" Shame jabbed a finger at each Sin in turn. "Tedious, predictable anger over the smallest slight against her; seething jealousy over every little thing she can't have; greed so intense he's started picking up empty beer cans just because they're shiny," Shame sneered. "And what's left? Raw arrogance in that one, self-induced powerlessness in that one, I've seen *that* one eat food scraps off the floor like the disgusting animal he pretends to be..." He grimaced. "And, of course, there's the slut of the realm."

A lot of things happened at once in the wake of that speech.

Lust began screaming promises to end Shame in ways that not even I had thought of. Envy joined them, draping her vines over Lust's shoulders and hissing insults so sharp, I was surprised they had not drawn blood. This was punctuated by a clattering of takeout boxes as Gluttony jumped on to the kitchen counter, where he took up a pouncing stance on all fours and snarled loudly. Sloth sat up. Pride vaulted over the couch to cross the room in a blur and pick Shame up by the collar of his shirt, shaking him vigorously. Wrath moved almost lazily, the air shimmering with heat as she drifted toward Shame. Avarice ripped empty beer cans off his body and threw them with enough passion to make up for his severe lack of aim.

I could not help but smile, pleased that the Sins clearly had the matter under control, now that they were all together again. Judging by the look on Shame's face, he seemed to realize that he had underestimated just how much the Sins cared about each other. Even if he could pick them apart when they were alone or in pairs, as a group, he was no match for them.

I took that as my cue to leave before I did more damage. I turned to the door, only to find Sloth standing in my path, regarding me with an icy stare that held no trace of its usual sleepiness.

I stood paralyzed for a moment before whipping a glance over my shoulder. Sloth's couch was now empty, so I had not hallucinated the Sin in front of me. I turned back to her, held up one finger, and managed to get one word out of my stunned mouth: "How?"

Sloth tilted her head. "I *can* move. I simply choose not to."

I remained poised with one finger raised and my head cocked to the side. "Okay, but…" I pointed from her to the couch and back again. "Why?"

Sloth gave me a wry smile. "If something's wrong on the mortal world and you came here looking for the source, it must be really, really bad."

I managed to drag a larger fraction of my vocabulary out of hiding. "I never said anything was wrong on the mortal world."

"You came back to Eternity after how many eons away, and you came *here*, to our den, and asked which one of us had the nerve to go against you. So you clearly think that a Force was responsible, and so there must be some non-mortal trouble happening on the mortal world. Then you threatened to bisect Envy, stared down Wrath, and had to be soothed by Lust, but only our collective fear really calmed you. Whatever's going on, it's got you bad." She tugged up the waistband of her pajamas over her fluffy belly and squared off against me. "So what happened?"

I considered not telling her, but if there was any Sin that I could trust a secret to, it was Sloth. She was far too lethargic to bother passing it on or finding a way to exploit it. At least, she usually was. This sudden surge of energy was new to me, and somewhat terrifying in its strangeness. "There was a soul jump." I finally said, trusting the shouting match on the other side of the room to mask my voice. "First we've ever seen."

Sloth cocked her head, eyes bright with interest. "What's a soul jump?" After a brief explanation, she gave a low whistle. "That's intense." She looked off for a moment, lost in her thoughts. "Something like that would need a lot of power on the mortal world, and whoever did it would probably need to be there at the time of the jump. Which is why you're here, looking for the one that did it."

"You are... very astute," I observed, and Sloth gave me a gleaming smile. I continued before she could grow too pleased. "Or perhaps involved?"

Sloth's laughter was little more than a quiet huff. "Please, Death, I don't get off the couch for anything less than the apocalypse. Even then, it's a fifty-fifty shot."

"You are up now," I observed.

She shrugged. "It could have been the apocalypse."

I had to admit, she made a fair point. Casting a final look behind me at the other Sins, all of whom were too busy arguing over who should be the first to hit a very regretful Shame to look our way, I asked Sloth how likely she was to share our conversation with the others.

Sloth yawned, the sleepy cast returning to her eyes. "I probably won't, unless there's a direct threat to us."

"This may threaten the mortal world *and* Eternity," I said quietly.

Alertness snapped back into Sloth as she considered this. "Chaos overspill from the mortal world?" she asked.

I nodded.

"Yuck." She scrunched her face in disgust. "Do you want my help?"

I gave a bark of laughter before I could stop myself. "Sloth, dear, what exactly can you do from your couch?"

"Okay, first, *rude*. Second, fair, but I overhear a lot whenever anyone thinks I'm sleeping and I'm really just dozing."

I could not imagine how often that actually happened, but I let the statement pass in silence.

"I'll keep my ear to the ground—" (I also let that pass, though I burned to correct her pronunciation of the word "couch,") "—and see what I can find out. Anything interesting, I'll find a way to get it back to you."

This time, I spoke sincerely. "I appreciate that."

Then a thought occurred to me. "You *will* actually let me know in time for me to do something about it, right? You won't sit on it for weeks?"

"Was that quip about the size of my rear, Bone Butt?" Sloth asked sweetly.

"Call me that again, and I'll carve your rear right off of you," I replied with just as much poisoned sugar in my tone.

Sloth eyed my scythe and quirked the corner of her mouth into a smirk.

"Really, though," I said, "*will* you let me know?"

"Maybe," Sloth said. Then she slumped to the floor at my feet, curled into a ball, and began to snore.

"Fantastic," I grumbled as I stepped over her.

I slipped out the door as another series of shouts erupted from the Sins jostling around Shame. The door clicked shut, leaving me with blessed silence. I paused just long enough to admit to myself that I really did need to see the Riders next. Sloth had been right, after all: a soul jump would have required a lot of power on the mortal world, and the Apocalypse Riders were some of the strongest Forces in Eternity.

I did not make it very far from the Sins' home before the door crashed open behind me. I turned to see Pride and Wrath throw Shame out. It was an impressive throw. The manmade Force shrieked as he sailed through the air. He landed facedown on the path and came skidding to a halt at my feet. I twitched my robes away.

"AND *STAY* OUT!" Pride screamed. Then he slammed the door shut.

The mere existence of Shame is not enough to justify an Apocalypse Ride.
-- excerpt from the Contract of Mortality, Addendum 4
authored by Justice, countersigned by Life

- 10 -

eft with no culprit to apprehend and Shame motionless at my feet, I spent a few moments studying his limp form. I wondered when he would move. Manmade or natural, he was still a Force, and a little flight through the air should not have kept him down. And yet, there he was. Lying on the ground. Next to my feet. Possibly injured. With only me around.

Normally, the lack of witnesses around me would have been a prime opportunity to try to get rid of him for good, but I felt a twinge of guilt worm its way across my mind, asking me why I had not helped him up yet.

Was I really so cruel? the guilt whispered to me, trying to find a weak point to feed on.

Yes, I answered before it could burrow deeper. Then I turned around and made myself walk away. The guilt faded with each step.

Shame was fine; his assumption that he could exert his power over me and make me feel embarrassed or even ashamed of my own nature was not. He had already tried to feed off of me once today, and I was not about to give him the chance to succeed when his

91

failure was so much better for my personal health.

I tried to focus on mentally preparing myself for my rapidly approaching visit to the Riders. I knew it would be difficult on a number of levels, and I knew it would help if I went to them with some semblance of a plan in mind. I tried to think of one, but that nagging feeling of guilt would not completely die.

I halted, and heard another set of feet stumble to a stop behind me. I did not turn around. I simply waited, but there was no further sound. I set off again, and now that I was listening for them, I heard the footsteps resume. I stopped again, and so did the Force behind me.

I gritted my teeth and turned just in time to see Shame spin around and angle his face towards the stars. He pretended to study them with great interest.

"Really?" I asked.

Shame looked over his shoulder, as though surprised to see me watching him. "Can I help you with something?" he asked, his tone making it clear that he had no intention of helping me whatsoever.

"Why are you following me?" I demanded.

"I'm not," he said. Amusement colored his voice. "We happen to be going the same way." He scraped his foot along the path and took a few sauntering steps towards me. "And I just happen to be walking a little bit behind you."

"I believe that is the definition of following," I observed.

Shame's mouth curved into a predatory smile. "Dearest Death, are you inviting me to walk with you?"

"No." I turned around and set off again.

Shame refused to let me go. To my great irritation and frustration, he caught up with me in only a few strides. I promised myself I would not look at him, would not give him the satisfaction of seeing me struggle as I urged myself to get away from him. That was a far-gone wish at that point, however.

As I walked, my scythe tapped out a steady rhythm on the path. Shame observed this for a few moments before fixing his full attention on me.

"Is this the fastest you can go?" he asked.

Yes, that's why I historically rode a horse.

The thought had surfaced in my mind unbidden, and I recognized the layer of embarrassment that coated it thanks to Shame's presence. The little fool was still trying to extend his influence over me. I clamped my jaw shut and refused to answer him.

Shame, however, had once again sensed a weakness, and now he picked at it. "I suppose it would take an awful lot of concentration and power to make yourself move, given that you have no muscles. Or ligaments."

Neither do several other Forces, I wanted to point out, but I knew that would only encourage him.

"How *do* you make yourself move?" he asked.

At that point in my existence, moving was as natural a process for me as breathing was for the mortals. It had the same weakness, too: if I started thinking about it, I suddenly had a lot of trouble doing it. I'd purposefully given the mortals that minor problem so that I would not feel so alone every time I accidentally turned myself into a pile of bones draped in what looked like a ragged black blanket next to an overly dramatic farming tool. Of course, I had not experienced that particular embarrassment in several millennia, and I was not about to let Shame steer me into it now. I concentrated on the tapping of my scythe as I walked and tried to drown his presence out. I thought of Life, waiting for me back on the mortal world, and Destiny, fighting to keep the chaos under control while I tried to find the one responsible before we lost everything.

"Why *are* you here?" Shame asked, demonstrating an eerily adept ability to infiltrate a line of thought, even when his victim refused to engage with his questions. "Earlier, you said you made a mistake." We went another few steps. "You came to try to fix it, so clearly it was something the Big Three could not handle on their own." He waved his hands in a dramatic flourish as he said this. "But you came here alone, which means you feel responsible."

I slowed to a halt, and Shame stepped in front of me. I could see something shifting in his face, something truly evil coming to the surface as he honed in on a whiff of someone else's pain. He thrived on this, and I could see his teeth sharpening and his mouth stretching wider as he prepared to feed.

He was Shame, and he always knew where to strike.

"If you're responsible, then it was something you did," he continued. He ran his tongue over his sharpened teeth, leaving them wet and glistening in its wake. "Or maybe, something you refused to do. Either way, it was *your* fault, and now you have to clean up the mess before you doom us all." He took a step closer, landing well inside my personal space. Meeting his gaze was like falling into a hot, slimy pit of pure self-loathing. "But you'll fail," he snarled, "and what good are you if you can't even keep the mortals in check?"

I do believe that the thing I hate the most about Shame is that he is impossible to destroy. The mortals have a nasty habit of reviving him and keeping him around, even when he's off the mortal world and prowling around Eternity, and he heals far too quickly for any of us to get any real satisfaction out of our futile but regular attempts to destroy him.

That said, I did feel a little better after I finished mangling him. I left him in the center of the path and cleaned the blade of my scythe on one of my sleeves as I continued on. I did not look back, choosing instead to enjoy the silence I left in my wake.

Upon the demise of a body, whether by natural or other causes,
Death must harvest the body's soul, distill the soul's power, and
return said power to Life.
-- excerpt from the Contract of Mortality, Rule 2

- 11 -

fter I'd shaken off Shame, the hike to the lair of the Apocalypse Riders was uneventful. It had been a long, long time since I'd been there, but I would never forget the way. Too many things would never let me.

The white path began to change under my feet as I drew closer, becoming a twisted, narrow lanyard of four colors that refused to resolve themselves into a pattern, and yet they kept suggesting that there was some sense of order to their madness, if only I could spare the rest of infinity to tease it out.

Once, this part of the path had been as uniformly wide and white as the rest, built from carefully laid stones that gleamed in the starlight. That was before much of it was stolen by some of the Virtues. They were smart about the theft, taking pieces from the edge of the path and still leaving the Sins and Riders with enough order stones to protect us from the chaos roaming the wilds of Eternity. Then the Virtues had decided that they needed more, so much more, and they had struck while we were distracted by... petty things, I suppose, although they had not felt petty at the time. Perhaps I had simply handled them poorly.

Desperate to make amends for my negligence, I had helped rebuild the path in the wake of the theft and the uneasy settlement Justice helped us reach, but we had needed to pull in new materials that did not fend off the surrounding chaos as efficiently as the order stones did. It wasn't enough. It was the best anyone could do. And that was the complete, unsatisfying truth; I had helped lay the original path, after all, and I knew the restrictions on our resources.

Back when chaos still dominated our existence, I'd learned to fight back, and I had taught the younger Forces to do the same. We had defined our natures and learned to execute control over ourselves, and from that strength, we forged the first order stones. Stark white against the darkness of chaos, these stones gave us a much-needed anchor in Eternity, and helped us find safety in a void that only wanted to tear us apart. The more we anchored ourselves, the stronger we became, and the more order stones we were able to forge and lay. We had also learned that our power was finite, however, and there was a limit to how many of these stones we could make. By then, however, more Forces had been born and made their way to our haven, and we carved a home out of Eternity. We each claimed our own territories, shaping them as we pleased, and connecting them all with a path of white order stones. That path kept the chaos at bay, and kept us all from isolation. And for a time, everything was right.

Then the Virtues had come, and hungry chaos had followed in their wake.

And thanks to them, very few Forces could safely come the way of the Apocalypse Riders now. Fewer still dared to try. The Riders found that they preferred it that way. I could not say that I blamed them.

I did not need Shame near me to feel a fresh spike of guilt as the ruined path under my feet reminded me of all of this. The colored stones pressed hot against my bones as I walked, each step demanding, *Why?*

I did not have an answer to the relentless question. I should have noticed what the Virtues were doing, but I'd already begun to focus my attention on a budding creation with Life, and our blossoming romance. He was patient and forgiving where my previous partner was not, and I'd allowed happiness to blind me to the danger cracking the world around me.

I would be lying if I said that I had not seen the mortal world as an escape from the pain and anger of my loved ones as I waited for them to cool down and forgive my negligence.

I had not meant to stay away for so long. I knew what coming back now would look like; I had helped rebuild the path, yes, but I had not recovered the stolen order stones, I had not been able to help Pestilence regain her corporeal form after the chaos floods devoured it, and I had not stayed to absorb the Riders' pain when they could not lash back at the ones who'd hurt them. Justice had fought to ensure the Virtues' safety, and I—recognizing the looming disaster the destruction of more Forces would bring—had agreed with him. He and I rebuilt what we could by taking power from the guilty Virtues and using it as the foundation for the new path. This depletion of their strength made it nearly impossible for the Virtues and Blessings to come near the Riders and Sins again, let alone venture far from their newly fortified territories. But this did not undo the damage that was already done.

I saw the evidence of this all along the multi-colored pathway that twisted and meandered around what had once been part of the everwood forest, but now was nothing. Back when Justice and I had lain the new path, the undying trees had still grown in this area. They'd been worse for wear, but once we'd drained the last of the chaos out of the area, the trees were still standing. I had taken that as a good omen, thinking that this place would heal. It had not. Evidently, the chaos had leeched too much power out of this part of the forest. While I had been away on the mortal world, the everwood trees had crumbled to dust. There were still a few jagged stumps here and there to remind me of what once was, and to caution me against abandoning this place again. I'd heard tales from Forces visiting the mortal world of what had happened to the forest out by the Sins and the Riders, but until I was walking the cracked and crooked path that wove its way around trees long gone, I did not realize how unprepared for the destruction I really was.

I would not say that I regretted making the mortal world with Life, but I did regret not coming home earlier. If I had tried harder, if I had made the reapers sooner, *before* my duties had become overwhelming, I could have been here. It was a lie to pretend otherwise.

As I walked on, the sky darkened and the stars dimmed, until there was only one blistering pinprick left overhead to guide me. I knew I had reached my destination when the mountains that always sat in the distance were suddenly within reach, and the path began to slope upward again. Thankfully, compared to my trek to the Sins' home, my uphill climb to the Riders' lair was mercifully short.

The path dropped me at the mouth of a cave. There were no ornaments to announce who lived there, but the pervading sense of doom was more than enough to compensate for that. When I stepped inside, torches flared in front of me, illuminating the four tunnels. Each branch was carved in stone that matched the colors of the torches marking them: white, red, black, and pale yellow.

Or there should have been pale yellow. Those torches had not lit with the others, and I noticed that the yellow cave had a sizeable pile of rocks built up across it, blocking anyone from entering. I was certain I had not left my entryway that cluttered when I'd left for the mortal world all those millennia ago. Clearly, this was no longer my home.

Not that I found this entirely unjustified, but the hostility would certainly complicate my attempts to gather information about the soul jump.

Ignoring the urge to clear the stones from my yellow cave, I instead focused on the other torches. I briefly wondered which of the other three Riders would be the easiest to deal with, then realized that this was not the right question to ask. I needed answers, and that meant summoning a Rider who would actually talk to me.

I moved to a red torch. I thrust my hand into the flames, wincing as they flared brighter, growing until they licked the ceiling of the antechamber.

I pulled my hand back before my bones could crack in the heat and shook off the sparks, hoping that I had caught War in a stealthy mood. Sometimes, he liked to use quiet intimidation tactics.

A sudden menacing glow at the far end of the red branch informed me that this was not going to be one of those times.

War made his dramatic entrance by suddenly appearing as a silhouette against the light. He lifted his massive arms above his head to show a longsword gripped in his hands. Then he bellowed a challenge and came barreling down the corridor, each crashing footfall sending a shower of dust and pebbles to the ground. As he charged towards me, his hulking form resolved itself into a shell of interlocking plate armor topped by a horned helmet. He swung the longsword in a glittering arc and screamed all the way down the tunnel.

I drummed my fingers on my scythe and waited for him.

War came tearing out of his cave, his armor gleaming red and silver in the light of the torches. He stopped so close to me that he nearly trampled my toes, whirling his sword over our heads and shouting at the top of his lungs, "WHO DARES INTRUDE UPON THE—" He froze, the sword jerking to a halt. "Death?"

"Hello, War," I greeted him. "I see you're going through a medieval European phase again."

"The classics never die," he rumbled from behind his visor. Two eyes like red-hot coals stared at me from the depths of his helmet.

"I beg to differ," I said mildly.

War gave a booming laugh, then peered at me through his visor. "You seem… different." He lifted his hand and leveled it against the top of my hood. "Shorter."

I pushed his hand away with my scythe. "Still just as deadly," I promised.

War's laugh crashed off the cave walls again as he wrapped one arm around my shoulders to drag me close and crush me against his chest. He lifted me off the ground, scythe and all, in a one-armed hug that threatened to snap my spine. "My darling!" he roared. "I knew you would come back to me!"

My bones creaked as I sputtered out a request to be returned to the ground.

War acquiesced and dropped me. "Are we to ride together again?"

"No," I snapped. I was bent over, one hand trying to sooth my poor spine while the other readied itself on the handle of my scythe, waiting for me to decide if I could get in one good swing of the blade before War could counter the attack. I decided to let the opportunity pass.

"No riding?" War asked, sounding disappointed. He rebounded immediately. "Ah, you have finally realized your feelings and come back for *me*, then!" He opened his arms and stepped toward me again.

I backpedaled faster than I knew I could move. "No, War. No riding, no reunions, definitely none of *that*—" I waved my scythe between us, "—just *talking*."

War stopped before he caught me again. "Talking?"

The black torch flared in its sconce as a thin shadow

stalked into the room. "I know it's a difficult concept for a thundering oaf like you," the wisp of darkness sneered, "but do try your best to keep up when a guest as *esteemed* as Death comes knocking."

I groaned. I'd been hoping I would be able to get War to tell me about the Riders' presence on the mortal world (and how much farther Famine and Pestilence were willing to carry their grudge against me) before the other two Riders realized I was there. Famine and I had no shortage of friction following the order stone theft and my refusal (or failure, according to Famine) to recover what had been taken from us. As for Pestilence and I… well, our troubles had started long before that, back when she had been my partner. That was a long time ago, but our somewhat amicable break had been soured by the theft. I suppose I should have known better than to hope for a quick visit with War alone, all things considered.

"Greetings, Famine," I said with as much neutrality as I could muster. "May your hunger never be sated."

The shadows fell away from Famine, revealing a bone-thin figure not unlike my own, except theirs sported dark skin, thin lips stretched over a wide mouth, and a pair of functioning eyeballs. They stood looking at me for a moment, their petite features screwed up tight in thought, then they unhinged their jaw to bare their double rows of jagged teeth at me.

I did not make the mistake of taking the gesture for a genuine smile.

"What brings Death to our door," Famine hissed, "if not to sound a Rider's call in the hopes that we may deign to answer?"

"Yes, Death," War chimed in. "Aren't you ready to destroy that horrible mortal world yet?"

I bristled at this, but before I could respond, another torch flared. I tensed as I heard Pestilence approach.

"Death is running with those mortal-lovers Life and Destiny now," the white Rider rasped as she joined us in the antechamber. Her permanently incorporeal form buzzed angrily as the swarm of venomous insects that made up her bulk shifted around the filthy whirlwind at her center. "Until the mortals see fit to destroy themselves, Death will be chained to them."

"I helped build that world," I growled at Pestilence.

"You were not made to build," she snapped back, "only destroy."

"Bold words from one who can only bring disease and decay."

"I know my nature, and my place," Pestilence droned angrily. "Just as you once knew yours, before you abandoned everything and willingly built your own prison."

My earlier guilt forgotten, I lunged for her, swinging my scythe. Pestilence dissolved around the blade, her bitter laughter echoing across her fragments as she scattered. She swirled around me, her winds tugging at my robes and blowing grit against my bones.

"You left us," Pestilence said as she churned through the air. "You broke the four and snapped our power, all so you could rule your mortals. And what has that given us?" She reformed next to Famine, back into a whirling swarm of insects and debris. "Nothing but an occasional chance to taste our own strength."

Famine bared their teeth again, and in that moment,

I realized how small I was next to the other three Riders, now that I had sacrificed some of my power to the creation of the reapers. They towered over me, and in sharp contrast to War's playfulness, Famine and Pestilence looked ready to test me, to see if I was still stronger than them.

I knew that I was, but I did not want to give them the chance to challenge me.

I cracked the butt of my scythe down on the ground. "I do not recall you complaining the last time you were on the mortal world," I said. "All of you have run unchecked across that planet plenty of times, always growing stronger for it."

Famine bared their fangs in response. "You left us under War's leadership," they hissed.

That surprised me. "I have no recollection of doing that," I said.

"It was implied," War rumbled. He slapped a gauntlet against his armored chest. "After Death, I am the natural leader!"

I rounded on him. "*You* seized control over the Riders?"

"You weren't here to stop him," Famine snarled.

"Have you any idea what it's like to be at War's beck and call?" Pestilence droned.

I gave her a slow, pointed look. "You are aware of what I do on the mortal world, right?"

"Death always follows me!" War boomed gleefully, answering me before Pestilence could. "And now they are here to follow me again!" He clapped his arm around my shoulders, catching me in a vice grip and making my bones rattle. "Whether we ride or not,

Death knows that their place is with me!"

My anger found its footing then. I placed my hand on top of War's and pried my robes free of his grip, then whipped my scythe around and swung the blade towards his neck. War quickly stepped back and dropped his head, catching my scythe against one of the horns of his helmet. There was a terrible screech, and the horn fell away, shorn clean through by the blade. The curved horn clattered across the cave floor. There was a heavy silence in its wake.

"My place," I growled, "is where *I* say it is. I may clean up after all of you—" I swung my scythe around to point at each of the Riders, "—but I follow no one."

"You followed Life away from us," Pestilence droned quietly.

"By my mercy, Pest, I *just* said—"

"Both are true," Famine cut in.

There was a quality to their voice that I had never heard before, and that stopped me. It almost sounded as though they were nervous. Or afraid, perhaps?

"You made your choice," Famine continued, keeping their gaze on me. They barely parted their lips to speak, now keeping their teeth sheathed and their voice soft. "And it was your choice to make, but you left us, and it's hurt us far more than you could know." Their gaze flickered to Pestilence, who drew in tight around herself in embarrassment.

That stunned me into silence. I did not know what to say.

War, however, did. "I suppose it has been a bit… difficult, shall we say, without you here." He waved toward the pile of rocks sealing off my tunnel. "There were traces of you everywhere, always reminding us that you picked Life instead of your Riders."

I turned my head to each of them. I looked to Pestilence last, and though she would not meet my gaze, I let mine linger on her. "It is possible," I said slowly, "for me to love more than one. You have always known this."

Pestilence swirled uncomfortably. "But you didn't leave us before. We thought we were enough." Her buzzing became angry again. "Now we see that Life will always be more important than us."

My own anger returned to a rolling boil. "I have been working so hard to be able to leave the mortal world. I was never supposed to be there for this long, but—"

"But your precious mortals and precious new partner demanded it," Famine scoffed.

"*But there was no one else* to reap the souls." Before I could think better of it, I gripped the edge of my sleeve and tore a patch of cloth free. "For millennia, I have felt trapped there, and I have been doing everything I can to break the chain that binds me." I balled the cloth in my hand and raised it to my mouth. It was larger than what I normally used, and I knew this would be unpleasant, but in that moment, I did not care. I stared down the Riders and said, "I have wanted nothing more than to come back ho—back *here*." I swallowed the cloth whole, and felt it slip toward my core. It leeched away a fragment of my essence, of my power, but that was enough. The pain was always a little worse with each new reaper I created, but I had always told myself that I could bear it, if it meant being able to leave. To come home. I opened my mouth as the newborn reaper fought to free itself, letting the shadows spill from between my teeth. They swirled in the air, fighting with the light from the three torches, until they coalesced into the sleek equine shape that I'd perfected and come to love.

The reaper whickered as it beat its leathery wings. It was considerably larger than any of its fellows back on the mortal world, easily the size of my arm instead of a little larger than my hand. The reaper circled overhead, buffeting us with the wind of its passing. It raked its hooves through the air as it completed a few passes of the cave before alighting on War's shoulder, stamping its feet a few times as it sought balance on the smooth surface. Its hooves rang against the metal, filling the otherwise silent cave with a discordant melody.

I leaned heavily on my scythe as I recovered from the loss of a piece of myself. "You see?" I asked, my voice ragged. "Nothing... but work."

Pestilence drifted closer to the reaper, which lashed its tail at her approach. "It looks like your horse," she droned. She tried to keep her tone neutral, but I heard the echoes of awe and remorse.

"I assure you," I said, drawing myself upright again, "that was intentional."

She finally turned her attention to me. "You have truly missed us, then?"

"More than you could ever know," I said, and I meant every word.

She thought about those words for a long time. "Why now, Death? Why have you returned, and why do you seem like you do not intend to stay?"

"You would have me?" I asked.

"Do not evade my questions," Pestilence droned, but there was no heat in her voice.

I accepted her offer of a truce. "Something has happened on the mortal world. Something terrible enough to threaten its existence, and Eternity's as well." I waited to see how the Riders would react to this statement, but other than a small uptick in their curiosity, they did not respond. "I need to understand how it happened," I said. "Otherwise, I may not be able to fix it."

Famine crossed their thin arms as they considered this. They exchanged a look with Pestilence before turning back to me. "I do not pretend to wish to see the mortal world preserved," they said, "but I can promise that whatever it was that broke your plaything, it was not of my doing."

"Nor mine," Pestilence said.

I looked back and forth between them, trying to decide if they were lying. Ruinous and terrible though they were, I had never known any of my Riders to be deceivers. They were proud of their power, and would never hide it from me. I had seen that firsthand on the mortal world whenever they came to run across the planet and leave destruction in their wake; I always knew their work when I saw it.

I had guessed incorrectly again, it seemed, and wasted precious time chasing a nonexistent lead.

For their sake, I kept my disappointment out of my voice when I said, "I believe you."

Pestilence's attention lingered on me for several moments. "Whatever questions brought you here," she finally said, "you are free to pursue the answers as you see fit. I will not interfere."

"Nor will I," Famine said.

I nodded to them, and they took their leave. Before they disappeared, Pestilence hesitated at the mouth of her tunnel. She seemed to consider something, then flew across the cave until she had enveloped the unlit torch near my blocked branch. When she pulled away, a small yellow flame was burning bright.

"When you are ready," Pestilence said, "you may come home." Then she whipped herself away.

Famine remained long enough to inform me that they would not be making any sort of housewarming gesture, such as clearing away the boulders from my cave while they waited for my permanent return. Instead, I was free to do that myself. Then they, too, were gone.

That left me, War, and a very unbalanced reaper in the main cave.

I reached up and coaxed the reaper off of War's shoulder, taking it in my arms as best I could. It was not heavy, but the larger wingspan made for an awkward grip, and it took some fumbling before I had a comfortable hold on it.

War gave a grateful sigh when the reaper lifted its last hoof off his armor. Then he laughed again and plucked the reaper from my hands.

"A wonderous little creature!" he said, holding the reaper up to examine. It snapped its teeth against his gauntlet and struggled out of his grasp. "Ha! I like it."

"Of course you do," I said as the reaper fluttered to rest on the cave floor. "Its presence means that someone is about to die."

"Oho!" War exclaimed, turning fully toward me again. "And who have you come to kill now, my darling? Surely not me, now that you've let Pest and Famine go unscathed."

I winced inwardly. "I would not say that they're unscathed."

"Well," War said, his eyes on the reaper as it trotted over to sniff curiously at the boulders piled high in my cave's entrance, "they're angry."

"Are you not?"

War looked at my blocked tunnel for a long, silent moment. "I found an outlet."

I huffed a begrudging laugh.

"What happened on the mortal world?" War asked. "Pest and Famine are sentimental fools, but they're right. You are here for answers to questions you don't seem to fully understand yet."

Silently, I wondered what upheaval had happened in this realm for the Sin of laziness and the Rider of violence to both become so perceptive. I kept the thought to myself. "Someone overstepped their limits on the mortal world," I said simply. "I'm here to make them pay for that."

"Sounds like something Justice would say."

I winced before I could stop myself. "I am keeping Justice on a need-to-know basis for now." I shifted my grip on my scythe. "I would consider my visit here as something he does not need to know about."

War's burning eyes crinkled as he grinned. "I trust you have some suspects to chase down, then?"

"Well, I thought it might have been one of you.

Hence the unannounced visit."

"But instead of a culprit, you found us licking our wounds."

I gave him a pointed look. "Do you *ever* actually do that?"

"Perhaps if anyone ever managed to wound me, I would."

My gaze drifted to the missing horn on his helmet. "I did not mean to hurt any of you," I murmured.

War sighed. "I know, my darling. And so do the others, even if they won't let you see it."

Ah, War. My brilliant tactician and hulking brute wrapped into one devastatingly beautiful herald of the apocalypse. I allowed myself a moment of tenderness and placed my hand on his shoulder. "I am sorry," I said, "but if I'm ever to come h—come back again, I need to fix this."

War gave his armor a shake and drew himself back up to his full height. "As well you should! We can't have some whelp of a Force getting the best of a Rider now, can we?" He ushered me to the mouth of the cave. "You go out there and make them understand what it means to cross one of us." Before I could step away, he caught my hand and ran his thumb across my knuckles. His voice was softer when he asked, "Is there any way I can I help?"

"Look after that new reaper for a bit, would you?" I said, tilting my gaze at said reaper over War's shoulder.

It looked back at me and lashed its tail.

"It would be my pleasure!" War said.

The reaper arched its neck and whickered unhappily.

War shifted back into my line of sight, gently directing my attention back to him. "What else can I do to help you, my darling?"

"Do you know who would want to defy me?" I asked, mostly out of amusement and partly out of hope that he might actually have an answer for me. "Other than Pest and Famine, I mean."

"A Virtue, maybe?" War suggested after a thoughtful pause.

I shook my head, remembering the solid wall of chaos on the mortal world. They may have stolen order stones and allowed a chaos leak to do serious damage to the territories of the Sins and Riders, but a Virtue never would have willingly manufactured chaos on the mortal world.

"Then, no," War said, "I'm afraid I can't think of anyone." His eyes glowed a little more brightly. "Perhaps I could help you look?"

I thought about this for a long moment, but I could not see War assisting me in my promise to Life. He did not lack finesse, but there was a degree of subtlety I wanted in this investigation that I did not think he could achieve. He did not have the patience for it.

"No," I said. "Not this time."

War sighed again, but he nodded his acceptance and let me go. "I'll be waiting for your call, my darling," he said. Then he gave me a wicked grin. "It shouldn't be too long, with the recent advances in warfare the mortals have been making."

I made a noise of disgust and pulled my hand free. When I had walked quite a ways, I found my footsteps slowing until I finally stopped. I hesitated before turning back for a final glimpse of the Riders' cave. Of my home. War was still standing in the entryway. He gave me a cheerful wave.

I surprised myself by lifting my arm and waving back.

*Example countermeasures against a potential chaos overspill
include but are not limited to: [...] methods of containment
that would otherwise be deemed reckless and/or dangerous.*
-- excerpt from the Contract of Mortality, Addendum 2
authored by Death, Life, and Destiny, countersigned by
Justice

- 12 -

Now that I had determined that the mastermind behind the soul jump was not among the Sins or the Riders, I found myself at a bit of a loss. The Riders may have been the heralds of total destruction, and the Sins could bring out the worst in the mortals if their power went unchecked, but Riders and Sins alike had always been honest and open about their intents, myself included. We were never deceitful.

Of course, that meant that I was out of suspects. All I had left was the nagging suspicion that maybe Life had been right, after all; maybe I had not needed to come back to Eternity to fix things. I still believed that it would be drastically easier to save the mortal world if I found the culprit in Eternity, but so far, all I had really done was injure Envy, threaten War, sort of (I think) make up with Pestilence, and waste a solid amount of time.

Maybe it was time to admit defeat and return to the mortal world. There, I could try to help Destiny contain the chaos, maybe even find a way to cut through to the source and stem the flow. Then everything would return to business as usual, although I would need to closely oversee the reapers as they harvested souls, making sure that each and every one of them did their job correctly. Who knew when I would be able to leave again?

And that was if we even found a way to stop the chaos. If we didn't, I did not like to think about what that much chaos could do to a Force like Destiny, who was young compared to the rest of us and not as stable in her own nature. I knew she could hold her own for a while if she had the mortal world to work with, and Life would be there to help if the chaos became too much, but even with Life and I both behind her, we would not be able to protect her from that much chaos. The only way to save us all was to cut off the source.

No, I could not give up just yet. But I still needed to figure out what to do next.

I mulled this over for a few minutes before coming to the conclusion that perhaps this situation required less certainty and more creativity. The more I thought about it, the more I was sure that some inspiration was what I truly needed. I set off again at a brisk pace, determined not to lose any more time.

This, of course, was another easier-said-than-done task that I had set for myself. Inspiration was notoriously difficult to find, after all.

Still, if I managed to catch her, there was a good chance that I could end this quickly. Elusive as she was, Inspiration usually let me have one of her sparks when I asked for it. The only difficult part was actually being able to ask for the spark; one cannot beg a favor from a

Force that is not present.

I knew that Inspiration lived far away from the Riders, somewhere between the Sins and the Virtues but not quite in the neutral territories proper. By design, the exact location of her unanchored home was impossible to pin down, but one could find it easily enough if they held the markers in mind.

As I made my way back towards the more stable areas of the path beyond the Sins' territory, I began to seek out the patch of land that vibrated between luck and intent. It was subtle in its signature, but unmistakable in its uniqueness. Sure enough, the air grew steadily warmer as I approached the correct spot, until a sudden plunge in temperature told me that I had gone too far. Quickly, I backtracked until the air grew heavy with heat again, and then I shuffled back and forth, determining where the hottest place was. When I found it, I stood still and waited.

After a few moments, the air shimmered, and a slim branch in the path revealed itself. The smaller path led to the base of a volcano that seethed with smoke and vibrant embers, staining the path red with their glow. But the entrance to the branching path was blocked by a closed gate carved from the strongest of order stones, too powerful for even me to break through and too high for me to scale. A sign hung across the gate, with curling, sprawling letters that spelled out, "Not home. Back later."

So very helpful.

Unfortunately, there was nothing to be done. Inspiration was not the kind of Force to put up a sign and then hide inside her home, hoping that her visitors would be too put off to approach. She had learned the hard way that I was not such a visitor the last time I had come around, and to my knowledge, she has not tried that trick since. Obviously, I still tested the gate to be certain, using my scythe to push against the order stones and rattle the lock. The gate creaked but did not move.

I decided to leave a note for Inspiration, letting her know that I had stopped by and would be back later. I scratched the words on to the sign with my scythe, ending with my signature. That was official enough to hint at how serious the matter was.

When I stepped off of Inspiration's private path, I felt the air snap closed behind me as her home disappeared. The air was cool around me once again, and I found myself savoring it as I got my bearings and tried to determine my next move, now that this one had not panned out.

I was still positioned somewhere between luck and intent. I knew that I had plenty of intent, but that had not gotten me anywhere useful thus far. So, I decided that it was time to try my luck instead, and pay a visit to the twins.

The total amount of souls that Life may distribute across the
mortal world at any given time shall be limited to three billion.
[Note from Justice: This places a restriction on Life that would
violate Rule 6. Per creation and purpose of the mortal world,
he must be allowed to grow.]
-- rejected addendum to the Contract of Mortality
authored by Death, countersigned by Destiny, vetoed by
Justice

- 13 -

The twins' home was trickier to find than Inspiration's, but with the small mercy that even with the constant fluxes of their territories' locations, these three particular Forces always lived near each other. I kept to the general vicinity of Inspiration's home, traipsing back and forth and feeling out the shifts in the air as I moved, searching for something other than heat this time. There is no wind in Eternity, but anyone could feel the tremble of concentrated chaos lingering off the path. Knowing the twins and their general lack of fear (or, more accurately, lack of good sense), they were bound to be somewhere close to one of the denser spots.

I had just about flushed out where I thought they might be when a spark of light ripped across the air in front of me, burning a bright green line across my vision. I gave an involuntary "Ack!" of surprise as I stumbled off-track and broke my concentration.

I groaned, knowing I would not have much time

before I lost that location and had to feel it out all over again. I looked up to see the green spark trailing out a lazy, incomplete circle over my head, waiting patiently for my response.

Grumbling, I reached out and thrust my hand into the center of the circle. The spark dove in front of me again, this time moving fast enough to catch its own tail. I raised my arm to shield my face against the flare of light that spilled out from the completed circle. The light dimmed when the connection solidified, and I lowered my arm to see the face of a very frazzled-looking Life peering back at me.

"Death," he breathed out with clear relief. "Thank creation I reached you."

"Have I ever not answered when you've called?" I asked. Not waiting for the obvious and only answer, I continued, "This is not a good time, however. I'm on my way to see the twins, and you know how much they hate keeping their home in one spot."

"The twins?" Life asked. "You've found reason to think they're involved?"

"Well, no," I admitted, "but I know it wasn't a Rider, and I sincerely doubt it was a Sin, considering what they were up to when I dropped in."

Life's deep green eyes widened. "You've already seen the Sins?"

"And the Riders, yes. They were the obvious suspects."

"And?" he asked.

"And nothing," I said, not completely succeeding in keeping my tone neutral. "The Sins were the Sins, and the Riders were angry with me for… a lot of things, but

I believe they're innocent in this."

"I see," Life said. He looked off and fell into silence, frowning deeply. I knew that he did not particularly like any of the Sins or the Riders, but he was diplomatic enough not to say anything against them now.

I wished I had more to tell him. Even just the inkling of a fresh suspicion would have made me feel better about the time I had already wasted in Eternity. Instead, I had chased dead ends and demonstrated that it just might be possible to hide from Death, after all. I waited for Life to chime in with an idea, but it became increasingly clear that he was following his thoughts somewhere I could not go, and he was not going to offer me the relief I desperately wanted at that moment.

"Was there something you needed?" I asked, jerking his attention back to me.

Life started as though guilty of something, but recovered himself. "Destiny is having a lot of trouble tracing the source, so we were actually hoping *you* had something for *us*."

"Ah." It was my turn to feel guilty. "Nothing yet. I'm sorry."

"But you're going to see the twins now?"

"If I can find them, yes."

"Do you really think that's a good idea, at this point?" Life asked.

The hard edge in his voice immediately put me on the defensive. "Unless we can suddenly cut through tainted chaos we don't understand, I can't do anything useful on the mortal world," I said tightly.

"I know," Life said, and I heard the effort he put in to softening his tone. "But you do still have responsibilities here. You can't abandon them to run around Eternity."

"I am doing no such thing," I shot back, making no effort to put any sort of gentleness in my own tone. "I am looking for the one who switched two mortals' souls. I feel the need to remind you that this is a massive problem for us all the way around."

"I know," Life said flatly. "And so does Justice."

I froze. "Is he there?"

"He was," Life said. "He had a lot of questions for us."

"About...?"

"The Contract breach, the tainted chaos, where you were and why you had run off... You know, the big stuff that's on everyone's minds right now."

My grip on my scythe tightened until my hands shook. "I trust you told him that I was trying to find answers?"

"Of course," Life said. "And no, I didn't tell him where you were, but I should warn you, he figured out that you were off the mortal world and back in Eternity pretty fast. He'll be looking for you, once he gets back there."

My grip relaxed, but only marginally. I was not certain how long I could evade Justice. If he found me, he would either take me back to the mortal world, or insist on coming with me as I continued investigating. He was an excellent judge, but only when he had a definitive culprit in front of him. Without one of those, he would either be useless to me, or dangerous. The last thing I wanted was him deciding that my reapers were at fault before I found a shred of evidence that could definitively prove that they had not been involved in the soul jump.

"I'll have to move fast, then," I said. "Find everything I can before he finds me."

A flash of sympathy and concern crossed Life's face. He leaned in closer and kept his voice low when he spoke again. "I don't mean this cruelly, Death, but what if there is nothing for you to find, and it really *was* your reaper that did this?"

I shook my head so hard, my hood snapped in the still air. "Taking a soul before its time would have been one thing, but my reaper *didn't do that*. It came back with the wrong soul, because that soul was already in the wrong body." My earlier defeatism was all but forgotten. "A Force did that, and I'm not going to stop until I find out who."

"But you already said it wasn't a Sin or a Rider, so…?"

"So it was someone else!" I snapped. "Virtue, Blessing, neutral, who*ever* it was, I will find them."

"Okay, okay," Life said, backing off again. "It's just…" he sighed and looked over his shoulder at something I could not see. I glanced at his surroundings and realized that he was in Destiny's room. In the pause, I heard the furious typing of her labor. "I don't think we expected finding the source of the chaos on the mortal world to be this hard," Life said.

"It would be a lot easier," Destiny shouted, "if I knew what I was looking for!"

The fact that Destiny was still firing angry comments at us instead of falling into despair gave me fresh hope. Not a lot, but enough to make me feel better.

"If we knew that," I said in response, "I wouldn't need to be here, would I?"

The typing did not let up, but one of Destiny's hands appeared over Life's shoulder, flashing me a rude gesture. As it disappeared to rejoin its companion in trying to destroy her keyboard, Destiny said that at least one of us had better make ourselves useful by bringing her a large amount of pizza.

"I believe she means you, my dear," I said to Life. I started to say goodbye, but Life kept talking.

"I'm sorry," he blurted, "about what I said earlier." He gave me a small, sad smile. "You would never abandon me, right?"

"Of course not," I said, the anger gone from my voice.

"I know you still have work to do, but... Are you coming home soon?" he asked.

I hesitated. "If I can find the one who did this, then yes," I said. "Otherwise, there's still a little time, and I intend to use it to find whatever I can." A thought occurred to me, and I raised my voice. "There *is* still time, right, Destiny?"

"A little more than half a day," she called back, "but I'd prefer if you didn't cut it close."

"Will do what I can," I promised.

The background moved around Life as he took a few steps away from Destiny. In a low voice, he said, "Hurry back, Death. I don't like the idea of you out there alone if the Riders are angry with you."

I remembered Pestilence relighting my torch and Famine hesitating before they left, teasing me but lingering all the same. "I will be all right," I told him.

"I'm far more worried about Justice and trying to get to the twins at this point."

"Remind me again why you are bothering with them?" Life asked as he drifted back toward Destiny.

I felt a shift in the air around me, a sudden release in pressure that signified a large chaos spot moving on. Time was up, and now I would need to find it all over again. This put an edge into my reply. "For someone to have performed a soul jump so perfectly, *something* must have aligned for them. At this point, I'm wondering if a solid bit of luck didn't put them in the right place at the right time to make this happen."

Life opened his mouth, but Destiny beat him to it.

"If that's true," I heard her say, "and you can find out how much was involved, that could help me narrow down the search for the source. It won't do much to counterbalance all that chaos already swirling around out there, but it'll be something, at least."

"I'm certain luck is only part of the equation," I told her. "There were several different traces of power in that chaos, and it would have taken more than luck for anyone to do this." A thought bloomed across my mind, and I felt my resolve harden again. "I haven't found the culprit yet, but maybe I can track down enough of the signatures from the tainted chaos to let you trace the source on the mortal world." I hesitated as a thread of doubt wove its way across my mind. "I was so sure a Sin had been involved, though," I murmured.

"Well, you did check," Life said. "Now you know for certain that they weren't."

"Things with them were a little… strange, though.

Perhaps I'll stop by their territory again before I leave, if Justice hasn't found me by then."

"Why?" Life asked. He was frowning again. "And strange how?"

I grimaced, remembering Shame's presence and attempt to overpower me, followed by Envy's innocent teasing and the way that had ended. "You don't want to know."

"Death—"

The chaos shifted again, withdrawing further away from the edges of the path. I took a couple of steps after it before I could stop myself.

"I need to go," I told Life. "Let me finish up here. I'll be back soon."

I waved my hand through the glowing circle, breaking the connection before Life could speak again. I knew that he worried so much because he cared so intensely, but sometimes, I wished he would let me work.

- Part Three -

Bargaining

Chance and Fortune are not allowed to throw comets and other things at Earth just because they are bored. [Note from Justice: Rule 6 technically allows for things like this, but I'm sure I can get them to help with the cleanup. That alone should dissuade them from pulling another stunt like this.]
-- rejected addendum to the Contract of Mortality authored by Death, countersigned by Life, vetoed by Justice

- 14 -

Thanks to Life's unscheduled check-in, the patch of chaos I'd been tracking had slipped so far away from the path that if I wanted to find it again, I would need to do the unthinkable: step off the path.

I could survive the wilds of Eternity. I'd done it before. But I had been stronger the last time I had needed to fend off raw chaos, and I was not keen on the idea of testing my durability. Also, there was always the chance that something could go wrong. Better to come back later, when the chaos was in a more cooperative mood and I would not need to search blindly for the twins.

Of course, that left me without a clear way forward. I turned my face starward, thinking that the sight of the familiar, unchanging constellations would spark my memory and remind me of another Force that I had reason to be suspicious of. If Inspiration had been home and I'd been able to get a spark from her, this tactic might have worked. Instead, the stars revealed that I was not the only Force who had recently returned to Eternity.

I saw his black wings against the night, and a flash of gold as he cast his awareness about, seeking something. Seeking *me*, really. There was no sense in being coy about it.

Justice was back from the mortal world, and he was one glance away from finding me.

"Oh, destroy me," I groaned.

I knew only one way to lose him. So I turned, and lunged off the path.

I was immediately swallowed by darkness, which might have unnerved a lesser Force. For me, it was like revisiting a distant memory. Granted, it was an unpleasant memory, and I would have preferred to forget it. If I wanted to shake Justice off my trail, however, I needed to risk reliving my days of being torn apart, and keep moving forward. At least now there was a chance I would run into the twins.

I kept my gait slow and a firm grip on my scythe as I walked. There was nothing to see, and I had to let instinct guide me. My instincts took me through a few lesser pools of chaos, too shallow to pose any real danger if I kept my wits about me, but I felt their cold presence sucking at my feet and tugging on my robes and scythe, trying to coax me under as I waded into them. Instead of balking at their touch and veering on to a different route, I simply kept moving along as straight a line as I could. Experience had taught me that as long as I followed a highly ordered route and did not let myself be distracted, I would not be overcome by the chaos. Of course, that's easiest done when one is not being stalked by a massive swell of the stuff.

I felt it roll across my path every now and again, sending out ripples of chilly confusion and interest. Its visits were not so frequent as to suggest a pattern to its movement, but they were enough to let me know that the chaos sensed my presence, and it was hungry. I had to pause twice when the chaos swell came far closer to me than I would have considered ideal, waiting for it to pass when it failed to find me. We played this game long enough that my nerves were frayed; I could not help but wonder if I really was still strong enough to fend off that much raw chaos. On the mortal world, I'd had the shadows to shield myself. Off the path in Eternity, everything was darkness, and all I had to defend myself against the chaos were my scythe and my diminishing ability to restrict my rising panic.

I do not know how long I wandered through the dark, my attention riveted on the chaos swell as it ricocheted around me. In hindsight, I should have expected what came next, but I was busy weighing my diminished power against my fear of being devoured, and I did not realize I had stumbled into another chaos pool until it caught my foot and pulled me down.

I was fortunate; the larger swell had moved away, and I kept enough of my wits about me to keep my scythe free as I fell. My initial surprise was slammed aside by eons of conditioning, and my mind flew through the rules that governed my existence. I called up all the things that made me *me*, and I came up short, buried hip-deep in the icy chaos pool. It lapped greedily at my torso, reaching for my core, but I had caught myself in time. Now I just had to free myself before it leeched me dry from the waist down.

I began the slow process of freeing myself, repeating *I am Death, I am the end* in a steady mantra. I stole my freedom back one painful shift at a time, wriggling myself free where I could and cutting the chaos with my scythe when it refused to let me go. I began to rise out of the pool, never quite brushing a bottom but feeling it become shallower and shallower with each repetition of the whispered words. I had just managed to free my knees when a fresh wash of coldness hit my skull, and I froze.

The chaos swell came so close then, I could smell the absolute nothingness of it, somehow rancid and pure all at once. The chaos pool that had snared me trembled as the swell rolled past, as though it were excited by the prospect of merging with the larger mass. I kept very still. I did not allow myself to think about what would happen to me if this smaller pool called to the swell, and let it sweep us both up.

Lucky for me, the swell rolled on, and I cut myself free from the pool and moved away as quickly as I dared.

There was only one positive to nearly being trapped and swallowed by not one but *two* patches of chaos: it meant that I was getting close. The twins had always flirted with danger, as though being immortal meant that they were also indestructible. They kept themselves tethered to the safety of the path by a thin ribbon of order stones, but it was such a flimsy anchor, it slid from place to place, as though by its own will and whim. Sometimes, I doubted that it even existed, and the twins merely *said* that they kept themselves connected to the main path as a means of placating the rest of us.

I certainly did not find their strip of order as I pressed on, but I was, finally, rewarded for my trials.

After escaping the hunting swell and stumbling through one last chaos pool, my outstretched fingers brushed against a wall of stones. I pressed my hand firmly against the rough surface, and the darkness around me melted away. I looked down to see that I was standing on a very, very thin branch of the order stone path. I looked up to see the most precariously built structure in existence, held up by sheer luck alone; it certainly was not obeying any laws of physics, immortal or otherwise.

To say that the "building" (for lack of a better term) was very top-heavy would have been an understatement. It was shaped vaguely like a pyramid, somehow resting on one of its points. Towers with holes that served as windows jutted off at impossible angles from every side of the structure, and I thought I saw a lowered drawbridge before the building tilted under the pressure of my hand and rotated that side out of sight. Strips and beams of everwood ran through the structure at seemingly random intervals, but the bulk of the building was made out of what looked suspiciously like chaos stones.

Knowing the twins, I should not have been surprised that they'd taken to mining the denser forms of chaos around them, simply because there was a small chance they could do it successfully.

I also should not have been surprised to have found

them while they were in the middle of an argument. Truth be told, I do not believe there is enough luck in all of Eternity to find the twins when they are *not* bickering about the potential outcome to whatever foolish gamble they have just cooked up, and this was no exception. Judging by the heated voices drifting down from the upper parts of the building, I had caught them just as they were getting fired up.

I decided it would be better to get my visit over with than prolong it any further.

Making certain I did not step off the path again, I drew back a few paces from the fortress and called for Chance and Fortune.

The arguing abruptly cut to silence. A few moments later, one of the twins popped their head over the edge of a balcony that had no business resting at that angle. The other's face appeared in a large hole in a wall that looked like it connected to nothing. Both peered at me curiously.

Identical in their youthful appearance with midnight skin, bright yellow eyes, and straight, starlight-colored hair that hung to their waists, I was not certain which twin was which. Despite their striking coloration and graceful builds, the twins were strangely bland-featured, with nothing to set them apart other than their natures. Even that was subtle at best.

However, as long as Chance and Fortune proved willing to help me and did not try to suck me into whatever bet they had going, I did not need to know who was who. I simply wanted to get the information that I needed, and get back to the main path.

I knew that was a foregone desire when the twins' yellow eyes lit up with recognition and their faces split into identical grins.

"Death!" the one on the balcony called. "You're just in time to settle a bet."

"Of course I am," I muttered. Louder, I called back, "I'm afraid I don't have time for that right now. I need to ask you two a question."

"A trade, then!" the twin in the wall said. They leaned over the edge of the stones, bending dangerously far out to get a better look at me. The whole structure swayed dangerously, and the twin on the balcony shot an irritated look at their sibling. With that small gesture, I knew that Chance was speaking to me from the window. "An answer for an answer," he called, his hips pressed against the edge of the wall.

"You *are* here at the perfect moment," Fortune added, resting her arms on railing of the balcony. The structure swung back toward some semblance of equilibrium.

"I really don't have time for this," I told them. "There's a problem on the mortal world and I—"

"It won't take long," Chance whined from the wall. He twisted around to look at his sister. "Best four-hundred-and-seventy-three out of nine-hundred-and-forty-five wins it all."

"Deal!" Fortune called back. "Okay, Death, time to settle the bet."

"I do not recall agreeing to play this game," I shouted up at them.

"But you came just when we said we needed an outside opinion," Fortune said. "Good luck brought you here, and it would be bad luck to turn away now."

I failed to see the logic in that, but the twins were impossible to argue with. It was faster and easier to just go along with whatever asinine thing they were betting on at the moment. So I reluctantly consented.

"Excellent," Chance said. "Now, this is very important, so listen closely."

There was a pause so dramatic that I lost my patience.

"I'm listening!" I shouted.

"If we flipped a coin right now," Fortune said, "would it land on heads or tails?"

This time, the pause was on my end.

"Is this really what you two are betting on now?"

"Heads or tails?" Chance and Fortune demanded in unison.

"Destruction give me strength," I groaned. Then I very patiently informed the twins that with their luck, the most likely outcome was that they'd flip the coin and the impact would break this me-defying structure they had somehow cobbled together out of what looked like pure chaos and threads of hopecloth.

The twins exchanged a look.

"You know," Chance said, "we never did consider the probability of that outcome."

"Truly something to think over carefully and analyze thoroughly," Fortune said.

"Indeed."

They held the look for another moment.

"Or we could flip it now?"

"Let's flip it now!"

"HOLD IT!" I shouted.

Fortune paused, the coin already in her hand. "Death," she said patiently, "we really need to settle this, so if you don't mind…"

"An answer for an answer," I reminded the twins. "So before you flip the coin and then disappear to catalogue the results in whatever nonsensical database you two keep—"

"How did you know about the database?" Chance asked.

"—you're *going* to answer my question."

Chance and Fortune made twin noises of disgust before drawing out an irritated *fiiiiiiine* in unison.

"Thank you," I said. I drew myself up to my full height and took a firm grip on my scythe. I knew I had to be direct with them, and I could only hope they understood how serious I was when I said, "Did you two give a lot of luck to another Force?"

"No!" Chance called immediately. He turned his attention back to Fortune, who readied the coin in her hand.

"Chance," I said, keeping my voice as steady and imposing as I could, "think very hard about this. Have you given anyone a *lot* of luck, or sent a particularly large amount to the mortal world? Far, far more than you've ever given out before?"

Chance frowned at me, then turned to look at his sister. She returned her brother's gaze with equal bewilderment.

"We don't give luck to anyone," Fortune said.

"Especially not mortals," Chance added.

I nearly threw up my hands in exasperation. "I know for a fact that you two send plenty of luck to the mortal world, both good and bad. Or did you think I never noticed that comet that took out the dinosaurs?" I was becoming furious just thinking about how long it had taken to clean up after that mess.

"But it's true," Chance protested. "We don't *give* anyone luck. Not Forces, and not the mortals."

"We like to throw it on to the mortal world and see what that stirs up," Fortune chimed in, "but we never pass it to anyone specifically." She cocked her head, considering. "Would it even be luck at that point?"

"More like fate," Chance agreed. "And that's Destiny's territory, not ours."

I held up my hand before they could follow that branch of logic (or whatever the twins operate on) any further. "There's something happening on the mortal world, and I think—no, I *know* that a lot of luck was involved. Whether you two meant for this to happen or not, I need you to tell me if that's true. Have you sent more luck than usual to the mortal world?"

"No," Fortune said with total finality. Then she exchanged another glance with her brother as I began to turn away. "Although, we never did find out what happened to that bit that went missing."

"What's this now?" I asked, whipping my attention back to them.

"Some of our luck went missing a little while ago," Chance said. "We thought maybe some chaos ate it, but the chaos has never taken that much before."

I felt a tightness wrap around my spine. "How much are you missing?"

"Tah-tah-tah," Fortune said, holding up a finger. She pointed down at me. "We've answered *two* of your questions now, and the bargain was one for one. That means you have to stay and settle our next bet."

I started to protest, then paused and looked at the brazen challenge to gravity the twins had built. "All right," I said, "but only if my prediction about the coin toss does not come true."

The twins giggled their acceptance of my terms, and Fortune flicked the coin high into the air. As it spun, Chance drove himself even further out of the window to watch. I took a few large steps away as the structure tipped again, and Chance nearly fell out the window. He threw himself backwards to compensate. The building swung back the other way, and Fortune stumbled with the sudden shift, disappearing from my sight. The coin winked through the air before landing with a soft *tnk* on the balcony railing, and then the entire fortress came crashing down.

When the dust had settled, the rubble began to shift. Eventually, Chance and Fortune shoved the chaos stones and broken pieces of everwood off of themselves, and sat blinking amid the ruins of their fort. They looked at each other, and then at me.

"A lucky guess," I said.

The mortals shall possess free will. Life and Death may override this, but only insofar as extending or shortening the mortal's intended lifespan in a genuine effort to preserve balance and protect the integrity of the mortal world's existence.
-- excerpt from the Contract of Mortality, Rule 4

- 15 -

After a few more guessing games in exchange for more information from the twins, a shouted threat to end the pair of them if they did not give me a straight answer, the onset of the worst headache I had ever experienced, and a trip to the twins' hidden mines that sobered all of us, I was back on the main path. There was a solid lump of luck hanging from a cord around my neck, reluctantly given to me by the twins. We had tried to work out some way to illustrate how much luck had been taken from their mines, but once it became clear that they could not convey the amount they had lost without a physical representation, I had to insist on taking a comparable piece with me. It weighed heavy against my chest, knocking my ribs with each step I took. I watched it thoughtfully as the gold and silver surface winked in the faint starlight. Considering the twins dispersed their luck in flakes across the mortal world, this was a massive amount that I was carrying. Its surface felt cool to the touch and while it did not seem to exude any real power, it somehow felt… volatile.

I knew that I needed the luck to help me evade Justice *and* track down the mortal that was spitting chaos back on Earth, but I'd be glad to be rid of my new accessory as soon as possible.

I was also a little surprised that the twins had known exactly how much luck to give me, but they had amazed me further after taking me into their hidden mine. I knew of no other Force who had been down there, save for the twins themselves and our mysterious thief. Chance and Fortune had shown me the veins of good and back luck running through the chaos stone, and the spot where someone had pried out a solid chunk of pure good luck. There had been no giggling then, and the twins had been oddly somber when they asked me what I intended to do when I found the culprit.

They must have found my answer satisfactory, for they had nodded and then gone to another vein, this one a swirling mix of impure luck. The twins had taken extremely complex measurements that I could not even begin to comprehend before carefully carving out the sample. They had secured the excavated lump of luck to a cord before handing it to me. They promised that what I now carried with me was balanced enough not to interfere with my investigation. Or at least, they gave me their version of a promise, which involved Chance betting that the luck would bring me minor inconveniences while Fortune claimed that I would have nothing but small miracles from now on. I took that to mean that I would have a perfectly normal mix of the two. Or so I hoped. It did me no good to worry about it either way.

The twins made me swear that in return for lending me this luck, I would bring it back to them unharmed, and tell them every last detail of my experiences while carrying it. They wanted to know everything, no matter how minor it may have seemed at the time. I caught the identical gleams in their eyes and understood that, as always, settling their bet was to be their price.

I knew that when I returned the luck, it was going to be a long, exhausting visit, but for Destiny's sake and for the survival of the mortal world and our own realm, I agreed. Chance and Fortune escorted me back to the surface, bid me farewell, and then scampered back to their collapsed fortress, already planning new ways to rebuild it.

I took the thin ribbon of white order stones back to the main path, careful to keep to the branch's safety. I may have had some good luck around my neck, but there was bad luck there too, and I did not want my first experiment with the balance to involve raw chaos. One near miss was more than enough.

When the twins' path dropped me back at the main walkway, I gave the skies a thorough scan and listened closely for the sound of Justice's wingbeats. I saw and heard nothing. I must have shaken him off by trekking across the chaos fields, but I knew that it wouldn't be long before he returned.

Turning my attention back to the path, I found that I had arrived very near the place where I had originally stepped off. The air felt warm around me, signaling that I was once again close to Inspiration's home, and

I had not needed to search for it this time.

I imagined one tick in Fortune's good luck column as I set off to find Inspiration's volcano, hoping that I would find the elusive Force at home now. I quickly found the branch in the path, but came to a halt at the gate again, seeing that it was still closed and locked. The sign bearing Inspiration's original message along with my response was still in place, but beneath my signature, a fresh bit of curling script read, "Sorry I missed you. Had to head out again. Busy day!"

The black ink was still wet in the starlight.

A low growl of frustration escaped me before I could stop it. I begrudgingly added a tick to Chance's bad luck column as I added my own spikey message: "Been by twice now. Patience and time running out. Need to talk."

I signed it with a little more vigor than I needed to, carving deep into the wood and grumbling about the balanced mix of luck hanging around my neck and the sheer audacity of it to drop me in front of Inspiration's home *after* she had already come and gone. I understood that a gift of mixed luck was the safest thing the twins could have given me, but that did not mean that I needed to be happy about it.

Back on the main path once again, I considered who I should visit next. The stolen luck from the twins had been a nasty but enlightening surprise, and I could not help but wonder if there were any other Forces that were missing something. I was sure that the Sins and the Riders would have told me if something had been stolen from them (Avarice especially), but just in case, I decided that I would swing back around to them before I left Eternity again. Much like the order stones all those eons ago, there may have been something missing that they weren't aware of yet. For the time being, I was still searching for a culprit, and with no other leads, I knew that there was only one way forward for me.

I had to go to the other end of the path.

I could have delayed the inevitable and traipsed around the neutral territories for a bit, checked to see if anything was amiss in that area, but I knew that I did not have the time. There also wasn't anything in the neutral territories really worth stealing, if thievery truly was becoming a problem in Eternity once again. There simply wasn't enough power in the neutral territories for anyone to set their sights on.

I did not count the twins and Inspiration as neutral Forces. Their unanchored homes fluxed between the Virtues and the Sins, the Blessings and the Riders, but they kept themselves off the path and guarded themselves very well. Anyone who would steal from them would have needed to be committed to the task, not striking out on a whim. And I already knew Forces who had done that once before.

In spite of what I had told myself earlier, it simply made sense to head into the Virtuous lands, no matter how badly I did not want to.

And I really, *really* did not want to.

As in Eternity, Forces that are directly and completely antithetical to each other may not occupy the same place and time on the mortal world. [Note from Death: This is already a natural law of existence and is therefore not physically (or metaphysically) possible. I find this redundant and unnecessary.] [Follow-up Note from Life: Maybe it is, but better safe than realm-ripped-apart-because-War-found-a-workaround levels of sorry.]

-- excerpt from the Contract of Mortality, Addendum 5 authored by Life and Destiny, countersigned by Justice

- 16 -

ometime later, I found myself sitting in Peace's library, feeling more uncomfortable than I ever remembered. That included my early eons spent being ripped apart and smashed back together by pure chaos. At least that pain had only been physical. It was nothing compared to sitting in an armchair so under-stuffed I was nearly drowning in the upholstery, and choking down green tea with cloying amounts of sugar and milk while listening to Peace drone on and on about all the things he believed were wrong with the immortal Forces around us.

Truth be told, I had not intended to visit Peace at all. He had nothing worth stealing, but he was on the way to the Virtues, and he did spend the majority of his free time trying to ingratiate himself to them. He was never very successful in that endeavor. Based on his mood,

I'd caught him in the wake of a fresh rejection from the Virtues. If I sat back and let Peace talk, perhaps he would reveal something about himself, or the other Forces. I could swallow a little tea in exchange for a potential clue.

When I'd shown up at Peace's door and told him that I was hoping for his help with something, he had scoffed and launched into a list of theories about all the things that could have caused me to come to him, and why they had so predictably gone wrong. None of said theories were plausible even by the greatest stretch of the imagination, but I knew that if I wanted any actual information out of Peace, I had better not interrupt. I may have been willing to admit that I needed Peace's help, but I had not told him anything beyond that. It wasn't that I didn't think he could be discreet; I *knew* he would not be. I also did not want to give him another thing to pick at for the rest of our existence, however long or short that proved to be.

So, I tried to keep myself from disappearing inside his armchair, drank the minimum amount of tea required to be polite, and watched for the pair of glowing doves that kept trying to deposit a crown of olive leaves on my head. Sure enough, the infernal white birds approached me again, and I shooed them away with frantic hand waving in the airspace immediately above my skull. The doves retreated with reproachful coos, coming to rest on one of the curving bookshelves. They settled in to wait for me to let my guard down.

Safe for the moment, I looked around the library again, watching the other doves flit back and forth across the circular room, darting from shelf to shelf in streaks of feathers and light. I did not understand the purpose of having so many birds, considering the books seemed to organize themselves according to whatever bibliophilic system had caught Peace's whimsy at the moment. The leather-bound tomes floated out of the shelves and silently re-slotted themselves into place, sometimes drifting so far upward that they disappeared into the deep blue haze that concealed the upper parts of Peace's library from my gaze. As if the doves and the millions upon millions of books were not enough, olive leaves and branches decorated almost every surface, from actual olive branches resting on the low table in front of me to the still life paintings on the walls and the abstract sculptures of olive leaves that served as bookends on some of the shelves. There was also a massive fireplace in the library, with a bright, cheerful fire inside, but it made no sound. Peace preferred it that way.

I watched Peace stoke the silent fire as he continued to prattle on about the other Forces. Tall, thin, and varying shades of olive from his toes all the way to his wispy, brushed-back hair, Peace was dressed in a white robe not completely unlike the one I'd seen Pride wearing earlier. I considered telling Peace this, but knew that would only lead to trouble.

"And Wisdom," Peace said as he replaced the poker and took the seat across from mine, close to the stifling warmth of the fire, "thinks she is so smart with her banks of knowledge, but does she have anything like this?" His eyes—pure, shining black from edge to edge—skimmed the room. He gestured at his collection of books and smiled, proudly displaying his flat, even teeth. "I think not!"

Sensing an opening, I clawed at it. "That's actually why I came to you first," I said, struggling to keep my voice pleasant. Between his incessant chatter and the over-sweetened tea, I was finding it hard not to turn my scythe upon myself and find some temporary relief in oblivion before I reformed somewhere in Eternity (preferably somewhere far, far away from that awful armchair). "Wisdom may be helpful in some regards," I said, "but this situation requires more… cleverness, shall we say."

Peace sniffed and settled back in his seat. "I have often said that Wisdom compensates in information for her severe lack of wit."

Ah, so Wisdom turned him away this time, I thought to myself.

"Indeed," I said aloud. In that moment, I was thankful that I did not have eyes. They would have betrayed me by rolling so hard, they might have popped out of my skull, and I would not have faulted them for it. Within days, Peace would be singing praises of the Virtues again, Wisdom included, as he tried to worm his way into their good graces. At that moment, however, I knew that I had my best chance at getting information out of him. "I come to you regarding a problem on the mortal world," I continued.

Peace sputtered into his tea and delicately hit his chest as he cleared his throat. "That horrid little place?" He held out his cup and saucer, and several doves immediately flocked to collect them. When his hands were free, he crossed one leg over the other and sat

147

back again with a dismissive wave. "That pathetic, filth-encrusted dimension you call the mortal world has been nothing but a problem since its inception."

I somehow managed to restrict the impulse to point out that all of Peace's doves and olive branches had been taken from said filth-encrusted dimension. I took another sip of tea to give myself time to think of all the problems it would cause if I destroyed Peace. The Riders would thank me, certainly, but War would run unchecked, and that was the last thing any of us needed. "Indeed," I said again, opting to play along with Peace's line of thinking in the interest of finishing with him quickly. "But you see, something's happened there that none of us have ever seen before."

"Ah," Peace said, leaning forward with fresh interest. "Hence why Wisdom would not be able to help you."

"Precisely." I considered my tea again but decided that I'd drunk enough that it would not be rude to put it down. I reached for the table, but several doves nearly attacked me in their frenzy to collect the fragile cup and saucer.

"So," Peace said, not bothering to conceal his smugness now that he knew for certain that he had the opportunity to show up Wisdom, "what is it that I can do for you?"

I kept my attention on the doves as they flew away, searching for the pair that waited to ambush me with the olive leaf crown. They were still on the shelf, but I saw them tuck their wings and settle back down, as though they'd been preparing to fly. I could not be certain, but I swore one of them glared at me. Not daring to look away from the scheming birds, I said to

Peace, "I was wondering if you had noticed any of the other Forces acting out recently, or paying more attention to the mortal world than they normally would."

I was so focused on the doves with the crown that I did not immediately realize that Peace had not responded. When I turned back to him, he was regarding me with a cold stare.

"I am not your personal sentry," he remarked. "I do not spy on my fellow Virtues, nor do I suspect that any of them would ever bother with that horrible mortal world any more than *you* deemed necessary. Or have you forgotten that Contract that you and Justice were so eager to bind us with?" He conveniently did not mention that he and every other Force who used the mortal world had willingly signed the Contract, or that the Virtues had a history of acting out. Instead, Peace raised his head a little so that he was looking down at me with his flat black eyes. "And I do *not* concern myself with the activities of those evil Forces you seem so fond of."

This remark I did not let go by unchallenged. "They are not evil," I said quietly. "They are simply true to their natures, which stand opposite to yours."

Peace waved his hand dismissively and closed his eyes, leaning his head back against his armchair. "Their natures are exactly the problem. Those lesser Forces cause all sorts of trouble. Surely one of *them* is to blame for your little issue on the mortal world." He smiled again. "In addition to all the other problems it already had, of course."

"I do believe I am done here," I said, pushing myself

to my feet. I reached for my scythe, only to make a disgusted sound when I saw that olive leaf wreathes had been twined around it. Several doves looked at me smugly as I began to pull the leaves off.

"You know what you have to do," Peace said.

I turned to see him watching me again, his eyes hard.

He took my silence as an invitation to continue. "Destroy that wretched mortal world, *and* those evil Forces you let run amuck." He tilted his head and held up one hand, as though he had solidly won whatever debate he thought we had been having. "Perhaps then my fellow Virtues and I could do some good work, for a change."

I lost what little patience I had left then, and decided that compromising my own nature in order to stroke the ego of a pain in the tailbone like Peace was not worth it. "Bold words," I said, pulling the last of the olive leaves free and dropping them to the ground, "from a Force who only exists in the absence of his antithesis, and then dares claim that he possesses any real power at all."

"Say whatever lies you wish," he snapped. "The fact remains that my fellow Virtues and I will always be stronger than those heathens you're so friendly with."

"You're not even a real Virtue," I shot back, "no matter how many times you call yourself one."

Peace leapt to his feet then. I turned to meet him, anticipating that this would be the moment that he told me to get out, but then I saw the flush of crimson blooming across his face.

"Come now, Peace," I said quickly, trying to soothe him before it was too late, "why don't you prove me wrong and—"

Peace opened his mouth and began to shriek then, loud and piercing enough to make me wince and send the doves into a frenzy. Red washed over his skin as he screamed, bathing him head to toe in violent scarlet, and then he was gone, vanishing with a thundercrack of concussive air, and leaving War standing in his stead.

War and I stared at each other as the doves flapped and cried around us, dodging books as they fell to the floor with heavy thuds. Several books bounced off of War's armor, and one particularly heavy tome landed in the fire, which now popped and crackled the way fire was supposed to.

As the last books fell and the doves found places among the shelves to hide and wait for Peace's return, War cleared his throat.

"You know, my darling," he said, "if you've decided that you did want my help after all, there are easier ways to call for me."

I put my hand over my face and turned away.

"Don't worry, I get it," War said, "this wasn't intentional, and you're not looking to start a Ride. I knew when I got pulled out of my lair that this was purely a counterbalance thing. I'm guessing you ticked off Peace enough that he snapped me over here. Good for you, Death. It's just going to be a far walk back for me, is all."

I heard him push a few books around with his foot.

"Before I go, do you think Peace would mind if I did a little redecorating?" War asked thoughtfully. "This is a good start, but I really think I could do something interesting with this space."

I walked out of the library in silence, hoping War did not see my smile.

Suitable consequences for a breach of contract include but are not limited to: Limitation of power. A Force's power may be restricted until the breach can be rectified and any and all damage repaired....
-- excerpt from the Contract of Mortality

- 17 -

I knew that War meant well, but I truly did not believe he could help me. I also believed that, now that I had accidentally summoned the red Rider, he would try to follow me. So, I set off for the one place he dared not tread. I was not keen on going there either, but I could not afford to have War trailing behind me, upsetting the other Forces I intended to speak with. They were more likely to flee when they saw his red armor approaching than willingly spend a moment in his presence, and War regularly made no effort to rectify this. It entertained him to no end to witness the effects he had on other Forces.

I also suspected that being near War physically hurt some of the other Forces. Temperance in particular had seen their tolerance for War deteriorate rapidly over the last few centuries, to the point where Temperance had developed a truly unfortunate allergy to the red Rider. Side effects included difficulty breathing, spontaneously bleeding, and loss of all motor functions. All in all, it was better for Temperance to stay away from War, and they were not the only Force to have a natural aversion to him.

With the Sins and Riders momentarily absolved from blame for the soul jump and nothing to show for enduring a visit with Peace, it was looking more and more likely that I would need to pay a visit to the Virtues soon. I knew it would be a far easier visit without War trailing behind me.

In order to shake War off my trail, I needed to go where he was afraid to follow, to the place where thoughts and fears became reality, whether one wanted to give them power or not. With all the trouble swirling around me, I was more than a little wary of going there myself, but I did have another reason driving me to visit Dreaming's den.

The walk from Inspiration's home to Peace's library had given me time and space to think over how this soul jump had happened. Not the exact method of the swap and the Forces involved (I was still puzzling over that), but how this had happened without Life, Destiny or I sensing another Force on the mortal world with us. We all have our signatures, and at the very least, I should have sensed the surge of power that would have come when another Force landed in the mortal realm. Especially if they had come with stolen essences in tow.

Nothing had been out of the ordinary in the time before the soul jump. We had not even had a visit from another Force in years. All had been quiet, and none of this made any sense.

Yet *some*one had facilitated the soul jump. And *some*one had stolen luck from the twins. Perhaps I could figure out who if I borrowed some of Dreaming's power.

Dreaming lived firmly in the neutral territories, off a branch of the path that curved away from Peace's library and flirted with the chaotic areas the twins migrated around. Unlike the entrance to the twins' home, however, Dreaming's den did not move. I found it easily enough, but I still hesitated before stepping on to the dreamscape.

This was an odd piece of land, forever covered in low, dense fog that glowed white under the cold stars. It was also alive, and hungry, just like chaos.

Given half the chance, the dreamscape would extend its borders as far as it could reach, driving every other Force out of their homes before chasing them across Eternity. It had appeared shortly after the first order stones of the path were laid, back when I and the other oldest Forces had discovered our capacity for rational thought. The dreamscape had been drawn to us, as though enchanted by our newfound capabilities. In reality, it wished to devour us, although we had not realized that until it was too late. We lost one of our fledgling number to its hunger, and with her went her name and her place in most of our memories. Once she was gone, the dreamscape had crept after the rest of us, stalking us across Eternity, until Dreaming was born and pulled the mists back. They tamed the dreamscape, and took much of its power for their own. Dreaming claimed that permanent patch of land for their home, which the rest of us were happy to give in exchange for protection against the twisting fog. How Dreaming actually held the dreamscape in check and fed off its power, I did not know, but I knew that in exchange for the dreamscape's absolute obedience, Dreaming could not leave its mists.

Thankfully, that rule did not apply to the rest of us, and we could come and go as we pleased. We kept a wide berth purely out of choice and a sense of self-preservation.

Of course, self-preservation can only take one so far when worlds are on the verge of collapse.

With that pleasant thought in mind, I stepped into the dreamscape.

The fog was so thick around me, I swore I could feel it brushing against my bones. It swirled and eddied, teasing me with shapes and shadows. I tried to ignore them as I walked on, calling out for Dreaming as I went. They did not respond, but the dreamscape did.

The shadows began to coalesce around me, transforming into dark, dead things so rotted that it was impossible to tell what had once been flesh and bone from what had been root and branch. The dead things jutted up around me in sharp, severe angles, forcing me to take a winding path forward. I saw a soft glow in the distance as I picked my way around the disease and decay, and I hurried on, thinking I had found Dreaming.

The glow grew as I approached. It darkened in intensity, transforming from a soft orange to a violent, blazing red. I stopped when the smoke began to roll over me, and then the flames came, jumping from corpse to corpse, devouring all in their path. There was something off about this fire, however. I could feel its heat and hear the jaws of its flames snapping through bone and branch alike, but it looked like something more than wildfire. Something alive that danced on the edge of my awareness, if only I could understand it. Something so familiar and yet…

A rain came then, cold and deliberate. It fell in a steady downpour, extinguishing the fire and washing away the ash and rot. My mind cleared along with the dreamscape, and I realized that I had been so mesmerized by the fire, I had reached into it. The flames had singed the tips of my fingers, turning the bones black. The rain did not wash this away. As the downpour slowed to a drizzle, I curled my fingers closed, and tried to calm my shaken nerves.

Dangerous as an existence in Eternity was, I was not used to facing my own certain demise, and I found that I did not like the taste.

By the time the rain had stopped, I had brought myself back under control, and I was standing calmly as I waited for my savior to appear. A new wash of color bled across the thick mists of the dreamscape, this time shifting between soft pastels, but there was a streak of dark blue worrying its way through the swirl. Eventually, the colors came to rest before me, shaping into an ageless and genderless face with delicate features and narrow, unseeing eyes. The dark blue streak settled across the blank eyes as the face turned to me.

Such fury and fear you bring to me. Dreaming's words echoed gravely through my skull. *Dangerous even for you, Death.*

I uncurled my fingers and studied the blackened tips again. "Believe me, I did notice that."

A thoughtful wash of pale green flickered across Dreaming's face. *Why did you bring this nightmare to me?* they asked.

I saw several reasons to give Dreaming the full truth, not the least of which was that the dreamscape was bound to reveal my secrets if I tried to suppress them. So I told Dreaming everything, including my suspicion that someone was trying to steal from other Forces, potentially even Dreaming themselves. Perhaps their power had enabled the Force responsible for the soul jump to hide from me, or been involved some other way. The dreamscape eagerly illustrated the details in the background as it fed off of my consciousness. I watched the dark blue streak across Dreaming's face slowly expand as I spoke and the dreamscape shifted with my words. By the time I was finished, the color had widened from a thin band to a solid mask over almost all of Dreaming's face. The blue bled at the edges, seeping into the shifting whorls that made up the rest of Dreaming's being.

I knew Dreaming would not be able to help me long before they said, *I am sorry, Death. I fear I cannot help you.*

I still did not like hearing the words, even if I knew they were coming.

I do not influence the dreams once I release them, Dreaming continued. *I can send pieces of the dreamscape to the mortal world, but I cannot control what happens to them beyond that.* They hesitated, and the dark blue mask gave way to a purple flush of embarrassment. *I am nearly powerless over the dreams once they are cut from the dreamscape, and they are truly beyond my reach once they have entered the mortal world.*

I nodded, trying to hide both my surprise and my disappointment. I was relieved that such a mysterious Force as Dreaming had not intentionally been part of the soul jump, but now, I could not shake the feeling that a dream had somehow been involved. Standing inside the dreamscape, the mists swirling all around me, I felt the ebb and flow of its power, and it felt so familiar, so seared into my recent memories, that I suddenly became certain.

I wondered how a dream would have fit into the method for the soul jump. The dreamscape moved to respond to my thoughts, and the beginnings of an idea came to me.

"Could a dream be used to deliver something to the mortal world?" I felt out each word carefully as I spoke, testing the idea against my own doubts along with Dreaming's. It was the only thing that made sense to me, though. How else could so much luck have come to the mortal world without Life, Destiny, or I noticing it? But if it had been wrapped in a dream and disguised...

The dreamscape eagerly rushed to illustrate the concept for me, concentrating around the lump of mixed luck I wore. I batted the mists away, still shaken by my earlier encounter with the dreamfire.

Dreaming watched this interaction play out in silence, their colors swirling with agitation. *The dreams should not be able to carry anything,* they finally said. *Like their parent dreamscape, once they find a host, they only reflect what is already inside the host's thoughts.*

I considered this, but wasn't quite willing to let go of the idea just yet. "What if someone else hijacked one of your dreams? What if they twisted it to their own purposes?"

Extremely doubtful, Dreaming informed me. *I may not be able to control them, but I do track the dreams all the way to the mortal world. I have never lost one before.* They glowed a proud mix of pinks and yellows then, bright enough to turn my gaze away.

"What about once they are on the mortal world?" I asked, holding up my sleeve to shield myself from the brightness. "You said you could not control them. Can you still track them?"

Dreaming's pride faded as quickly as it came. *No,* they said, turning a pearlescent gray. *I cannot see them once they leave this realm.*

"So it would be possible for someone to steal a dream from the mortal world, then?" I turned back to Dreaming and watched them closely as they thought this through. "And once they had it, they could try to change it to suit their needs?"

I suppose it must be, Dreaming finally admitted, *but it would take a lot of power to exert such control over the dreamscape, even a tiny piece of it.*

"How much power?"

I don't know, Dreaming admitted. *But to catch the dream and then control it? More than many Forces are known to possess.*

Struck by this, I began to consider Dreaming's words in context with everything I had learned earlier that day. I could feel the dreamscape straining to respond to my churning thoughts, but Dreaming moved to quell it.

"Wait," I said, and Dreaming turned their attention

back to me. I spread my arms out, sweeping them across as much of the dreamscape as I could. "May I?"

Dreaming frowned, and a fiery orange bloomed around the edges of their face. Clearly, they also remembered the dreamfire I had accidentally called forth. I assured Dreaming that revisiting that nightmare was the last thing I wanted.

If you will let me interfere should I sense danger, Dreaming said, *then I suppose I could let you try.*

I agreed without hesitation.

Dreaming bowed their head and loosened their restraints, although I could still sense their power lingering as they prepared to subdue any nightmares I unleashed, accidental or otherwise. I could not be ungrateful for that, however, as their home had nearly destroyed me on a number of occasions, and that was excluding the wildfire at the start of my current visit. My blackened fingertips tingled at the memories.

Turning away from Dreaming, I let my thoughts unspool across the dreamscape, solidifying as they saw fit while I ran through everything I knew.

I thought about the damaged soul first, taken before its time. In response, a reaper coalesced on the dreamscape before me, small and dark as it stood beneath the dying light of a severed soul. The soul's mortality cords hung ragged, true to my memory, their ends swaying in a nonexistent breeze. I wanted to keep the reaper and the damaged soul in the background of my thoughts as I worked my way through my ideas, and the dreamscape obliged, moving them into the distance as several gray threads appeared before me, tangled and snarled and impossible to separate.

I thought back to the corrupted chaos I had run into on the mortal world, pulling its taste and smell out of my memory. I had not recognized the first signature under all of the corruption, but now that I knew that luck was involved, it was easy to pull that piece away from the others. It flashed gold, and slipped free of the tangle.

With that came new focus on the remaining threads. One was definitely rotten, or perhaps fermented from being held for so long. When I focused on this particular signature, I caught an underlying whiff of dampness and potential, the same unique scent that the dreamscape's mists carried. This, I decided, *must* have been a stolen dream. But even if it wasn't, that still left me with three other threads I had not identified yet. The dreamscape shifted to accommodate my realizations and uncertainties.

The golden thread coiled and knotted itself until it matched the size and shape of the lump of luck hanging around my neck, but it was the pure gold of good luck rather than the metallic mix I wore. The thread I had identified as a stolen dream became the same color as the thickest of the dreamscape's fog, then shaped itself into a fluffy white cloud.

The remaining threads twisted discordantly as I considered them, but try as I might, I could not figure out what they represented. I had been away too long from Eternity to remember what everyone's unique essences felt like. The missing signatures I had sensed in the chaos on the mortal world would have to remain a mystery, but I still pulled at my memory, certain that if I thought long and hard enough, I could figure them out. The gray threads kinked and knotted, until I finally let the mystery go. I simply did not have the time. So I shoved them and the lump of golden luck inside the cloud the dreamscape had created for me.

Next, a figure rose up from the fog, bright and shining.

But there I stopped, puzzled.

For a Force to have stolen essences and carried out the soul switch, they would have needed to jump back and forth between Eternity and the mortal world, and I already knew that had not happened. No one could shield themselves that completely from me, let alone Life and Destiny as well. One of us would have sensed someone coming and going from the mortal world that frequently. It would have drawn our attention too easily.

And I already knew that no Forces other than Life, Destiny and I had been present on the mortal world during the time of the soul switch. All three of us had been in the kitchen of our shared apartment, happy, relaxed, but not distracted to the point where we would have missed another Force's entrance.

How, then, had the soul jump been executed? Who could have been there to see it through?

I went over the discoveries I had made at the reaping site, removing the chaos-touched police and neighbors from the memory for the time being. Instead, I imagined the apartment as it must had been, moments before the soul swap, and let the dreamscape build the tiny rooms before me.

There was the immaculately clean living area off of the kitchen, and the small, orderly bedroom, and that bathroom that somehow managed to house all the necessities of the mortal who had lived there. The moment my thoughts touched on him, he appeared, young and healthy and whole, going about whatever it was young men of his age did in their apartments as they got ready for the day. I felt nothing but raw curiosity as I watched him go about his mortal life in his mortal home on the mortal world.

Mortals.

I was instrumental in their creation, but I had taken such little interest in the things they did with the bodies I gave them. I had only really needed to focus on their expirations, and even that became overwhelming. If I had paid a little more attention to them, perhaps I would have come to my next conclusion earlier, and saved myself a lot of time and trouble that day.

But because I had taken the mortals for granted, I had assumed that another Force had come to the mortal world and messed everything up. Once I slowed down and finally made myself really think about the soul jump, I realized that maybe, just maybe, a Force would not have needed to be there, after all.

The dreamscape worked to reflect my new idea, and produced a second human with the face and shape of the old man I had found at the reaping site. His expression was eager and hungry, sharpened by my own distress at overlooking such a basic possibility. I was not afraid of this mortal man, but I knew that if I did not find his soul soon, he could destroy everything.

I felt the dreamscape tugging at my thoughts, and I let it take them, turning myself into a spectator as I watched the true method behind the soul jump play out.

The young man was in his apartment, dressed and ready for his day. There was a knock on his door. He answered, and the old man came through, holding a mysterious weapon that I could not quite make out, but I thought that it must have been some sort of blade. It flashed gold and white, but also muddied colors that I could not identify; the signatures I did not yet understand.

The old man used the mystery blade to attack the young man, driving it deep into his chest to carve through the mortality threads. He ripped the young man's soul out of his body before turning the blade on himself and slicing his own threads, and then the vision went muted and fuzzy before me.

Apologies, Dreaming murmured. *Too fatal for me.*

I felt a twinge of annoyance at having my explorations halted, but my scorched fingertips itched, reminding me to tread carefully in someone else's home. I also knew that something was missing from the theory I'd illustrated through the dreamscape, so I let the scene dissolve.

That is a… fascinating yet disturbing theory, Death, Dreaming informed me as the last few pieces melted back into the mists. Dreaming's colors gradually shifted from sickly paleness back to their normal shades of pastel, with a teal tint of curiosity now.

"I know," I said grimly. "It is the only thing that makes sense, though."

Dreaming did not contradict me. They had seen my thoughts illustrated in full color by the dreamscape, and knew every last thing that had cycled through my mind as I worked through them.

How would a mortal have known how to do any of that? they asked. *And where would they have gotten such a weapon?*

"That's where I'm afraid your dreams may have come in to play," I said.

But nothing tangible can be sent through a dream, Dreaming informed me. *Even if another Force managed to twist a piece of the dreamscape to their own purposes, a weapon like that could not have been housed inside.*

I reached inside my hood and scratched the back of my skull. "What if the dream was used to pass distilled essences from Eternity to the mortal world?"

Distilled?

"I break down souls on the mortal world to return them to Life. Other Forces have done something similar before."

I am aware, Dreaming said, *simply unsure of how possible that would be.* They were quiet for a long moment, their colors swirling as they worked through their own, private thoughts. *I suppose it would be possible,* they finally admitted. *But who would want to do this, Death, and why?*

"Those are questions I do not yet have answers for."

I looked out across the dreamscape, and the reaper and severed soul I had pushed aside earlier were brought before me again. I looked again at the ragged ends of the mortality cords, and again at the bone scythe on my reaper's tail. Only a weapon forged from my power should have been able to cut a soul away from its body, but that had not happened. That was perhaps the most disturbing aspect of all of this. If it was not me, and if it was not my reaper, then what had severed the mortality cords?

I saw the mysterious weapon again, and the old, rogue mortal who wielded it. He *must* have gotten all or part of that blade from a Force, that much was certain, but the idea of him being able to use it on his own? That sent a ripple of fear through me. Not at the idea of one rogue mortal, no. *That* I could handle, bizarre, unidentified blades aside. But one mortal causing this much chaos and undoing all the work Life and I had put into the mortal world? That was what scared me. That was what would bring Justice down upon us, upon *me* for not only letting this happen, but for evading him and wasting time in Eternity, even if I was making progress now. And what would happen to the mortal world if I could not find the culprit in time? We would need to place all our hopes on an Apocalypse Ride, and trust that ending the mortal world would destroy the chaos, too. If it didn't…

Death!

I broke free of my thoughts just in time to see the shape of the nightmare before me. It loomed huge and dark, a frozen tsunami of chaos that dripped hunger and rage. I stood under it, helpless, watching the wave crest and begin to tumble, and then a spear of pastel light cracked through. The chaos screamed and shattered into a million glittering shards that slowly faded away, leaving me in the cool mists of the dreamscape once again.

I did not realize that I had been shaking until I suddenly stopped. I looked down to see that Dreaming had pooled some of their light under my feet, providing me with a stable patch of warmth to stand on. The colors shifted between agitated pinks and concerned blues.

I'm sorry, Death, Dreaming said, *but it is dangerous for you to stay here any longer.*

I held my scythe close and nodded. "I understand."

Dreaming shifted and turned their blank eyes to the side. I followed their gaze and saw the mists part, revealing the white path and the dark, unchanging sky of Eternity beyond the edge of the dreamscape.

I knew that I should leave, but I remained still for a long, quiet time, holding my scythe and trying to understand why the answer to this mystery eluded me so. I knew all of the other Forces. I should have been able to see who would have wanted to do this to me. I was more than disappointed with myself for failing.

Sobered, I turned back to Dreaming and thanked them for use of the dreamscape. A tentative wash of light blue crept over their face when they said that they had enjoyed my company in spite of the nightmares, and wished that I had been able to visit under better circumstances.

I hope you find your answers soon, Death, they said.

I doubted that hope would get me very far at all, but I appreciated the sentiment all the same. Dreaming saw me out, and I tried to think of my next move without disrupting the dreamscape. I need not have worried; Dreaming had such a firm grasp on the dreamscape after my last nightmare, the mists barely moved as I passed them. Dreaming left me at the edge of the path and bid me a final, wistful farewell.

As I walked away, I decided that maybe hope could take me somewhere, after all. He was an insufferable optimist, but Hope was one of the kindest Forces in existence, and truthful to his core. And with Justice out looking for me somewhere in Eternity, this was the best time to visit his partner. I could swallow a little sunshine if it meant straight answers and nothing threatening to destroy me.

It wasn't until after I had left the dreamscape and felt a few wistful tendrils of mist cling to my robes that it occurred to me that Dreaming might have been lonely. I could not remember the last time a Force had willingly crossed into the dreamscape to visit them. That gave me an idea. I did not know if it would do any good, but I reached out and summoned the reaper I had created back in the Riders' lair. It came on silent wings, slower than they usually did on the mortal world, but still at my beck and call. I whispered to it, and the reaper whickered in response before trotting fearlessly into the dreamscape. It was swallowed immediately by the mists. All was still, until the dreamscape lit up with joyous streaks of pastels, which caught the silhouette of the reaper as it raced across the dreamscape, baying happily.

As I watched this, I begrudgingly admitted to myself that maybe, perhaps, in a very abstract sort of way, Destiny had been right; my reapers could, *sometimes*, be a little cute.

A Force may never make his/her/their existence known to the mortals.
-- excerpt from the Contract of Mortality, Rule 3

- 18 -

ope lived deep inside the Virtues' territories, where everything gleamed under stars that somehow seemed to shine brighter than they ever had over the Sins' or Riders' homes. The path ran thickest here, the dark everwood forest standing strong and the chaos of Eternity held at bay by short but impassible walls of order stones piled along the edges of the path. Lesser Forces might have found this impressive, but the sight only reminded me of the Virtues' decision to steal the order that had been so carefully laid down where the Sins and Riders had once lived. Wisdom and Courage had led the effort, citing the need to protect "their" youngest and most vulnerable members—Hope included—against growing chaos, but none of the Sins or Riders had accepted that excuse. Of course, by the time we had learned that they intended to act regardless of whether we gave our consent or not, it was already too late.

I picked my way over the path, sticking to the shade of the everwood trees that grew along the edges of the path, and in large clusters throughout the center. The colors of their warm trunks ranged from pale honey all the way to deep mahogany, but all of their leaves were black. I hesitated for a moment beneath one golden tree with a split trunk, resting my hand against the smooth bark and looking up at the dark leaves. I had met Justice under this exact tree in the tense days following the aftermath of the order stone theft. He had agreed to see me without hesitation. We both knew that something had to be done to rectify the damage.

Technically, there had been no casualties in the wake of the Virtues' thievery, but between Pestilence's loss of her corporeal form and the flood of chaos into the Sins' and Riders' lands, War had been threatening total destruction of everything within his reach, and I knew that I could not have stopped him. Truthfully, I had not *wanted* to stop War, but I also knew that unleashing him would have thrown Eternity out of balance, and we could not have afforded that with raw chaos lapping at our doors. I called on Justice for an alternative solution. He came to our meeting ready to rectify the wrongs against the Sins and the Riders, but he had also already fallen in love with Hope, and would not see the young Force threatened by the chaos that surged against the freshly built walls.

In the end, it was decided that some of the order stones would be returned to the Sins and the Riders, who could tolerate the chaos far better than any of the Virtues could. The Riders further lent more of their order stones to the Sins, and with Justice's help, new materials were crafted to keep the Riders safely tethered to the other Forces. The path bridging the territories was rebuilt, and I talked War down from his battle lust with the promise of a new world where he could flex his strength, if he had the patience to wait. Already, I had been calculating ways to keep balance and bind power in what would eventually become the Contract of Mortality.

None of us ever forgot what the Virtues had done, however, especially when the aftermath birthed not only Peace from the quelling of War, but also Chance and Fortune in the heart of the chaos that had been left to grow in the absence of the order stones. The Virtues claimed that good things had come from their actions. The Riders dared them to test what results their next actions would yield, and the two factions had avoided each other ever since.

Such was the eventful era that had dawned with Hope.

And yet, in spite of all the trouble his arrival had caused, none of us had ever found it within ourselves to resent Hope. He was too earnest and too kind for anyone to wish him any ill will, and in the end, even Envy was glad he was so well-insulated from the chaos. Sins and Riders alike became sworn enemies of the Virtues and their Blessing allies, but they were all glad that Hope was protected, myself included.

Still, visiting Hope did mean that I ran the risk of running into another Blessing or a Virtue, so I made my way carefully through their territories, keeping as quiet as I could as I cut across their lands to get to Hope. The silent everwood forest helped shield me from detection, but there was one Force I knew I could not evade. I sensed her watching me from the trees as I moved, yet I knew I had no reason to fear her. Not anymore. Even if she wanted to reveal me to another, she couldn't.

Once, she had been called Secrecy. She had aided the Virtues in their thievery, making it possible for them to sneak undetected into the Sins' and Riders' territories to steal the order stones. If I had been paying attention, I would have been able to find them. I would have been able to stop them. That's what I still tell myself to this day, but even I know that will never be anything more than a lie. Secrecy had been strong, then. Strong and cunning and terrible, enough to get Wisdom and Courage past my notice, but she had paid dearly for her involvement in the theft.

Left behind to cover the trail of the Virtues, Secrecy had been caught by one of the first chaos waves. She was lucky that it was a weaker swell that had hit her, but it had robbed her of her abilities and transformed her into something else.

Now, she roamed Eternity as Silence, present but fragile, with no real power of her own. She still stalked Forces from time to time, trying to remind us of what she once was, but she could never hold us, or do anything other than make us appreciate the quiet. Some Forces liked her better as Silence. For my part, I had promised her that if I ever caught her, I would break her.

I felt her following me as I moved deeper into the Virtues' territories, staying a safe distance away but keeping pace with me, too. I briefly considered chasing her off, but my visit to the dreamscape had instilled a new sense of urgency in me, and I decided to leave her be. At least until she was close enough for me to take a quick swing with my scythe.

I was about to step out from beneath the large everwood tree when I heard the soft but steady wingbeats above me, and I froze.

My abrupt halt caused Silence to drift closer to me than she had intended, and she had just enough time to twist herself into a soundless scream before I slammed into her, wrestling her into a shield between myself and Justice as he alighted on the ground not ten paces from us. Silence struggled against me, but I held her fast and let the blade of my scythe touch the translucent, lavender edge of her amorphous form. She stilled then, and we both watched as Justice stretched and shook his onyx-feathered wings.

Heavily muscled and easily much taller than I had ever been, even before my reapers, Justice was a formidable Force. Like Life, he had a somewhat human appearance, with dark skin and the fine proportions of an endurance athlete. However, his ears were large and pointed, and they swiveled as he sought out the smallest of sounds. His wings were longer than he was tall, making him a fast flier and nearly impossible to outrun. And his eyes were wide, unseeing pools of gold from end to end, with golden lines spiderwebbing out across the rest of his face. Justice relied on his hearing for his flights and for hunting down trouble, so with Silence between me and him, I was safe.

That did not mean that I allowed myself to so much as relax my toes as I watched him turn his head left and right, seeking me out. He took a few tentative steps in my direction, and I felt Silence shiver, but she did not try to break free.

Justice frowned. "Is someone there?" he asked, his

voice deep and sonorous and inviting me to tell the truth.

I clamped my teeth shut and held on to Silence.

Justice listened for a few more moments, then sighed and turned away. He cocked his head as he turned his ears, hands on his hips as he considered the empty path and groves of everwood trees. Other than Silence and me, there was no one else for him to find. So Justice spread his wings and jumped back into the sky.

I listened to the beating of his wings as he climbed higher. Once the sounds of Justice's flight had faded away, I counted to one hundred, then let my grip on Silence relax. She tore herself free and slithered away from me as fast as she could, but I barely registered her departure.

That had been far, far too close a call for my liking. I clutched at the lump of mixed luck around my neck and wondered whether that had been good or bad luck just then. Most likely, it was both.

The one good thing about Justice's impromptu appearance: I now knew where he was, and what direction he was heading in. And he had taken off for the other end of the path, back towards the Sins and Riders. Maybe that meant I had a little more time before he found me again. I hurried on my way.

I reached Hope's home without running into any further trouble. He lived in a small cabin built of everwood and order stones beneath a mighty mahogany everwood tree. His home was surrounded by a wide ring of order stones on all sides, and was positioned well away from the edges of the path, which

I could not even see at this point. His lands butted up against Justice's territory (obviously), which invited the idea that Justice could have easily doubled back and stopped for a visit with his partner after nearly catching me. My steps slowed. As I approached the cabin, I listened closely for Justice's deep voice, but all I heard was a soft song drifting out of the cabin.

Hope was alone for the moment, then; he only sang when he worked, and he only worked when he was not with Justice.

My spine relaxed as I lifted the thick cloth that served as the door to Hope's home and peered inside.

The cabin was divided into two rooms, the smaller of which held the threads and finished cloths that Hope created. The larger room, the one I looked in to, housed Hope's loom, carved from golden everwood. He sat at the giant instrument, singing quietly to himself in that rich, sweet voice we all loved as he wove a new hopecloth. I knew that when it was finished, he would cut it up and send the scraps to the mortal world, where they would take hold wherever they could, sometimes for better and sometimes for worse.

I had never seen Hope's work before it had been cut, however, and I found myself pausing to admire the craftsmanship that went into his weaving. This particular hopecloth was deep blue with shimmering white threads woven into a seemingly random spread across it, giving it the appearance of a night sky on the mortal world. I caught the careful pattern of the threads, however, and picked out several constellations that the mortals had once revered. While those stars had never held any influence of their own, I could feel the power radiating off of the incomplete hopecloth. I reveled in this for a moment, letting the sensation roll over me, but the strength of it cut deep into my recent memories, and a sinking suspicion took hold of me. That was why I had gone to Hope, but I had not expected to be proven right so soon.

My mood was so palpable that Hope's voice actually caught on a sour note, and he paused in his work, confused. Then he turned on his stool and saw me standing in his doorway.

"Death!" Hope said with a wide, genuine smile. "I did not know you were back. Please, come in." He rose to greet me, ushering me inside with gentle gestures and open arms.

I stepped into the room, and did something that I rarely did with another Force, including Life: I held my arms open, and allowed him to embrace me.

Hope, courteous as he was, knew to hold me gently and release me after a few moments. His eyes were honey gold set against golden brown skin that looked more like polished wood than flesh, and his curling hair was a mop of shining, golden curls. I sometimes wondered if his hair was made of the same stuff as his fine threads. He cut a handsome figure, something that his partner enjoyed but always swore was secondary to Hope's personality. In short, Hope was a charming Force, and even I could not help but smile in his presence.

When Hope stepped back from me, he offered me the only seat he had—the one at his loom—and asked what had led me to his home.

I politely declined the seat and said that I wished

better circumstances had brought me to him. "There is a problem on the mortal world," I told Hope, "and unfortunately, I believe your work was involved."

Hope tilted his head in confusion. "My work?" He looked at the unfinished hopecloth on his loom. "I don't see how that's possible. I certainly have never wished to cause trouble on the mortal world."

"I know, Hope, but I have reason to believe that someone may have stolen your cloth."

Hope was startled by this, then laughed uncomfortably. "I've always shared my hopecloths freely. Why would anyone ever need to steal it?"

"Perhaps because they needed far more than even you would have given," I said. I lifted the cord around my neck and showed Hope the solid lump of luck it held.

The young Force squinted at the silver and gold pendant, then drew in a sharp breath. "How did you ever get that much luck?"

"A lot of guessing games and one very serious migraine," I said, letting the luck drop back against my chest. "The twins told me that someone had stolen a piece of pure good luck from them, same size as this mixed one they gave me."

Hope's eyes went wide. "Who would do that?"

"That's what I am trying to find out."

He nodded, but his face shifted into a regretful expression. "I wish I could help you," he said, "but all of my hopecloth is accounted for."

"Really?" I asked. "All of it?"

He nodded again, this time emphatically and proudly. "I keep careful records of my work, especially when another Force asks me for a piece. If they come too often, I try to help them find a solution to whatever problem it is they're having instead of letting them rely on my cloth to get through it."

"Of course you do," I murmured without malice.

I should have known better. Who would ever steal from such a pure Force? Perhaps the culprit had waited for the hopecloth to be cut and scattered on the mortal world, then gathered it there, when no one was watching. Or maybe I was mistaken, and hope had not been part of the equation at all.

And yet, the feel of the power from the half-finished hopecloth had felt so familiar…

"Death?" Hope asked, touching my arm lightly.

I jolted out of my thoughts.

"I asked if you would like to see one of my latest hopecloths." He gave me a shy smile. "I'm quite proud of it. I think it's one of my best works."

Absently, I agreed, and let him lead me to the smaller room. I cast one final, lingering look at the cloth on the loom before following Hope over the threshold.

The walls of the smaller room were packed from corner to corner with mounted spools of thread. In the center of the room was an octangular everwood chest with several drawers on each side. Hope made for the chest, chatting about thread colors and his sources of inspiration as he went.

"I'm so glad you're here to see this," Hope said as he opened one of the drawers. "I was actually thinking of you when I tried a new pattern with the black threads, and I think you'll really like—" He pulled up short, staring into the drawer.

Part of me wished that I really had been wrong about the hopecloth, that there was nothing tying this Force to the soul jump. He did not deserve that. As I watched the color drain from him, leaving him ashen gray all over, I knew that I had been right after all.

Hope lifted the cloth out of the drawer in silence. He turned to me and shook it open, letting it unfurl gracefully around the massive, ragged hole that had been cut out of its center. From the fraying, snarled edges of the hole, a jagged blackness radiated out across the hopecloth.

At first, I thought this was the new pattern Hope had been telling me about. Then I saw the blackness shift, spidering up toward Hope's fingers.

"Drop it!" I snapped. I jumped to Hope's side and swatted the cloth out of his hands before he could move.

Startled, he shied away from me, and I moved between him and the chaos-contaminated hopecloth on the floor. I pushed it further away with the butt of my scythe, then turned to Hope and caught his hands. I examined them carefully, searching for the smallest sign of chaos poisoning. I was relieved to see that he was untouched.

"I don't understand," Hope whispered. His eyes were riveted on the ruined hopecloth.

"Unfortunately, I do," I muttered.

Before I explained, I needed to take care of the contaminated hopecloth. I sent Hope back to the other room, and then spent a few minutes centering myself, taking extra time just in case something went wrong. I recalled the terrifying moments of being stuck in the chaos pool while a swell hunted me as I sought out the twins, and I took every precaution in preparing myself for what I needed to do. When I was ready, I swung the blade of my scythe around, cutting through the spidery chaos. It writhed and screeched as is it was pulled free of the cloth. Thankfully, it was only a trace amount of chaos, and absorbing it into the blade of my scythe took only a brief concentration of effort and a minor flexing of my power. I barely felt the ebb in my energy as the chaos became trapped in the blade, forming a thin, spikey vein of black across the pale surface. I would need to release it later if I did not want to severely damage whatever I used the blade on next, but for now, the chaos was safely contained.

When I rejoined Hope in the other room, I had the ruined hopecloth in my hand. "Would it be all right if I kept this?"

Hope was at his loom again, staring hard at his unfinished work. He nodded at my request, but did not turn around.

I approached him slowly and put a hand on his shoulder, my dream-scorched fingers resting lightly against him. "This was not your fault," I told him.

He sighed, still not looking away from the blue hopecloth. "Perhaps I should pull back on production for a while."

I gave his shoulder a gentle squeeze. "Until I've learned who did this, that may be for the best."

Hope dropped his head. His voice was very small when he said, "I never thought my hopecloth could be dangerous."

"Don't you dare go against your nature and lose yourself over this," I told him firmly. "You are so important to all of us, and I can tell you for certain, the mortal world would fall apart in no time without you. Eternity, too. Yes, someone took your hard work and twisted it to fit their own ends, but that does not mean that it is not worth continuing." I softened my voice. "You've done so much good for us."

It took a few moments, but Hope finally looked up at me and smiled again. "Thank you, Death."

We parted ways with another embrace, holding each other a little longer this time. Hope decided to take a short break from his work, spending the newfound free time with Justice. He agreed not to mention the theft of the hopecloth until I had flushed out the culprit, understanding that sending his boyfriend into a vengeful rage would not help the situation. I suggested that he also see about borrowing a lock for his chest from Peace, who so intensely disliked the idea of anyone intruding on his library and disturbing his possessions that he had multiple locks in place. (I suppressed a smile as I remembered War's earlier musings on rearranging his counterpart's decorations.) Hope promised me that he would visit Peace, but perhaps when Justice was free to accompany him. He grimaced at the thought of going alone. (This time, I allowed myself to smile fully.)

Hope set off for his partner's home, and I snuck across Temperance's land with the ruined hopecloth slung across my shoulder like a sash. With two confirmed elements and measurements of their quantities and qualities to work with, Destiny's chances of finding the source of the chaos were far better than they had been this morning.

I knew it was still not enough, but I also knew two more things after my visit with Hope.

First, the hopecloth had been cut by a blade forged from chaos. Nothing else would have created those ragged, poisoned edges, and judging by what I'd seen at the reaping site and the ragged ends of the mortality threads, there was a very high probability that the same blade had been used in the soul jump. That had to be the mystery weapon, then: a chaos blade fortified by a massive amount of luck, a dangerous amount of hope, and something else that I had not yet identified.

Second, I knew that whoever had done this had robbed Hope. Judging by the execution of the cuts and the fact that the ruined cloth had been left at the scene of the crime, the culprit had taken as much as they thought they had needed, then fled. That did not speak to any vindictiveness towards Hope (truly, who would ever harbor that?), but it did suggest an indifference to the effect the act would have on the hopecloth, possibly even on Hope himself. This meant that I was looking for someone who did not fully appreciate what Hope did for us all, most likely because they did not need any shreds of hope in order to operate at their full power.

I wasn't quite sure how this all led back to wanting to enable a soul jump on the mortal world, but I did know that it was time I visited the Sins again. I had some new questions for them.

*Example countermeasures against a potential chaos overspill
include but are not limited to: one or more creator Forces
leaving the mortal world for the length of time necessary to
summon help and/or locate a solution to the threat [...]*
-- excerpt from the Contract of Mortality, Addendum 2
authored by Death, Life, and Destiny, countersigned by
Justice

- 19 -

I managed to get back out of the Virtues' and Blessings' territories without running into one of them, although it was a near miss with Temperance, and the silence resettling around Peace's library announced that he was back home. As sorely tempted as I was to see what War had done to the place, I skirted around Peace's territory and followed the path back toward the Sins' domain, keeping a careful watch for Justice as I went. I had just passed the edges of the dreamscape when I walked through a warm patch of air.

I paused, wondering if the Sins could wait a little while longer. Then I doubled back, seeking out the hot spot. Maybe it was the shredded hope I was wearing, but something urged me to check for Inspiration one last time. At the very least, I would know if Inspiration had seen my second message or not.

As it turned out, she had. When I found the branch that led to the smoldering volcano, the sign was gone, and the gate was open. I nearly tripped over my own robes when I saw this, but I caught myself in time and set off as quickly as I could.

I had to travel to the other side of the volcano to reach Inspiration's front door, and I was risking a severe case of falling bones by the time I got there. I had not run, but the brisk pace had set me bouncing on my feet, and it was all I could do to keep myself distracted from my own bone structure. I accomplished this mostly by imagining myself commandeering one of those mobile snow skimming vehicles from the mortal world and seeing if I could modify it enough to enable it to run in Eternity, where gasoline was a nonexistent commodity. It certainly would have made the trip around the volcano much easier. So would riding my horse, but I would not allow myself to summon my steed.

When the door finally came in sight, I wasted no time. I charged up to the dark slab of everwood set into the side of the volcano, and knocked. Very, very hard.

A moment later, the door opened, and Inspiration stood before me, regarding me in silence. I watched her take in the heavy way I leaned on my scythe, the ragged hope cloth across my shoulders, and the lump of mixed luck hanging around my neck.

Inspiration took a step back, and waved me inside.

The door closed with a heavy *thud* behind me.

- Part Four -

Depression

*Destiny must pay the landlord rent, in full and on time, alone,
whenever the need arises. [Note from Justice: I do not know
what a "landlord" is, but I'm sure I don't need to in order to
understand that this is a petty dispute that you all can resolve
on your own. Try to sneak another one of these in here, and by
destruction I swear I will send Shame to live with you.]*
-- rejected addendum to the Contract of Mortality
authored by Death, countersigned by Life, vetoed by Justice

- 20 -

Inspiration sat in a carved stone chair, gazing thoughtfully at nothing in particular in the aftermath of my explanation of all the events that had brought me to her home. After learning of the theft of raw luck and the vandalized, stolen hopecloth, I was willing to bet that Inspiration had lost a spark or two to the thief. I had told her everything, hoping to expedite the grand reveal and get back to Life and Destiny before Justice could drag me back. Still, we would not benefit from false evidence, so I gave Inspiration time to think while I studied the interior of her home with interest.

I had never actually been inside. Before the mortal world, I had usually dealt with Inspiration somewhere in Eternity when we had chanced upon each other on the main path. The closest I ever came to her home before this was the gate. Having made it all the way past the front door, I found myself in a massive cavern that was much too large to fit inside the small volcano I'd seen outside. I sat upon a smooth stone platform colored that particular shade of gray that spoke of a perfect, safe balance between order and chaos. Inspiration's furnishings were all carved from that same stone, with intricate patterns etched along the surfaces. From what I could see, her entire living space was contained to this one shelf of rock that jutted out over the heart of the volcano. Molten rock bubbled far below us, painting our surroundings a deep shade of orange. Despite the pool below and the lavafalls that fell from a ceiling so high I could not see it, the air around us was cool and pleasant.

I was studying the lavafalls, trying to determine the purpose of disguising one's home as a tiny volcano that only hinted at the barest fraction of their true dwelling, when everything suddenly shifted from warm reds and oranges to shades of blue.

I turned to see Inspiration studying me, or more specifically, gazing at the hopecloth and the luck I wore. At least, I assumed that was what she was looking at. Inspiration wore a long, white hooded cloak that concealed her entire body. Her face was nothing more than a pool of shadow beneath the hood. The cloak had an iridescent sheen to it, often throwing flashes of shimmering red and blue whenever Inspiration moved. Around her covered head, four flames circled and danced, leaving tiny embers in their wake. Most of these burned out and disappeared, but every so often, one would flare to life and shoot off into the unknown, compelled to spark someone's creativity. These flames and their sparks had been red a few moments earlier; I was not surprised to see that they had shifted to blue to harmonize with their surroundings.

I sat on my hands to keep them from reaching for any of the sparks. I had the feeling that even just one of them could help me see something that I was missing, but after seeing the damage my mysterious thief had done, I was not about to take from another Force anything that was not freely given.

"I do have to admit," Inspiration finally said, her faceted voice whispering across the room, "it's likely that one of my sparks was involved in this."

I felt a surge of vindication at the words, but a grim one. "I don't suppose you'd be able to tell how said spark was used?"

Inspiration's flames wobbled on their orbit before settling back on track. "Unfortunately, no. Once a spark is caught and flames into an idea, it's gone."

"How fitting," I grumbled. I grit my teeth as I shifted my perch on the vaguely chair-shaped bit of rock Inspiration had steered me into. I had been so tired from my hurried walk around the volcano that I'd accepted the offer without thinking. My feet were glad for the chance to recover, but my tailbone and lower spine were less than pleased with this arrangement. "If you can't track your sparks, there's no way to tell how many of them may have been involved in this mess."

"I did not say I couldn't track them," Inspiration put in.

I stopped trying to find a nonexistent soft spot on the boulder and perked up. "Do tell."

Inspiration's flames widened their orbit as she considered her next words. I watched her wrestle with herself, trying to find the right language.

"My sparks are pieces of me," she finally said, and I could hear in her voice that while this explanation was not quite right, it was the best she could do. "I feel them when they leave, and I know when they have taken hold in someone. I usually cannot tell who is touched by a spark when they go to the mortal world, but I *can* feel it when they flare and fuel someone's thoughts, and when they simply burn out before they have the chance to catch."

Inspiration turned her hooded face towards me again, trying to determine if I understood. Thanks to my visit with Dreaming, I had a better grasp on the concept than I would have otherwise. I nodded my encouragement for Inspiration to continue.

"I can also feel the difference between a mortal catching one of my sparks, and a Force catching it. When a Force takes a spark… it's duller. Less intense. The mortals crave the sparks more keenly, and when they find them, their euphoria burns hot."

This was less clear to me, but the bit about feeling a difference between a moral and a Force claiming a spark caught my interest. I asked if she could ever tell which Forces had claimed her sparks.

Inspiration's fires wobbled again and shifted back to red, along with the lavafalls. "I have come to know one specific Force when she catches my sparks. Her claiming carries a distinct signature, like… the taste of satisfaction and excitement wrapped around a core of determination." Inspiration's dancing fires burned a little brighter, becoming shyly euphoric, if I had to put an emotion to them. Her voice was full of admiration when she said, "I know that Destiny finds many wonderful uses for my sparks."

I smiled inwardly at Inspirations obvious crush on my roommate. Several questions regarding this flitted to the forefront of my mind, but I hammered them into oblivion before they could spill out.

"Have you felt any other Forces taking one of your sparks recently?" I managed to ask instead.

Inspiration nodded, her flames returning to their neutral state. "There was an odd spark that was taken by a Force not long ago. This one stood out because it came after a rush of only mortals catching them for the longest time. I cannot tell you who took it, specifically, but I know that it was not Destiny. That I am certain of, particularly since the spark was taken long before it reached the mortal world."

This was not especially helpful information, as it was not unusual. We Forces caught Inspiration's sparks all the time, when we could find them. And yet, Inspiration had called the spark "odd." I knew that had to mean something more.

"It was so strange," Inspiration continued at my prompting. "While a Force did take a spark while it was still in this realm, I never felt it flare into an idea. I assumed whoever found it must have been trying to save it for something, but now that you have told me of the soul jump, I wonder if the isolated flare I felt a few days ago was linked to the switch."

"Isolated flare?" I asked.

"Yes, from a mortal absorbing a spark. I couldn't figure out where it had come from, as the mortals cannot save my sparks, and I have not felt another

Force take a spark from this realm since the one that disappeared. Before you told me about the soul jump, I thought perhaps that Destiny had returned and claimed a spark to save, and she simply chose not to visit me."

There was a questioning lilt at the end of this last bit, and Inspiration's fires twirled hopefully around her head.

"Destiny has not left the mortal world for years," I said. She was not bound to the mortal world in the same ways that Life and I were, but she had not seen much reason to leave. I knew that, in many ways, she preferred the mortal world to our home realm, but I saw the comfort and encouragement Inspiration took from my words, and I decided not to tell her about Destiny's location preferences.

"I doubted it was really her," Inspiration said, encouraged that she had not been snubbed. "She's never saved my sparks before, but I simply could not think of anyone else who would have wanted to keep one for so long."

I turned this over in my mind, trying to fit together everything I had learned during my visit home. "Do you know how long it takes a dream to ferment?" I asked.

Inspiration was caught off guard by the question, and her fires slowed and shifted momentarily to violet before burning red again. "I could hazard a guess," she offered uncertainly.

"Could one of your sparks survive long enough to be planted in a fermented dream, and then released into a mortal?"

Inspiration dipped her head in cautious agreement.

"And how much power would it take to keep one of your sparks burning for that long?"

"I suppose that would depend on where you were," Inspiration said after a moment of consideration. "Here in Eternity, not much. On the mortal world…" She trailed off and shrugged her thin shoulders. "Far more than I could sustain."

This snagged on something in my mind, on some jagged piece of the puzzle that I could not quite see the full shape of. I needed something to give me clarity and let me understand what I was still missing. Something, say, small and fiery and currently pleasantly easy to access.

I slid off the boulder, immediately feeling relief in my backside. I took a moment to savor the lack of rock pressing against my tailbone before turning to Inspiration and respectfully lowering the blade of my scythe to the ground. "Might I beg a spark from you?" I asked.

Inspiration's fires spun merrily before me. "Of course, Death." She tossed her head, whipping her circling flames off their customary orbit. A spark flew off of one of the fires and sailed towards me. I caught it in my hand, feeling it pulse against my bones. It was warm to the touch, but not enough to burn me.

"You are aware of how my sparks work?" Inspiration asked.

"Intimately," I said, raising the fresh spark to my mouth. "I swallow this, and it gives me a new idea."

Inspiration vigorously shook her head.

I paused, wondering if I'd gotten a vital part of the

process so wrong for so many eons. "I am not supposed to swallow it, am I?"

"Well, that's one of the less popular methods I've seen," Inspiration said, "but my sparks do not bring *new* ideas to anyone. Not even the Forces. All they do is ignite what is already inside." Her fires flickered and danced more wildly, which I took as amusement. "This is why they are sparks, after all. Nothing more."

I lowered my hand. "Then, that means, if one of your sparks *was* involved in the soul jump," I said, carefully walking myself through the idea as it formed, "whoever initiated all of this would have needed to already know that a soul jump was possible."

"They would have," Inspiration agreed.

"So I'm looking for someone who knew how the souls were bound to their bodies." I lifted my scythe again and thumped the butt against the stone floor. "And how to sever those bindings. And someone with enough power to twist a spark to give the idea to a mortal." I froze, staring down at the spark in my hand. "Oh," I said softly, curling my dream-scarred fingers tight around the small glow.

I'd had a terrible thought at that moment. One that I was not ready to seriously consider. It was too wild for that. Too painful. And yet...

I could not think of anything else that made sense.

"Death?" Inspiration said, drawing me out of my distraction.

"Thank you for your help," I said stiffly, turning as an afterthought to give Inspiration the bare minimum of respect with a small bow before I took my leave. I suddenly wanted to be away from her, with time and room to think over what I had just realized. Maybe I could even convince myself that I was wrong. I desperately wanted to be wrong.

Inspiration would not let me go so easily. She rose from her seat and glided towards me, but did not reach out to touch me. "Are you all right, Death?"

"No," I heard myself say. "But I need to be, if I'm going to fix this." I held out my hand, offering the spark back to Inspiration.

She gently shook her head, sending shimmers of color down her cloak. "You keep that," she said. "You may find that you need it."

I looked down at the spark, seeing in its brightness all the chaos and destruction one of its cousins had brought down. All because of a little possessive jealousy. I doubted I would ever use it, but I still closed my fingers around the spark and bent it to my will, smothering its power until the spark was just soft enough to be reshaped. I poked a hole through the center and slid it down my finger, where it came to rest against my knuckle. It glowed a contented scarlet against the bone.

It had been so easy to reshape.

"If you don't mind," I said, "I think I'll give this to Destiny. She'll find a much better use for it."

Inspiration had the courtesy to insist that I could use the spark just as well, but it was half-hearted and she could not stop her fires from blazing with joy at the thought of Destiny holding one of her sparks again.

I considered advising Inspiration against romance of any sort, but I managed to bite back the words.

Instead, I turned and rushed out of her home, leaving her fires burning a baffled blue behind me.

In the event of the mortal world becoming unstable beyond repair, an Apocalypse Ride will require the support of either co-creator Life, co-creator Destiny, or arbiter Justice before it can be officially called, but as long as Death has the support of at least one other Force named in this Addendum, they may end the mortal world with a Ride, regardless of whether or not this Contract has been dissolved.

-- excerpt from the Contract of Mortality, Addendum 3
authored by Death, countersigned by Justice

- 21 -

I stumbled back on to the main path, caught in a wild whorl of anger and denial. The heat of Inspiration's home faded away, leaving me with the cold stars overhead and the swirling mists of the dreamscape off to my left, back the way I had come.

I was so frustrated with myself for not realizing the truth *before* rushing all over Eternity, but I also could not accept the idea that had come to me in the volcano. I was torn between wanting to act and put a definitive end to the culprit, and an intense need to prove to myself that I was wrong, that I could not have possibly overlooked so many things for so long, that I was simply tired and desperate and grasping at the flimsiest of ideas before Justice found me or the chaos overran the mortal world or both.

I could not let myself be paralyzed by angst and indecision. I needed to work through my emotions and focus on the facts, to sort my own desires from the truth. I needed space to think, and I needed to actually force myself to face those thoughts.

I turned before I could tell myself that it was a terrible idea, and walked into the dreamscape.

The mists swallowed me whole the moment I set foot over their threshold. The dreamscape remembered me, and it eagerly began to feast on my turmoil. Embers and flames raced at me through the mists, while screaming figures rose and died all around me. The world went dark, even with the wildfires charging towards me, and the screams threatened to rip me apart.

I took a firm grip on my scythe, and whipped myself in a fast turn, swinging the blade in a glittering circle. "Enough!" I yelled, and I pushed a little of my power into the cut.

The dreamscape hissed and retreated, momentarily leaving me on a patch of dry, gray ground surrounded by clear air. Then the mists closed back in, reaching for my fears and desires.

I swung my scythe again, driving the dreamscape back once more, but it prowled around me, as though it knew that I could not keep this up. So I cupped one hand around my mouth, and whispered the name of the last reaper I had made, the one I had gifted to Dreaming. I released the name just as the mists collapsed on top of me. I felt them lift me off my feet and worm their way inside my robes, reaching for my core, ready to take me the way they had taken my lost sister and left nothing of her behind but the faint sense of someone missing.

Then there was an angry cry, and the mists shattered as the big reaper beat its wings and lashed its tail, driving the hunger of the dreamscape away. I landed hard on the ground, in the middle of soft white mists that swirled calmly all around me. I waited, tensed and ready, but the dreamscape did not attack again.

I hauled myself to my feet just in time to avoid greeting Dreaming from the ground. They were an angry blaze of dark colors when they found me.

What stupidity drove you to bring an even stronger *nightmare here?* Dreaming thundered as they finished coalescing in front of me. Then they got a good look at me, or at whatever aura was trembling around me that the dreamscape had been so keen to feed on, and Dreaming's colors softened. *What did you learn, Death?*

I shook my head. "I need to make myself accept the truth before I try to explain it. I think the dreamscape could help me, if you'll let me try?"

The mists swirled silently around us as Dreaming considered my request. They were quiet for so long that I expected their answer to be no. I would not have blamed them.

There's too much power in you, Dreaming finally said. *I won't be able to protect you if you let the dreamscape take hold. Not when you're this distraught.*

"I understand," I said.

If you do this, Dreaming warned, *you are on your own.*

I hesitated only a moment before nodding.

An agitated whorl of deep blue passed across Dreaming's face. *I will stay with you until the end,* they promised. *Now close your self, and open your mind.*

I did not try to understand what that meant. Instead, I turned away from Dreaming, and waited.

The dreamscape did not stay quiet for long. It honed in on my frustration and confusion, but this time, rather than sending fires to devour me, the dreamscape began to parade figures before me. Familiar Forces I had already dismissed as innocent, but they marched across my vision all the same, reminding me why I could not ignore the truth anymore.

The Riders came first, astride their horses and led by red War, glorious and terrifying in his armor. His massive beast snarled as they rode past, the dreamscape echoing with the thunder of its hoofbeats. Pestilence followed on her pure white steed, but not the incorporeal Pestilence she had become after the chaos exposure that had ripped her from her body. Instead, she was the haunting beauty I remembered, white and fearsome, her skin streaked with dirt and her nails dark with grit. Her hair was long and tangled, and a crown of dead branches and rotting leaves sat upon her white tresses. She flashed me the wicked, alluring grin I remembered so well. But this was not Pestilence anymore. It would never be Pestilence again. A wave of black rose from the dreamscape and covered her, ripping away her corporeal form and leaving the swarming whirlwind in its wake. This form clung to the back of her dainty, impeccably clean mare, which whickered and cantered away, taking Pestilence with her. Before I could watch my last love disappear, Famine's mechanical horse plodded into view, so tarnished it was fully black from ear to hoof. Famine had once had expressed a desire for a real horse, but the rest of us had worried that they would starve the poor thing. We had given Famine a steed of living silver instead. They had promptly forgotten about it for a few centuries, then marveled at how smoothly the mechanical horse rode even after it had been left to rot, and never asked for a different horse ever again.

The Riders moved in a graceful circle around Dreaming and me, finally coming to rest in formation in front of us. I noted their order, incorrect now that I had left and Pestilence had lost her corporeal form. She should have led the way. Instead, she followed War with Famine bringing up the rear. It was so wrong that I could not help but think of the ghostly tread of my own pale steed, who should have stood proud and tall next to the other horses. The dreamscape shifted, and another equine form began to rise from the mist.

"No!" I said, and clamped down on the thought before it could rise any further.

The mist dissolved.

There was a flicker of color as Dreaming considered my distress, but they were kind enough to remain silent.

I focused my attention back on the remaining three Riders. I knew that each one of them had the power needed to twist a dream to their whim, and of all the Forces, they would have had the easiest time stealing essences from Inspiration and the twins. But the Virtues would have known if one of them had so much as glanced at their territories, and the sheer depth of the Riders' power would have made it impossible for them to keep their footprints out of the chaos on the mortal world.

I also knew that they had not lied to me. They were angry and petty and frightening and terrible, but they were also loyal and honest. I loved them for that, and somehow, after everything, they still loved me.

A soft glow suffused the dreamscape then, painting the Riders in beautiful light that showcased their power and strength. They shone brightly for a moment, regal and glorious. Then they turned their horses and galloped away. I knew that they were not real, but I ached to see them go, so badly that I could not stop the equine wisp of ashen mist that coalesced and tore off after them, fast and silent as a memory. They all vanished over the edge of the light.

Once the Riders were gone, the Virtues rose up in their place, too ethereal and untouchable for me to ever consider beautiful.

First there was Wisdom, emotionless and unyielding. Similar in build and features to Justice, Wisdom lacked his natural grace and energy, and looked as though she had been carved from banded stone. She did not move so much as she abruptly changed positions with no motion in between, which often unnerved a good number of us. She concerned herself with nothing but absolute truths and facts, and had no patience for anything else. Powerful, yes, but never one to operate on theories and guesswork, and until the soul jump had actually happened, none of us could have been certain that it was possible.

Next to Wisdom stood Temperance, smiling and simple and open in their friendliness. I did not spend long considering Temperance; they were powerful, but so often defined themselves by what they did not do, and never lashed out with any form of malice. If Temperance had been involved in the soul jump in any way, I had no doubt that they would have come begging for my forgiveness as soon as the first chaos ripple washed across the mortal world.

After them came Courage, towering and striking in her gleaming silver-blue gown. She wore no armor, but would face down War by herself if the need arose. And for that reason, I knew I could dismiss her as well. Courage could be strong, and inspiring, and even fearsome, but a complex thinker she was not. She lacked the capacity to plan something as intricate as a soul jump performed by a mortal's hand, and I sincerely doubted she could have stolen from other Forces without them knowing. Maybe the twins, if she'd walked into their mines while they'd been bickering about a wager, but she was more likely to announce her presence and intentions than to sneak through the shadows. It was only because of the Force formally known as Secrecy that she had been able to steal order stones from the Sins and Riders in the first place.

That left me with Justice, who I had avoided looking at until now.

The dreamscape had done me no favors, and had portrayed Justice easily three heads taller than he truly was. It kept his predominate features: dark skin; large, pointed ears; massive, onyx-feathered wings growing from his shoulder blades; gold eyes and the wild webs of glowing, golden lines on his face; and a body rippling with powerful muscles. But the dreamscape had magnified everything, until Justice was terrifying to behold. He sneered at me before his dream-dramatized face twisted in disgust, as though tasting all of my shortcomings and mistakes on his tongue. Still desperate for an alternate truth, I wondered if Justice could have caused the soul jump as punishment for some offense I was not aware of, but the act had violated the Contract he had helped write in painstaking detail. He never would have breached the Contract, not even if his very existence had depended on it.

As much as I wanted to pretend that one of them was to blame, I simply knew that a Virtue would never enable a soul jump and knowingly generate that much chaos on the mortal world.

The dreamscape seemed to agree, for it dissolved the Virtues one by one. Of course, Justice went last, and I could not help shifting uncomfortably when he turned his head towards me one last time. Though blind, his eyes seemed to stare me down, reminding me of all my wrongdoings, and my thoughts turned to Envy.

She coalesced before me, screaming in pain and horror at her severed vines, and in the dreamscape, everything was amplified until her cries threatened to split my skull and all I could see was her existence leaking out of the squirming vines I had cut.

Be at peace, Death, Dreaming's voice encouraged me, and Envy blurred into silence.

When she came back into focus, she was whole and standing with her familiar sly smile, eying my scythe and letting her vines creep wherever they wanted. The other Sins rose up around her, calm and confident now that they'd been divorced from Shame.

Which reminded me that I still did not know why Shame had been inside their home in the first place. But more important than that, was the bizarrely insightful comment that Sloth had made about the guilty Force needing to be at the reaping site when the soul jump had happened.

The dreamscape formed a misted version of the Sin of laziness next to me, and with a voice like echoes in water, she said, "You'd need a lot of power on the mortal world for that, and probably even have to be with the mortal at the time of the swap."

She had said "probably" without meaning anything by it, but if I had been paying attention, I would have understood everything then.

I still did not want to accept it. I knew it had to be true, but I *could not* accept it. The dreamscape churned as I struggled with my own denial, darkening and then glowing with another promise of a frustrated fire.

Death, Dreaming called to me, their voice heavy with warning.

I knew that there was only one way forward. I had to stop struggling, and accept it.

The visions dissolved around me, until nothing was left but a swirling eddy of color and light that slowly, painfully came together to form the Force I knew so well. The dreamscape made him smile at me. I stood staring back for so long that Dreaming flickered beside me, trying to catch my attention.

I don't understand, they said.

"I should have known from the start," I replied.

I did, after all, know of only three Forces with enough power over mortals and the mortal world to have done all of this. Of those three, only two of us knew how to slice a soul free from its body, because we were the ones who had created mortality. And of the two of us, only one would have set all of this up to scapegoat my reapers and convince me to stay on the mortal world forever.

I simply had not thought that Life would ever do this to the things we had made together. That he would ever do something like this to my reapers. That he would do it to *me*.

With the full scope of his betrayal finally illuminated, I expected to be furious, but I found myself strangely calm. There was pain, deep and aching, and I heard the dreamscape reverberate with my thoughts, painting them in clear, sharp detail to Dreaming. I felt them flinch away from the sheer strength of what I called from the mists, but I felt no danger around me. Finally having the answer had snapped so many things into focus, and showed me so many patterns echoing through the past, all the way to the inception of the mortal world. Things I had been blind to, and things that I had seen and chosen to ignore. Anger would not make any of those things go away, or fix what Life had broken.

Not yet, at least.

Not when I was still on Eternity, and he was out of my reach, on the mortal world. But that was only a temporary barrier. I just had to get back to the main path, where I could anchor myself and return to the mortal world. I could not do that in the dreamscape. It was time for me to go.

Dreaming understood. Nothing was secret from them in their own home, and they'd seen everything I had brought with me, whether I'd intended to reveal it or not. They escorted me back to the path, and I could tell they were trying to find the right words for what they had seen.

Death, they finally said, their colors muted and forlorn, *I am sorry for what you must endure. If you wished to visit the dreamscape again to work through anything...*

They trailed off, which was probably for the best. I might have taken them up on the offer and tested just how strong the dreamscape's visions were against my scythe. Instead, I said to Dreaming, "Take care of that reaper. It will get into mischief if it grows bored."

A swirl of yellow danced across Dreaming's face. *I will keep that in mind.*

Then we said goodbye, and I stepped out of the mists.

This Contract may be terminated at any time by the joint agreement of both creator parties. Upon termination of said Contract, the mortal world is to be destroyed by an Apocalypse Ride, as called forth and led by Death.
-- excerpt from the Contract of Mortality

- 22 -

The moment I was back on the main path, I slammed my feet into the order stones and began to orient myself against the stars. My distress made me sloppy, and it took me a few tries to properly anchor myself, but I finally honed in on the mortal world. I raised my scythe to take myself back.

"THERE THEY ARE!"

I jumped, the shout and the sudden, thunderous footfalls breaking my anchor and nearly sending me off the path. I recovered myself just in time to see a streak of pure white lancing towards me. Behind that was a red mountain of a beast, and after that came a deep black void that spat mechanical sounds. The apocalyptic horses bore down on me, their Riders perched on their backs.

I did not have time for them.

I turned away, frantically searching for the anchor point again. I ignored their calls and kept looking for the telltale tug of the world I had helped create. The Riders reigned in their mounts and circled me, begging me to wait.

"I will come back to you," I promised them as I lifted my scythe again, "but I need to return to the mortal world right now. I have to set this right!"

"Death, wait!" Pestilence said.

"I will come back!" I shouted, cutting her off. "I promise!"

But before I could bring my scythe down, I heard another sound over all of the snorts and footfalls and even the mechanical whirs of Famine's horse, so soft and delicate I might have imagined it. I knew I had not. I would have recognized my own horse's footsteps anywhere.

I dropped my scythe, throwing my arms over my head so that the sleeves of my robe fell across my face and suffocated my sight. "Send it away!" I snarled, fighting the rib-crushing urge to tear my sleeves away and gaze upon the wonderful, terrible being that approached me.

Even under the heavy footfalls of War's fidgeting brute, I could still hear the near-silent steps of my own horse. A deep ache seared through me. I longed to lower my arms and rush to my mount, to cast off the trinkets I had gathered that day and command the Riders to end the mortal world. To ride with them and bring total, perfect silence to everything.

I felt myself falling to my knees as I nearly begged the Riders to send my beloved horse away, my voice growing weaker and less convincing with each word, until I was moaning at them, pathetic and broken.

I did not hear the others say anything, but my horse's footsteps stopped, and then the urge to rip through the mortal world and put an end to everything receded so quickly, it left me dizzy and shivering. I waited a few minutes before lifting my head, giving myself time to calm down and muster the strength to stand again.

"How dare they," I said as I surfaced from my sleeves. "How dare they tempt me with—"

I broke off when I saw that Pestilence and War were still seated on their horses before me. I nearly flinched back inside my robes, fearing that my horse was somehow still there, even if I could not sense it any more.

War made no effort to spur his horse closer, but he thrust his hand towards me, the palm facing me. "I swear by all the blood I've spilled, your steed is gone," he said.

Pestilence shifted on her glowing mare, extending part of herself to me. "I swear by all the disease I've spread, your steed is gone," she said.

I was not certain that I believed them, but I did feel a warm wash of power as their words took hold. A red circle burned against War's gauntlet, and a silvery white one appeared silhouetted against Pestilence's angry whirlwind. The oaths settled over us like a blanket, heavy and thick, then dissolved without breaking. The circles faded.

They had spoken the truth, then.

I was not ready to forgive them.

"How *dare* you try to seduce me to ride?" I demanded. "The Riders are *mine* to call. I may come last, but that is because I am absolute while you are only temporary." I took a lunging step towards them both, and even War's horse flattened its ears and sidestepped away from me. "THE RIDE IS *MINE*."

War raised his hands in surrender. "We had no intention to summon an Apocalypse Ride," he said, nearly twisting the words in his haste to get them out. "I'm sorry! Truly and deeply, I am sorry."

"As am I," Pestilence added quietly. I could feel all of her attention riveted on me. "It really was not our intent, Death."

This stilled me, but my fury was still alive and thrashing. "Why would you bring my horse to me?" I snarled.

War lowered his hands to his reins. I realized that he was still wearing the same armor he'd had on when I saw him earlier, including the helmet I had dehorned. For some reason, this took the edge off of my anger.

"We thought you might wish to move faster, so we brought your horse with us when we set out to find you."

"I have no need to move faster," I said, the heat not fully gone from my voice. "I am returning to the mortal world to put an end to this."

"Death," Pestilence said, regaining her impatient drone, "there's something you need to hear."

"I don't have time," I said, once again anchoring myself to the mortal world. "I have to stop him before he hurts anyone else."

"But, Death—!"

I raised my scythe one more time.

And then a searing, blinding pain ripped through me, and I screamed. I fell to the ground, writhing in agony far greater than anything I had ever felt before. Not even raw chaos had hurt me this much. I felt myself coming apart, every bone snapping and my core tearing and there was nothing but the pain and the blistering stars over my head, cold and indifferent to my destruction. Then even they began to fade as darkness rushed in, and I thought I heard someone calling my name before it all echoed into nothing.

Suitable consequences for a breach of contract include but are not limited to: Removal. Continued abuse of power, especially for major offenses, may result in the removal of a Force from existence.
-- excerpt from the Contract of Mortality

- 23 -

I floated in silence for so long, I began to forget who I was. I felt myself dissolving at the edges, fading into the void that had birthed me. I tried to fight back, to remember, but it was just so much easier to succumb, and there was almost no pain then. I started to slip away.

Then I heard a voice, and somehow I knew that they were calling for me, calling *my name*, and I grabbed on to that voice and pulled myself back from the nothingness. Reclaiming myself was one of the hardest things I have ever done, and when I finally returned to existence, with the warm order stones of the path pressing against my spine and *Death* ringing in my core, I was so weak, I could barely move.

The world came back to me in bits and pieces.

First, the undying stars, gazing down at me with cold impassiveness from the dark sky.

Then, the ghost of the pain I had felt before, still rippling through me from skull to toe. It hurt to lie against the order stones, but I knew that they were keeping me connected to Eternity, to myself, and I pressed as many of my bones against the path as I could.

Finally, the red gleam of War's armor as he bent over me, calling my name and coaxing me back into existence. One gauntleted hand was pressed to my chest, and I only realized after he had been there for a while that War was siphoning off his own power and pumping it into me, giving me the strength I needed to hold on. I felt it pulsing through me as my core absorbed it all, feeding on instinct and the raw need to survive. That was dangerous. I tried to reach up to push War's hand away, knowing that my core would take and take until there was nothing left to give, but by the time I managed to move my fingers, War had already withdrawn.

"I couldn't let you leave us yet, my darling," War murmured as he sat back. He lifted something off the ground and pressed it into my hand.

My scythe.

My fingers curled around it automatically.

"What happened?" I managed to croak out. I tried to sit up, but War restrained me with a hand on my shoulder.

"Wait until my power has a chance to settle," War cautioned me. "The soul jump nearly destroyed you."

I frowned. "I know I'm not what I once was, but the soul jump was hours ago."

War shook his head. "No, Death, there was a second one."

Despite the heat of the order stones beneath me, I went cold all over. This time, when I tried to sit up, War braced me with an arm around my shoulders, and helped me rise. I felt a little better once I was sitting, but all I could do was sputter, "What did... *How* did...?"

War looked at me with something bordering on pity, but he knew better than to stare at me like that. "When you started screaming," he said, keeping his voice as gentle as a herald of destruction could, "Pest and I had no idea what was happening. You just dropped and then you started to crumble. We couldn't let you go. Pest held you down and I tried to hold you here, but that Contract breach nearly obliterated you." War paused and shuddered, his armor clanking softly. "Of course, we didn't know that was what it was until Destiny told us," he continued, shifting to a more matter-of-fact attitude. "Once we knew that, we knew what to do, and so, here you are." He patted my shoulder lightly. "I can accept creative favors as payment for my heroic sacrifice, to be collected at the time of my choosing."

I pushed his hand away. "Destiny was here?" I asked as I glanced around. War and I were alone on the path, save for his stamping brute of a horse.

"No, it was more of a long-distance call," War said. "You were a bit busy being unconscious and succumbing to the void, so Pest made the connection instead. Destiny was a bit frazzled from the new breach, but she was in way better shape than you. The best she could figure, this second soul jump hit you so hard because the Contract seems to think that you're no longer necessary, if the mortals can fling their souls from body to body." He hesitated before plowing on. "The Contract tried to eliminate you, Death. Pest and I wouldn't let it."

"It probably helped that I am much better at killing

than being killed," I noted dryly.

War huffed a laugh, but I saw how strained it was.

"Thank you, War," I said, and I meant it sincerely.

War seemed to glow in the wake of those two words.

I glanced around for Pestilence again, so I could thank her as well. My skull throbbed with the movement, reminding me that I had to go slow just when I could not afford it. I looked for the white Rider, anyway. She was nowhere to be seen. "Did Pestilence go back to the lair?" I asked.

"Ah, no," War said. "Destiny said the chaos on the mortal world had reached the breaking point, and she couldn't contain it on her own anymore. She'd reached out for you so she could beg you to go back and help her, but as I said, you were otherwise engaged, so I stayed here to keep you from crumbling to dust, and Pest went to see what she could do to help quell the chaos."

"Pestilence went to the mortal world?" I asked, my grip on my scythe suddenly tight and shaking.

War nodded. "She went as quickly as she could, and—"

"HOW COULD YOU LET HER GO?" I screamed. I grabbed for War and only succeeded in scratching my dream-scarred fingers across his red armor. My scrabbling hand closed around the remaining horn on War's helmet, and I used the purchase to pull myself to my feet. My scythe was in the air a moment later, and then I locked on to the mortal world again.

War was too stunned to stop me as I brought the butt of my scythe down. It crashed against the order stones with enough force to rattle my teeth and startle

War's horse.

Nothing else happened. I felt no rush of power. The world did not shatter. I was not catapulted across realms to return to the mortal world. And in spite of my desperation to get to Pestilence and keep her safe, I could barely stand. My legs shook as I slid down the handle of my scythe, falling to my knees on the path. "How could you let her go?" I whispered. My scythe clattered to the ground.

War's hand came to rest with uncharacteristic gentleness on my shoulder. "Pestilence won't be caught by surprise this time," he said. "She knows how to handle chaos now, and she's grown a lot stronger since she lost her corporeal form." He gave my shoulder a light squeeze. "She'll be okay."

I shook my head violently. "It's too dangerous for her there."

War's hand tightened on my shoulder before relaxing again. "I know you're worried about her, but Destiny's going to work hard to keep Pest safe. They came up with this idea to tether the chaos to the mortal plane and control it using Pest's power. See, if there's a new disease to explain all the weird things the mortals have been getting up to in the chaos flux, that puts some sense back into the world, and gives the mortals a way to fight back." War began to slowly rub my shoulder blade. "I mean, sure, Pestilence may go a bit overboard and create a plague that may not have a perfect vaccine, but she saw what the Contract breach did to you, and there was no stopping her once she'd made up her mind. And Destiny thinks that, together, they can lock the chaos to the mortal world and stop the overspill, maybe even calm it enough to find the source." His hand paused for a moment. "That's a pretty smart partner you have there."

I groaned and turned to face War. "My partner is going to destroy Pestilence on sight," I said.

War froze. "Destiny would do that?"

"Life," I said, my voice brittle with bitterness. "He allowed the soul jumps. He gave the mortals the ability to defy me. He did *every*thing, and if he finds Pestilence alone…" I did not want to finish the thought.

It was hard to imagine Life destroying anyone, but he had allowed not one but two major Contract breaches, the second of which had almost annihilated me. What would he do to Pestilence, if she succeeded in calming the chaos? He knew my history with Pest and what we'd once meant to each other. What we *still* meant to each other, if she was fighting chaos on the mortal world with Destiny. She was doing that for me.

"You have to bring her back," I told War. "Go to the mortal world, and find Pestilence before Life does."

War made a careful sound and shifted until he was on one knee before me. "If I could, I would, but you were fading so fast, Death. You needed me more."

I gazed at him for a long moment as his words sank in. War had given me so much of his strength, he must have been nearly as weak as I was. That was why he had not moved to stop me when I'd tried to return to the mortal world. And why he had not yet risen to his feet.

I pressed my face into my hands. "I don't have the strength to reach out to Destiny yet," I said.

There was a pause, and I heard War's armor clank as he moved. "I'm afraid I can't reach Pestilence, either," he admitted. "Which is probably for the best. We should not break her concentration while she's fighting chaos."

"So we are stuck here, waiting until we're strong enough to move, or until we hear from one of them again," I muttered.

"Well, my horse could take us somewhere else," War offered.

"There is nowhere else to go," I said, "until this plays out."

"That's not entirely true," another voice chimed in.

I snapped my head around. I found myself at a complete loss for words when I saw Sloth on the back of War's horse. A complicated tangle of rope kept her bound to the saddle, holding the Sin in place even as she pitched to the side, not bothering to expend the necessary energy to keep her seat on the red horse.

"Ah, right," War said. "Before the second soul jump and we almost lost you forever—" I heard the strain in his tone, despite his attempt to keep his voice light, "—we had a visitor at the Riders' lair."

This shocked my voice out of hiding. "*Sloth* came to *you*?"

War shrugged, clearly as perplexed by the happening as I was, and I had witnessed firsthand how fast Sloth could actually move. I had simply assumed that was the upper limit of her energy and she would not move again this century.

"I told you," Sloth said, rolling her head around to fully join the conversation, but she paused when she caught sight of me. "Nice outfit," she said as she eyed me up and down. "What is that, solid luck, hopecloth,

219

and a spark of inspiration?"

"I liked you better when I thought you were a burnt-out lump," I snapped.

"Always been a lump, just never a burnout," Sloth countered. "Anyway, like I said before, I *can* move. I simply choose not to."

"She demonstrated that quite efficiently after she showed up at our lair," War commented dryly. He gave me a brief rundown of what had happened after he'd gotten back from Peace's library, which he pointedly informed me was not a short walk on the best of days, least of all when the pedestrian was wearing full body armor.

"That was your decision," I reminded him.

War huffed something under his breath that I chose to ignore, then plowed on with the story of Sloth's sudden appearance.

According to War, there had been no preamble to Sloth's visit, no warning that she was coming. She had simply appeared in the main cave while Pestilence and Famine were teasing War about his impromptu summoning, said that she had something very important to tell me, and that I needed to come back to the Sins' den right away.

"Then she collapsed on the ground and refused to move," War said. "After we all stared at her in silence for what I thought was a *perfectly appropriate* amount of time, Sloth here suddenly woke up and said we had better find you if we didn't want you getting angrier than you already were. Then Pest suggested we take the horses, and we all rode out to find you. This one—" War jerked his thumb at Sloth, who lolled in the saddle and only managed not to fall thanks to the snarl of rope holding her in place, "—insisted on coming along for the ride."

Sloth gave me a sleepy smile.

"And what, exactly, were you hoping for, sweet Sloth?" I asked, reaching for my scythe. "The next apocalypse, maybe?"

Sloth's smile widened. "It's entirely possible that may still happen, especially if Life really is the one who started all this. I might've realized that if I looked a little harder, but eh, I do what I can. And you know, even if I don't get to see a full-on apocalypse, it'll be just as interesting if you and War are both coming back to the den."

"Why?" I asked.

Sloth's eyes lost their sleepy cast again, and her grin turned dangerously sharp. "Because his brother shares your taste in accessories."

Shame may not exert his influence over anyone, any place, or anything. [Note from Justice: Sorry, all. Rule 6 is very clear on this matter, and applies to all Forces, natural or otherwise. My hands are tied on this one.]
-- rejected addendum to the Contract of Mortality authored by Death, countersigned by Life and Destiny, vetoed by Justice

- 24 -

War's horse thundered along the path, rattling my bones with every step. I found myself yearning for the gliding gait of my own beloved horse, and it was all I could do to keep my focus on Sloth as the giant red beast carried us back to the Sins' den.

War had recovered his strength more quickly than I had, and he had placed me behind Sloth in the giant saddle before positioning himself in front. I clung to the Sin's soft fur as we rode, trying to keep my own balance as I listened to her story of Pride's involvement. Her voice would have lulled me to sleep if she did not keep trailing into silence, and I jostled us both every time she drifted off. It seemed that finding me had removed the urgency from the situation as far as she was concerned, and Sloth had given herself permission to return to her regularly scheduled naps.

The few pieces that I did get out of Sloth only

strengthened her claim that Pride had played a role in the soul jumps, but I could not determine the depth of his involvement. I knew that I wasn't wrong about Life orchestrating everything; Pride didn't have the knowledge or the strength to do the things the soul jump demanded, and I would have sensed him on the mortal world if he'd been there. But according to Sloth, a few hours after my visit to their den, Pride had tried to have a private, long-distance discussion with someone not in Eternity, and failed to realize that Sloth was in the room. She did not know who had initiated the connection, or who had been on the other end, but she'd heard enough. Apparently, Pride was more than upset that his contact had not carried through on a bargain they'd struck, even though Pride had delivered everything he'd been asked to "secretly borrow" from other Forces, which I translated to "steal" as I listened to Sloth's account.

Sloth agreed that it could have been Life that Pride spoke to, when I presented the idea to her. She also said that after seeing the luck, hopecloth, and spark that I wore, she was more than certain that Pride had stolen those essences. Especially since in the weeks prior to the soul jump, Pride had taken to wandering restlessly around the den, finally distracting himself with the fraternity house renovation of the interior, but he kept sneaking off to his room and being very conscientious about locking his door against Avarice's prying hands.

"Is that all?" I asked.

Sloth did not respond, and I gave her a rough shake. Her head lolled and she cracked one eye open long enough to give me an irritated glance.

I pressed her to answer me. "I thought you said you saw Pride with luck, hopecloth, and a spark?"

"I never *really* said that," Sloth said, yawning over the back half of her words. "But he did get weirdly lucky in finding all of those decorations without trouble, along with that restaurant that will deliver to our anchor point on the mortal world if you add a big enough tip. *And* he was weirdly optimistic up until about two days ago."

"Hold on here," I said, clinging to Sloth as War reined in his hulking horse in front of our destination. "Are you telling me we're about to accuse Pride of stealing from other Forces and helping to facilitate a soul jump based purely on a hunch you formed from your couch?"

"Kitchen floor, this time," Sloth said. "And that is absolutely what we're going to do."

War glanced over his shoulder to meet my incredulous stare. "I've ridden out for less," he said with a shrug.

"Of course you have," I muttered as I slid off of the horse. I stumbled as I landed, still not fully recovered from the second Contract violation, but I was grateful to be back on solid ground. I carefully shook out and rearranged my robes, checking to be certain that the mixed luck, hopecloth, and spark were all still intact and in place.

War did not bother untying Sloth before he swung his leg over the back of his horse and dismounted. Sloth pitched to the side, hanging limply off of the horse's saddle, but War did not look back. He seemed to have forgotten that she was there as he strode up to the entrance of the Sins' den.

I reached out with my scythe to gently cut the rope as War knocked on the door. He glanced back when Sloth landed with a soft *whump* on the ground, where she lay in a sprawl of limbs and rope.

"Ah, thank you, my darling," War said as he surveyed Sloth's limp form. "Seems I'm so excited to see my little brother, I'd leave my own sword behind if it wasn't strapped to my hip."

"I could have sworn Pride was older than you," I said as I nudged Sloth with the butt of my scythe. She did not stir.

"Yes, but I'm taller," War said.

The door opened at that moment, and before I could say a word, War slammed his way over the threshold and scooped up poor Pride, who barely had time to blink before he was several feet off the ground.

"BROTHER!" War bellowed, crushing the Sin in his embrace with enough power to make my spine creak in sympathy.

I moved to follow War inside, but felt a tug on my scythe. I looked down to see Sloth's hand wrapped around the handle. I tried to shake her off, but she would not release her grip on my scythe. I groaned, then dug my heels into the ground and dragged Sloth through the door in a series of short, sharp bursts of motion that left my bones shaking. The moment she was fully inside, Sloth uncurled her fingers and dropped flat against the floor.

I shook my head and turned to see War spinning in circles with Pride locked in his arms. I pressed my fingertips to my forehead in exasperation. "War, would you please put your brother down?"

"Come now, Death," War crooned. "Allow me my fun." He shifted his grip on Pride, and for a moment, I thought that he would actually grant my request. Then War tossed his brother into the air and caught him in a cradle of red metal and muscled arms.

With his lungs now free, Pride sucked in as much air as he could, then coughed at his brother, "Must you do this every twice-cursed time?"

"I'll stop when wars no longer carry the weight of the Sins!" War said, then roared with laughter. "And I carry my little brother most of all!"

"I'm older than you!"

"But I am taller!"

"That's not how this works! You're still *my* little brother!"

War rocked his brother in his arms, deepening the insult to Pride. "If I were the little brother," he said, "I could never ride my magnificent horse."

Pride flushed a deep, angry purple, but before he could fire off a retort, Envy popped her head around War's shoulder. Her eyes flickered to me for a moment, and I saw a bud of fear in her, but before it could bloom, she shifted her attention back to War and offered him a dazzling smile.

"What's this about size mattering, now?" she asked.

"Yes," came Lust's purr from the stairs. "Do tell."

"Darlings!" War cried, dropping Pride in an undignified heap on the floor as he whipped around to focus on the other Sins. "It has been *too* long!" He draped an arm around Envy's shoulders and steered her towards a couch, waving for Lust to follow.

As Lust gracefully descended the stairs, they caught my gaze and offered me a friendly smile.

"Feeling better?" I asked as they passed me.

"Much," they said. "Thank you."

"Happy to help," I said, then slammed the butt of my scythe on the floor, catching the hem of Pride's toga before he could crawl away. "I only wish there had not been anything to help with."

"Lust, darling, come join us!" War interrupted. He patted the seat next to him on the couch. Envy was already draped across his lap, looking very pleased with herself for having claimed Lust's preferred spot.

Lust gave me another smile and Pride a quizzical glance before slipping away.

I heard the red Rider mention the Trojan War as I turned my attention to Pride, who was desperately trying to tug his toga free. He fell still as I bent over him. I caught the scent of his fear mixed with his power, and in that moment, I knew that Sloth had guessed right; I'd found the final signature I'd sensed in the chaos on the mortal world. "I've made some very interesting discoveries since you and I last spoke," I said.

Pride looked up, ready to say something sharp to me, but whatever the words were, they died on his lips. He swallowed hard as his eyes moved over the trinkets I wore.

I touched the lump of luck dangling from its cord, drawing Pride's attention to that first. It glinted silver and gold in the light. "I don't like playing games," I said, never taking my gaze off of Pride, "but I endured them to learn that someone stole a lot of pure good luck from the twins. Enough, perhaps, to allow a mortal to wield a chaos blade without destroying two—no, *three* souls when he cut their cords of mortality and unbound them from their bodies."

I ran my hand over the ragged hopecloth next. "Of course, I didn't know for certain that it was a chaos blade until poor Hope tried to show me one of his completed hopecloths. He was devastated to discover that someone had cut out the middle and stolen it. That was a massive amount of hope that was taken. Maybe even enough to let a mortal believe that he could switch his soul into a new body and evade me, if only he had the means to try."

Pride shut his eyes. He looked very small, huddled in my shadow.

I snapped my dream-scarred fingers in front of his face, startling him into opening his eyes again. I brandished the dimmed spark of inspiration that I had fashioned into a ring around my finger. "I did wonder how the mortal had gotten this idea to begin with. But then I learned from Dreaming that it's possible to deliver distilled essences to a mortal through a dream, and then all that remained was a twisted spark to ignite the mortal's desire so that the wretched idea could take root."

I straightened and lifted my scythe off of Pride's toga. He made no move to get up. "There was still one piece missing, one last thing I sensed in the tainted chaos spawning on the mortal world, but Sloth was kind enough to supply the answer." I glanced at the dozing Sin, but she was as inert as ever. "All those elements certainly enabled the soul jump, but none of them *made* the mortal believe he could actually do it on his own. Not even hope could do that. No, he needed something far more potent in order to believe himself capable of such a feat. I believe this missing piece was never supposed to be part of the equation, but a Force could never handle another's essence as much as you did without marking it in some way."

I squatted down next to Pride and gently hooked the blade of my scythe around the back of his neck, keeping the pressure light so it would not cut his skin. I would let Pride come away from that encounter unharmed… as long as he did not try to move away from me.

"So that was the secret blend. A stolen dream, a twisted spark of inspiration, a ragged cut of hope, a solid lump of pure luck, and a touch of pride."

I was planning to let the Sin suffer for a few moments, to let the weight of his guilt and the confirmation that I knew he was involved crush down on him, but when Pride pressed his face into his hands and seemed to fold in on himself, the other Sins in the room suddenly whipped their attention to him, and Sloth shot up.

"Don't—!" she yelped at the same moment that Envy and Lust leapt up from the couch, but they were too late.

With a crack of displaced air and the sudden, viscous sensation of despair, another Force was pulled into the room, right next to the guilt-ridden Pride. I lifted my scythe from his neck and held it like a wall between myself and Shame.

The room went very still as Shame's eyes slid over everyone. He looked as bewildered as I felt, but he quickly covered his surprise with a sneer. "I'm back in this cesspool *again*?" he grumbled.

Pride surfaced from his self-pity to shoot a look of hateful disbelief up at his opposite. The other Sins echoed him, and even War looked tense. Then there was a soft thunder of footsteps overhead, and the rest of the Sins appeared on the stairs. They took one look at Shame and their faces broke into snarls.

Shame curled his lip right back at them.

"Well," I said, shattering the silence, "I suppose that answers my question about how he got here earlier."

"Just figuring that out now, are you?" Shame fired at me.

I pointed the blade of my scythe at him. "I can't kill you, but I *will* leave you in pieces again if you say one more word."

Shame eyed the blade, then shot me a silent glower before crossing his arms and regarding the Sins with open hostility.

I looked down at Pride. "Interesting that you don't disappear when he comes. I suppose there's less power in this dynamic than with War and Peace, but it's not what I expected."

Pride pushed himself to his feet and made a point of standing with his back to Shame. "It's because he's not a real Force." Shame made a face at Pride's back, but the jab landed true, and Pride seemed to draw strength from Shame's displeasure. The Sin stood taller when he said, "Not like the rest of us."

"There's our Sin back," I said, clapping him on the shoulder.

Pride smiled, right up to the moment when I

snatched his chin in my hand.

"But there's still something I don't understand," I said, my voice low and dangerous, "and you're going to tell me straight. No games, no trying to hide anything from me. Just the truth."

Shame popped his head over Pride's shoulder, mouth open and ready to spit more venom. I pressed the top edge of my scythe's blade to the artificial Force's neck. He shut his mouth with an audible click of his teeth.

"Did you know what you were doing," I said, watching Pride closely, "when you stole all of those things?"

"Yes." Pride swallowed around my grip. "Or at least, I thought I did."

"Why?"

"The last time I was on the mortal world, I was approached by… uh…" The Sin pressed his lips together, and I could see him weighing how likely I was to believe him. He took a shallow breath and braced himself for the worst, but I did not want him to say it, not with Shame over his shoulder.

"I already know," I told Pride. I let a little of my pain color my voice, so that Pride would understand that I really, truly already knew who had contacted him. "Now I need you to give me the truth. I need to know *why* you agreed to do all of this for him."

Pride shifted uneasily, and Shame's features took on their predatory sharpness. The artificial Force said nothing, but he did flash a wicked smile as he scented Pride's guilt.

I decided this would be much easier without Shame

trying to feed off of my interrogation. "War," I called, "do you think you could…?" I gestured at Shame.

War rose from the couch in one fluid motion, but before he could step forward, Lust was restraining him with a delicate hand on his arm.

"No," they said, their eyes hard, "I've got it this time."

Shame twisted around to give Lust a look that must have been intended to wither their confidence, but Lust squared their shoulders, cracked their knuckles, and then closed the distance to Shame so quickly that even I took a small step back.

I heard the muffled *thwmp* of an impact, followed by a moan of pain and another thud as Shame fell to his knees, and then Lust had Shame by the back of his shirt. They dragged him across the floor, wearing the same look that I had seen on Destiny's face when she needed to haul a trash bag full of old coffee grounds and the unrecognizable remains of Life's latest failed experiment out to the curb. "Sloth, dear," Lust said, cool as could be, "would you mind getting the door?"

Sloth leapt to the task, tugging the door open just in time to catch Justice with his fist raised, ready to knock on the everwood.

We all froze.

Shame was the first to move. He wriggled free of Lust's grasp, ducked his head, and ran out of the Sins' den, not even pausing to glance at Justice. This seemed to snap Justice out of his own surprise, for he lowered his hand and cleared his throat, offering the Sins a polite greeting. Then he slanted an ear in my direction before turning his blind, gold eyes on me.

"Do you have *any* idea," Justice asked me, his voice

deep and cutting, "how long it took me to find you?"

"I actually do," I said mildly. I did not mention the close call in the Virtues' territories, when I had used Silence as a shield, but we both knew that Justice had been looking for me since the first soul jump and Contract breach. That felt like eons ago.

"Then why?" Justice asked as he stepped through the door. He had to turn himself sideways to accommodate his wings, and duck to avoid hitting his head. "Why did you keep running from me?"

"I had some truths to find," I said.

"That's literally my job," he shot back, but there was no heat in the words.

Instead, I heard the resigned exhaustion in his voice, and I realized that the second Contract breach must have hit him hard. Maybe not eliminated-from-existence hard, but a little jaunt across Eternity and back would not have worn him out under better circumstances. It occurred to me that if I was to ever present Justice with the facts and prove to him who was really responsible for the whole chaotic mess, now was the time to do it, when he was too weak to exert his power over me and he'd be forced to listen before judging.

Few things are as soothing (or as numbing) as realizing that one's source of panic cannot actually do any them harm.

"Come do your job now, then," I invited Justice.

He scowled at me. "You did not answer my question."

"I hid from you because there were some things that I needed to see and understand for myself before I could accept the truth. I would be delighted to catch you up on everything I've learned, but I think you'll be particularly interested in this last piece of the mystery I'm about to hear."

Pride quailed beside me. I snared his toga and held him in place.

Justice tilted his head, his unseeing eyes staring through me and my captive Sin. His ears twitched in the silence that gripped the room. Then Justice gave a resigned sigh and moved closer, stopping just out of range of my scythe. If I had been less tired, I might have found that insulting. At that moment, I took it as a promising sign, and turned my attention back to Pride.

"Go on," I urged him, not unkindly. "Why did you agree to help him?"

I felt Justice's attention fix on my back for a moment before returning to the Sin.

Pride cast an uneasy look at Justice before glancing at the other Sins, all of whom now watched him with guarded interest. When Pride spoke, he tried to pitch his voice low, as though hoping that would keep it from carrying to everyone in the silent room. "He told me that if I got a few things for him," Pride said, "he would get rid of Shame."

"You should have known that was an impossible promise," I told Pride.

The Sin nodded. "I should have, but I thought that out of everyone, he would have been able to do it, especially with all those essences. All he wanted in return were the items he listed, and my silence. He said it needed to be a secret, or word might get back to Shame. He told me that I was the only one he could

234

trust with this." Pride frowned. "I suppose I should have asked why you weren't involved, but when you came here earlier, I thought maybe you knew after all and were here to end Shame for good, and he *hadn't* lied to me and fooled me into stealing all of those things, but…"

"But I didn't know, and you were tricked because he played to your pride," I said, making sure Justice heard my every word.

Life had known who to target and how to get exactly what he wanted. All to make me believe that there was something wrong with my reapers, and that I could not leave the mortal world. I'd known he had not wanted me to go, and that he resented my reapers, but this…

This was unforgiveable.

"Hold up now," War said, cutting across my thoughts. "What's going on here?"

Pride looked at me pleadingly.

I crossed my arms and waited. Justice stepped up next to me, adding the weight of his own interest to the pressure on Pride.

With a deep sigh, Pride faced his brother and his fellow Sins. "I was tricked into stealing luck, hopecloth, and a spark of inspiration."

Several of the Sins inhaled sharply at this. Sloth looked grimly satisfied.

Justice leaned towards me, until he his cheek was less than an inch away from brushing against my skull. "Hopecloth?" he whispered fiercely.

"I'll explain everything," I promised. "Just let him talk before you do anything."

Justice made an eerie sound in the back of his throat,

the kind of sound that promised violence and revenge. But he rocked back on his heels, rustled his wings, and waited.

I looked away from Justice to see War staring at me. "Who did this to my brother?" he asked, a deadly rumble rolling across his voice. He already knew the answer. I could see it in his burning eyes.

But the Sins...

They did not know. They did not know that one of their own had been manipulated into nearly destroying the mortal world, and our own. I forgave Pride for that. Or I would have, if he had warned me from the start instead of letting me wander through Eternity while chaos bloomed and stormed. He had put not only me in danger, but Destiny too, and now Pestilence. He would be punished for that.

"Life," Pride finally said. "Life asked me to steal these things for him, and promised that he would help me destroy Shame in return." He frowned and scratched the back of his neck. "I don't know what he wanted all of that stuff for, though. I thought he was going to make a weapon to kill Shame, but he never did anything with it."

"Yes, he did," I said, my voice quiet, but all eyes turned to me just the same. "Life gave the chaos blade to a mortal, and then let him loose to destroy mortality." I watched the growing horror settle over the Forces around me. "In short, Life broke the Contract, and now I need to go break him."

The Force Destiny will hereafter be granted the rights and privileges of co-creator status of the mortal world in exchange for her assistance in maintaining balance within said world.
-- excerpt from the Contract of Mortality, Addendum 1 authored by Life, countersigned by Death

- 25 -

War took Pride aside and had a long, quiet conversation with him while the other Sins gathered in a loose group around the couches, whispering to each other and throwing concerned looks at Pride. Even Sloth was engaged, having been carried to one of the couches by Wrath shortly after Pride's confession. Gluttony was the only one who was not speaking, but his eyes were bright and his lupine ears were thrust forward as he looked back and forth between Pride and the others, following the ebbs and flows of the disjointed discussions.

I watched their worry and frustration as I explained everything to Justice, from the way Life had tried to blame my reapers for the first soul jump and Contract breach, to tracking down the stolen essences and Pride's unwitting involvement in something this catastrophic. I argued that the Sin was not the one who should shoulder all or even most of the blame, even if he had been the one to steal from other Forces. There would need to be consequences for that, of course, but not on the same level that Life deserved.

I do not know if Justice was so worn out by chasing me across Eternity between two Contract breaches, or if he was actually swayed by my words, but I did not push the matter when, to my surprise, he agreed with me.

"I am far from mollified over what nearly happened to Hope," he growled, "but I would rather see punishment fall upon the one who encouraged the actions rather than his dim-witted tool." Justice crossed his arms and stared across the room at Pride. "Speaking of which, where did a Sin get a chaos blade to begin with?"

The question threw me. My first thought was that Pride must have forged the blade himself, but why would a Sin ever dive into chaos and risk themselves to craft a chaos blade? It would have been better (although perhaps not much safer or easier) for Pride to steal metal from Avarice and then craft the weapon in secret without Envy somehow sniffing out his private workshop. And even if Pride had elected to throw himself into a chaos field instead of trying to steal something from Avarice, how could he have held a piece of chaos in check and kept it from hurting him or his fellow Sins?

"Pride?" I called, and the room fell silent. "Where did you get the chaos blade you used to cut the hopecloth?"

Pride looked miserable when he said, "Life passed it to me in a dream. I sent everything back to him the same way. That should have been my first clue that everything was messed up."

"Yes," Justice growled, "it *should* have." The

Virtue's attention swung back to me. "What kind of punishment did you have in mind for War's little brother?"

"I'm *older*," Pride grumbled, the room still too quiet to stop his voice from carrying.

I did not acknowledge either the Sin or the Virtue, however. I was too busy staring at the top of my scythe, where the missing ornamental piece usually went. The small piece made from pure chaos. That morning, I had thought that it was hiding somewhere in my bedroom closet, and I had worried about a contained bit of chaos being lost on the mortal world. It had never occurred to me that I might have been stolen from, too.

"Conniving, greedy little seed of destruction," I hissed.

Justice looked at me in surprise. "I'll assume you are not talking about me, as that would be a very foolish thing to call me while I am standing next to you."

"Life stole part of my scythe and used it to make the chaos blade."

"Ah." Justice considered this for a moment. "I suppose that would have been considerably safer and faster than mining raw chaos to—where are you going?"

I was moving to a more private corner of the room. I trusted Justice to follow me whether I wanted him to or not, so I did not respond. Instead, I spent a few moments of silent effort gathering a few scraps of power. Justice was at my shoulder again by the time I lifted my scythe and gently tore a small hole in our realm with the tip of the blade. Light spilled out of the tear, making me squint as I pushed my arm through and reached across realms, trying to find Destiny. This was not an easy undertaking at the best of times, and right then, tired as I was, I felt the sticky, hungry pull of the tainted chaos as I stretched my fingers towards the mortal world. I gave the chaos several cautious, testing prods to confirm that it was not growing, merely beginning to seep through the gaps. That was not a great sign, but I steadied myself with the knowledge that I finally had everything that Destiny needed, I knew who to blame for the entire mess, and I had Justice on my side. That boosted my strength enough to let me punch through the chaos and tear into the mortal world. The connection opened with a sharp snap. I withdrew my arm to see Destiny's startled face peering back at me through the hole. Her attention flickered over my shoulder to Justice as he came up behind me, and she did not bother to conceal her surprise before looking back at me.

"Death? Are you—?"

"Where's Pestilence?" I asked, too upset and exhausted for anything more than terse demands.

"I'm here," the white Rider's ragged voice answered. A curl of dirty wind slipped into the hole.

My knees went weak with relief.

"Thank destruction you're safe," I said.

"It was just a little chaos," Pestilence said haughtily. "Nothing I could not handle."

Destiny shot her a disbelieving look, but knew better than to go against a Rider. She turned back to Justice and me instead. "We've managed to contain a good chunk of the stuff, thanks to Pestilence," Destiny informed us.

Pestilence gave a self-satisfied buzz before moving

out of range of my interdimensional tear.

Destiny tracked her across the room, clearly tense at the thought of anyone—especially a literal whirlwind of disease—disrupting her organized mess. "There's still enough out there to be dangerous," Destiny continued, "but at least we're not fighting a losing battle anymore. If Pestilence agrees to stay here, we can—"

"No!" I said, nearly throwing my head and shoulders through the tear to reach the two Forces just in front of me, and so beyond my reach. I felt Justice's hands close over my shoulders, stopping me before I could wear myself out with the effort of trying to travel across dimensions that way.

"Death, use your words," he cautioned me.

I pulled back and pushed his hands away. "It's too dangerous for her," I nearly yelled at Destiny. "For *both* of you!"

Pestilence's drone was shaded with confusion and anger when she returned to the tear. She buffeted Destiny out of the way so she could square off against me, and she barely gave Justice more than a cursory glance. "*We* are doing just fine," she snapped. "And before *I* showed up, poor Destiny here was on the verge of curling up in a corner and waiting for the chaos to come for her."

Destiny moved back into view and opened her mouth to counter that statement. Then she paused, shrugged, and moved away again. I heard the clacking of her keyboard join the harshness of Pestilence's droning a moment later.

"It's not the chaos that I'm worried about," I said

quietly. I shifted back and forth, trying to catch new angles through the tear and see if Pestilence and Destiny were alone, but the tear wasn't big enough. I leaned closer and whispered, "Pest, where's Life?"

"Not here," she snarled. She did not bother lowering her voice when she added, "Figures you'd ask about him while Destiny and I are the ones bleeding off power dealing with tainted chaos."

"Are you certain he's not there?" I pressed, too agitated to fire back at her.

"Yes!" she snapped, and Destiny sounded her agreement. "He went out hours ago, leaving poor Destiny here to fight off tainted chaos all by herself."

"So he does not know that you're there?"

Pestilence whipped dirt across the tear. "No, Death, he hasn't bothered to show his ugly face yet."

I was too tired to contain myself, and I sobbed with relief. It may not have been dignified, but it made Pestilence pause, Destiny slide back into view, and Justice give me a few awkwardly gentle but not unwelcome pats on the shoulder.

"Death," Pestilence said, "what did you learn?"

By the time I finished giving them a brief recap of my adventures and discoveries in Eternity, including Life's orchestration of the soul jump and duping of Pride, I had myself back under control. Destiny and Pestilence, however, were seething with not-so-silent rage. They fumbled over curses and insults to Life, building off of and trying to outdo each other.

"Creative as you both are," Justice cut across them, "I believe there are more pressing issues at hand."

I nodded vehemently. "You both need to leave the

mortal world," I told them. "It's not safe with Life there, and it's especially not safe for you, Pestilence. Come home."

"Home?" Pestilence asked, her voice a soft drone. "I thought the mortal world was your home now."

"I know you know me better than that," I said.

Pestilence held my gaze for a long moment. "Okay," she finally said. "I'll come home."

"I won't," Destiny put in. Before I could argue with her, she said, "There's still enough unbound chaos out here that it could spill into Eternity. If Pestilence is leaving, I need to stay back until it's under control."

I could not say that she was wrong, but I did not like it. "If Life was willing to do all of this to me, I don't want to imagine what he might try to do to you."

"He doesn't need to know that I know," Destiny pointed out. "And if Pestilence manages to go back to Eternity without leaving the apartment a total wreck, he'll never know she was here. Besides, if you can bring me all that stuff you found, I know I can pinpoint the source of the chaos and clear a path for you. If you can cut the source, I can contain the rest of the chaos, and then it will be safe for me to leave."

"I will come with you to the mortal world," Justice told me. "We'll move faster if we combine our power, and then I can help Destiny clean up the last of the chaos."

I failed to come up with any reasonable argument against the idea, and I reluctantly agreed to it.

"What are you going to do about Life?" Pestilence asked. Her buzzing ratcheted up to a frenzied pitch. "You're not going to let him keep you here, are you,

Death?"

Justice's ear slanted in my direction, informing me that he was equally interested in my answer.

"No," I promised Pestilence. "He's too strong for me to eliminate, but I will make sure he can't hurt anyone like this ever again."

"Really?" Justice asked mildly.

"Really," I said, and my tone was heavy enough to drive him back a step.

"How?" Pestilence pressed me.

I gazed at her in silence, and she gradually backed down as well.

"Be careful, Death," she said. Her whirlwind churned for a few moments. "I'll see you back home?"

"You will," I promised.

Pestilence moved out of my range of sight, but I heard the drone of her insects at the edge of the room as she paused, waiting. Destiny resettled herself in my field of view.

"How quickly can you bring me everything?" Destiny asked.

"That second soul jump took a lot out of me. Out of *us*," I said, pointing to Justice and myself, "but once I take care of one last thing here in Eternity, I think we can make the journey back."

"Be careful," Destiny warned. "Pestilence bound a lot of chaos, but there's still enough out there to make things dangerous."

I nodded. "I did not expect anything less."

We did not say goodbye. I let the tear snap closed, and then Justice and I turned back to the Sins.

The others had finished speaking at this point, and

those who were not staring at Pride were watching me. This included War, who steered Pride back to the Sins with one armored arm thrown protectively around his brother's shoulders.

"What's this 'one last thing' you need to do, my darling?" War asked as he approached.

He gave Pride a gentle push away, stepping between me and his brother. Pride drifted towards the Sins, who moved forward to intercept him. Lust reached out and took Pride's hand in their own, and squeezed it tight. They looked at me as though daring me to try to take Pride away from them.

"I know Pride was tricked into helping Life," I said, picking my words carefully, "but he still willingly stole from other Forces. He even left a chaos taint in Hope's home."

This startled everyone in the room, including Justice, who crossed his arms and scowled at me.

"You neglected to mention that little detail, Death," Justice growled.

"I did no such thing!" Pride protested.

"The chaos blade you used to cut the hopecloth," I reminded him. "It left traces on the cloth and they almost touched Hope." I quickly turned to Justice. "I swear on all the ends I've wrought, I stopped the chaos before it touched him."

Justice's eyes narrowed and his ears flattened, but aside from a low growl, he offered me no response.

War and the Sins were silent, all of their eyes wide and fixed on me.

"Life swore he tempered the blade when he gave it to me," Pride whispered. "It wasn't supposed to leave a taint."

I showed him the blade of my scythe, pointing to the marbled pattern of chaos absorbed from the ruined hopecloth.

Pride paled to a sickly off-white as he gazed at my scythe. "You held that to my neck," he said.

"I would have done more than held it if you had destroyed Hope," I said, "even by mistake."

"Which would have been nothing compared to what *I* would have done to you," Justice snarled.

Pride opened his mouth, then shut it almost immediately and dropped his eyes to the floor. "I would have accepted that," he said. He was shaking when he looked at me again. "But I did not destroy that Force, and I truly did not understand what Life wanted the essences for until… well. I know I helped breach the Contract, because I felt it when the first soul jump happened. And it made me so sick of myself that I summoned Shame."

Justice and I regarded Pride in silence.

The other Sins pressed in around him, and Lust placed themselves between me and Pride, adding to the barrier War had already established.

"He does not deserve to perish for this," Lust said. "Give him a chance to fix things."

"I can't," I said simply. "This has gone too far for Pride or any other Sin to set right." I held up a hand when War took a step forward. "Nor could another Rider undo what has been done."

All the Sins save for Lust looked fearful then, and Lust looked furious. Tears welled in their eyes, but they squared their shoulders and stared me down. "He does not deserve to perish," they said again.

"I agree," I said.

"As do I," Justice said, although the words were clipped.

I paused long enough for relief to wash over the Sins and melt some of the tension out of the room. Lust turned to say something to Pride, but he closed the distance between them and wrapped his arms around Lust, pressing his mouth over theirs in a deep, tearful kiss. Lust was caught by surprise, but quickly wove their fingers through Pride's hair and pulled him even closer. This prompted light laughing from the others, and I even saw Envy murmur to Wrath, "About destroying time."

When Lust and Pride finally broke apart and the Sins had quieted a little, I ruined the moment.

"There still needs to be a punishment," I said, and threw a meaningful glance at Justice, whose lips were set in an impassive line.

The room went still again.

But to his credit, Pride gave Lust another hug and a kiss on the forehead, then gently freed himself and stepped towards me. "I will accept whatever diminishment of my power this merits," he said, holding himself tall and looking at Justice and me without flinching.

Short of ending a Force's existence, curtailing their power was capital punishment for misdeeds. I'd done it before, after the Virtues had stolen the order stones, and I would do it again before the day was through. But with the current state of the mortal world and the careful balance constructed in and around the contract already under threat, I did not see a diminishment of any Sin's power as a benign action. This left me one choice, loathed as I was to take it.

"Your power cannot be lessened without destabilizing the mortal world even further," I said, "so instead, I'm afraid we'll have to amplify another's."

Justice stiffened. He fixed his full attention on me as he considered the idea, then he huffed a short, bitter laugh. "I suppose I could accept that," he said. "Even if it would punish more Forces than just Pride."

A ripple of confusion passed over the Sins, and then understanding snapped into place for Pride alone. "Actually, why don't you just end me." He came towards me and grabbed for my scythe, pointing to his neck. "One good cut, right here, take the head clean off."

I wrenched my scythe out of his grasp as Lust and War sprang forward to restrain him. Justice laughed more earnestly.

"What in destruction's name are you talking about, Death?" War asked as he lifted Pride off the floor and slung him over his shoulder.

Lust was momentarily taken aback by suddenly being presented with Pride's posterior, but they recovered smoothly and hurried around War to try to calm Pride as he struggled.

I met the confused stares of the other Sins as they watched all of this. "I truly hate to say this," I told them, "but you are going to need to make some space for your new roommate."

"HE'S NOT LIVING HERE!" Pride managed to bellow, clawing his way around War's torso until he was glaring at me from under his brother's arm.

"He's going to have to live somewhere if he's going to be a Sin," Justice pointed out mildly.

"Fine, but not *here*!" Pride snapped.

"I don't care if you shove him in a closet," I said, already working with Justice to tug on the power balances across Eternity, "but there's going to be an eighth Sin for a while, and you're all going to have to get used to it."

This statement was met by another silence, and then the room burst into a chorus of begging and pleading for Justice and me not to do it.

By then, of course, it was already too late, and when the door creaked open behind me, I did not have to turn around to know who was sticking their head inside. The intense feeling of loathing and embarrassment was more than enough.

"Hello, friends," Shame purred as the room went still. It was all too easy to imagine the sharp, unpleasant smile on his face as he flexed his newfound power and another wave of disgrace washed over us. "I think we're going to have a *sinfully* good time."

"All right, fine," Justice said in the wake of this, "he doesn't need to live *here*."

Wrath growled at me as she stalked to the door, shoved Shame back out despite his protests and attempts to undermine her with his power, and slammed the door. "We're getting a lock," she snarled.

"Peace has some very good ones," War informed her gravely.

The Sins took this piece of information quite seriously, speculating about how difficult it would be to steal a lock from him. At my stern look and Justice's rustling wings, they revised their plan to pestering Peace until he freely gave up a spare lock.

Justice nodded his approval to the Sins. "Much better."

Life must extract and distribute his essence in order to create the "souls" that shall bind to and inhabit the host vessels ("bodies") provided by Death, thus creating mortality.
-- excerpt from the Contract of Mortality

- 26 -

The Sins were considerably subdued as War, Justice and I took our leave. We were momentarily delayed when we opened the door to find Shame pressed against the everwood, trying to listen in on us. The Sins brightened considerably when War chased Shame out of their territory, bellowing promises of annihilation and wildly swinging his sword overhead as he ran after Shame. Justice made no move to interfere, and neither did I. The newest Sin vanished over the horizon before War could catch him, but we all knew he'd be back. He always came back. I left the original seven Sins with my sincerest promise that this was a temporary punishment, and I would reverse the amplification of Shame as soon as Justice and I both felt an appropriate amount of time had passed.

"That will probably be sooner rather than later," I confessed once War, Justice and I were alone.

"Much as I think Pride needs to reflect on his actions, I'm inclined to agree," Justice said. "I do not know how long I'll be able to stand that cretin running around with that kind of power."

War made a disinterested noise, which surprised me. I had expected him to be very invested in the removal of Shame's power. "Something on your mind?" I asked.

War nodded absently. "Just thinking about how many wars could possibly be started by an excess of shame."

"Not many, I'd imagine," Justice said.

"You may be surprised," War said. He thumbed the pommel of his sword before begrudgingly adding, "Or you may be exactly right. That is a very real possibility."

War's horse bayed a greeting as we approached. The red Rider took his mount's reins and gave the beast an affectionate pat on the neck. The horse snapped at his hand and stomped the ground.

"Where to next?" War asked as he swung up into the saddle and offered me his hand.

"Back to the mortal world," I said.

War stared at me for such a long, wistful moment that Justice politely excused himself and walked a few steps away. Not so far that I could forget that he was keeping track of me, but enough to give War and I some semblance of privacy.

War fiddled with his reins and watched me sadly. "You're finished here, then?"

"I have to put an end to this," I told him, "but I likely won't be gone long."

War tilted his head. "How do you figure?"

I ground the butt of my scythe into the ground as I said, "It is clear that there is a problem on the mortal world, even if it's not the one I originally thought."

War gripped the reins and gazed down the path, out at the dark lands that formed our home and the frozen stars that lit our existence. "I will be ready to ride if you need me, and I'm sure the others will answer your call, too." He turned his head to me again. "But remember, we are a last resort." He hesitated before adding, "You may still be able to fix things."

I looked at the veins of chaos spidering across my scythe blade. "Even if I can fix the mortal world," I said, "there is something there that will always be broken."

The giant red horse stamped its hooves again, and War whispered a few soothing words to quiet the beast. I ached for my own mount as I watched him, for the comforting, familiar presence of Pestilence and the mysterious but constant void that was Famine. I should have been there, all those eons ago, after the order stones were stolen and their pain was fresh. I should have always been there, and not been tempted away by Life and the promise of a new realm of our own making.

"You know," War said, still watching me, "after Sloth appeared at our lair and told us that you were on the verge of destroying the universe, Pestilence and I did come to an agreement on something."

"Well, if that's not a sign of doom, I don't know what is."

War snorted, then said, very seriously, "We both wish that the mortal world had worked out better for you."

I was surprised by this, and in spite of everything I knew about him, I wondered if War was lying. "Why?" I asked.

"Because we are never so happy as when you are happy," he said.

I did not know how to respond, and War was kind enough not to push me. Instead, he bent down and gave my shoulder a light squeeze. Before I could stop him, he poured even more of his power into me. It rushed through me, a river of strength that warmed my bones and straightened my spine. I felt my exhaustion wash away. War did not have enough in him to restore the power I'd sacrificed over the millennia to the creation of the reapers, but I closed my hand over War's and pushed him away long before he could begin to try to give that much of himself to me.

War swayed in his saddle as he gazed down at me, his hand still gripped in mine. His eyes burned a little duller due to his sacrifice, but the fire was still in his gaze, and I knew he was smiling at me beneath his helmet. "End this, Death," he said. "For all of us."

"I will," I said, and helped him straighten in his saddle.

He gave my hand one final squeeze.

"When you're ready," War said, "we'll be waiting for you."

Then he turned his horse towards the lair of the Apocalypse Riders, and with a brisk command and snap of the reins, the beast took off. The thunder of its hoofbeats faded as it galloped away, until the horse and its Rider were nothing but a streak of red swallowed by the dark.

I stood looking after them long after they were gone, trying to remember how it felt to truly be home.

- Part Five -

Acceptance

Should a mortal discover the existence of one or more Forces either through accident or intent, countermeasures must be taken to produce and distribute an acceptable alternative explanation for the discovered Force(s)'s presence.
-- excerpt from the Contract of Mortality, Rule 3

- 27 -

eturning to the mortal world took a lot out of me, even with War's donations and Justice combining his power with my own. The effort of bringing along the eclectic trinkets I had amassed in Eternity chewed up much of my recovered strength. It did not help matters that the chaos surrounding the mortal world sensed the essences I brought and tried to tear them away from me. I almost lost the spark to a chaos swell that closed over my hand, and another bit managed to fray the edges of the hopecloth before I noticed it. Justice helped me where he could, clawing at the chaos and giving me enough space to strike back with my scythe. Together, he and I managed to break through the barrier between realms and tumble on to the mortal world.

We were fortunate enough to hit the landing outside the front door of the apartment I shared with Life and Destiny, which was far, far better than I had hoped for. I was intensely relieved that Justice and I had not emerged on the wrong floor or in the wrong building, let along the wrong city. Relief was not enough to return my physical strength, however. I keeled over in the weak, early morning light, my skull pounding and my bones shaking all the way down to my toes. I clung to my scythe for support. Justice was not much better off. He slumped against the wall, panting and dry heaving and muttering something about destroying someone. I don't think he cared who, at that point.

At least dropping ourselves at the apartment had granted us the mercy of landing in a chaos-free zone. Destiny was working wonders around our domicile on the mortal world, and that gave Justice and I some time to recover.

Or at least, it should have.

As the shaking stopped and I tested my ability to stand on my own again, it slowly dawned on me that the pounding in my skull was not going away, and, therefore, was not a headache from fighting through the chaos. Also, I could sense two mortal heartbeats behind me.

Before I thought better of it, I turned around and saw a man and a child standing on the stairs that led up to the next floor. The man held a paper bag full of baked goods in one hand and his daughter's small fingers in the other. The girl had a fuzzy rabbit toy clutched close to her chest. Both were staring with open mouths and wide eyes, the man's in bewildered horror and the child's in candid wonder.

I felt a breach of Contract wrap around my skull, and begin to apply a light but pointed amount of pressure, warning me to fix this before it got worse. It was almost a pleasant sensation compared to what I'd felt in the wake of the second soul jump, but with every moment that slipped by, the pressure increased.

Justice must have felt it too, for his grumbling increased and he managed to groan, "What fresh destruction is this?" before turning around and freezing in place. "Oh," he said next, very unhelpfully.

The mortals blinked.

I blurted out the first thing that came to mind. "All-night dress rehearsal," I rasped out, gesturing wildly at my robes and the outlandish accessories I had picked up. "For a musical." I watched the mortals slide their eyes from me to Justice and his very large wings. "The makeup and costumes are hard to take off," I bumbled on, "so we wore them home."

The man and his daughter blinked again.

"You, uh," the man began, trying to not-so-subtly push his daughter behind him. The girl did not budge. "You two live here?"

"Yes," I said, and turned to the apartment door. With a sudden jolt of dread, I came up short. I did not have my key with me. And of course it was locked. I applied more pressure to the knob, and then I nearly sobbed with relief when the lock broke with a click and the door swung open. I had never been so happy to know that we had flimsy security.

"How'd you get here?" a high voice behind me asked.

I looked over my shoulder to see the child frowning at me, refusing to move in spite of her father's best efforts to tug her up the stairwell. "I've always lived here," I said, hoping that would satisfy her.

"We," Justice said quickly, shooting a smile in the general direction of the girl and not quite landing the gesture. "*We've* always lived here."

"Right," I said, tapping Justice's shin with my scythe until he shifted his smile a few degrees to the left, "we."

The band of pressure around my skull tightened as the little girl shook her head. "No, *here*," she insisted. "You weren't here, and then you were. I saw it."

"Oh," I said stupidly, "no, we… we ran."

The child cocked her head suspiciously. "You ran?"

"Yes," I said. "Up the stairs. Very fast." I tapped my robes lightly. "Cardio is very good for the heart." I only realized I had touched far too low a spot on my heartless chest when the father tensed even more. He looked like he was seriously considering how effective a weapon the fresh loaf of French bread in his grocery bag would be. I grabbed Justice by the elbow and edged towards the open door and the safety of the apartment. "Our costumes are very quiet," I said, hoping to distract him from the fact that I had forgotten where human hearts were located.

"Uh-huh," the man said slowly, clearly willing to accept this lie if it meant we never had to see each other again.

I pushed Justice inside and slipped over the threshold, fumbling for the doorknob. "I wear special slippers and, well, um," I stammered before finally closing my fingers around the knob, "goodbye."

As I whipped the door shut, I saw the father seize his daughter by the back of her pink overalls, hoist her into the air, and charge up the stairs.

The pressure did not let up on my skull.

"A *dress rehearsal*?" Justice hissed at me as we listened to the man's footsteps hit the landing above us and keep going.

"I did not hear you come up with anything," I growled.

"*I* would have simply erased their memories before they became too aware of us."

I looked at Justice. "And you did not do that because…?"

"Because you started *talking* to them and made it impossible for them to believe we were a trick of the light, or shadows meeting their over-active imaginations, or a weird pair of dogs, or *something other than what we are.* Mortals tend to pay far more attention to the things they shouldn't be looking at when those things are having conversations with them!"

Groaning, I stalked down the hall, leaving Justice to stomp after me. For a winged Force, he was far from light on his feet.

I reached out with my awareness, and sensed Destiny hard at work in her room. Pestilence was nowhere to be found. A little relieved but still haunted by all the things left to do, I let myself in to Destiny's room.

She had abandoned her human glamour and was floating in a dense cloud around her computers, operating them through some connection I did not understand. I felt part of her awareness swivel to me as I stepped up to her.

"Can you make a flyer for a fake musical that involves Justice and a bizarrely dressed version of me?" I asked as I began to remove the hopecloth from my shoulders. Justice gave a reluctantly amused huff somewhere behind me.

I felt Destiny's confusion and irritation spike through the air.

"Would you like that flyer before or after the chaos wave devours us and tears a breach between the mortal world and Eternity?" she snapped.

"We landed outside and two mortals saw us," I explained, sliding the spark ring off my finger and wrapping it and the lump of luck with the hopecloth.

"And Death *talked* to them," Justice grumbled.

Destiny snatched the bundle out of my hands, drawing it inside the shifting cloud of colors that made up her being. "I'll pencil it in for this afternoon, if we make it to then."

I muttered a thanks and asked if Life had been back yet.

"No," Destiny said, "but Pestilence left safely, and your reaper's still here, if that helps at all."

I peered over the back of the chair Destiny no longer occupied and found the reaper curled up on a pillow, fast asleep. The glow of the soul inside it burned bright.

"You know, it actually does," I said. "If nothing else, at least I know that one soul is safe."

"Can you save it?" Destiny asked.

Justice regarded me with mild interest in the wake of the question.

I did not bother answering. We all knew that souls were not of my making. All I could do for this one was keep it from losing itself on the mortal world. Under different circumstances, maybe Life could have set the soul back in its body, and maybe together, we could have fixed the mortality cords, but the violent severing of this soul had hurt Life to the point where he could not touch the soul again without feeling its pain.

I was glad. For the severed soul, that was far more protection than I could have ever offered on my own.

But Life still had retribution coming for him, and it was time he met it head-on.

"As soon as the chaos source is cut off," I said, "I am going to find Life."

Destiny went still. Her computers immediately shrieked warnings and alarms, and she quickly dove back into her efforts to contain the chaos that Pestilence had not been able to bind. Justice moved to help her, but he pulled up short when the ends of a pair of jumper cables launched out of the cloud that was Destiny and landed in his hands.

"Hook yourself up and give me a boost."

Justice's ears twitched. "You cannot be serious."

"You said you would help contain the chaos," Destiny snapped. "So clamp those cables wherever you're okay with Hope not touching anytime soon, and flex your power so I can amplify my reach."

Justice stood frozen for a long moment before bending down to secure the cables around his ankles. "I don't think I like you all that much," he informed Destiny as he straightened.

"I'd like you more if you stopped talking and started flexing."

Justice flattened his ears and growled, but did as he was told. I sensed the rise in the room as he fed power into the cables, and a golden glow suffused the air. Destiny's computer screens flared brighter, and her colors churned with fresh intensity.

"Good," she said after a moment, "now grab that

keyboard over on the bed and type exactly what I tell you, starting with this…"

I faded to the edges of the room as Justice took over one of the simpler but still complicated processes that required the dexterity of ligaments to perform. Gradually, Destiny's orders faded to murmurs as Justice picked up the rhythm of the process. Together, they headed off the worst of the chaos, although even I could see that Destiny's blockades remained close to failing. We had to find that rogue mortal and the chaos blade, fast.

But until Destiny could trace the source, there was nothing more that I could do.

Many tormented minutes trickled by, and then Destiny suddenly asked me, very softly, "What are you going to do to him?"

The question struck me hard. I knew what needed to be done, but I had not thought at all about how I would do it. I had the sense that, when the time came, I would either know exactly what to do, or be deserted by all rational thought. I did not know what that meant, save for one thing:

Life and I were over.

Justice cut through my turmoil with a heavy command. "You are not going to do anything to him, Death." I looked up to see Justice standing, the keyboard in his hands and the jumper cables still clamped around his ankles, but his ears were turned to me and his wings were shivering. "Not without me," he added. "I'll come to you once the chaos is under control and Destiny can spare me, and we'll deal with Life together."

My grip began to grind around my scythe. "I like to think that I would appreciate the help," I said, "but if I find him before all that happens, I cannot promise that I will wait for you."

"Then do not seek him out," Justice said.

I tightened my grip on my scythe and said nothing.

"Death," Justice warned, but I waved my hand to quiet him.

"I won't seek him out," I said, and felt the weight of the promise settle over the room.

After several more agonizing minutes of complex calculations and computing that I could not even begin to pretend to understand, Destiny gave me the coordinates of the rogue mortal's location. "Now that I know what tainted the chaos, I can drive a hole through it and give you a way in," she told me as I prepared to take my leave, "but you're going to be on your own once you're inside. Justice and I won't be able to help you there. We can keep the chaos from interfering too much as you deal with the mortal, but that's as far as we can go."

"I'll be all right, now that I know what to expect," I said, then paused. "Although, if I could have that mixed luck back, that would be better than nothing."

"You sure you want to take that gamble?" Destiny asked.

My mouth twisted into a dry smirk. "The twins would never forgive me if I didn't."

Reluctantly and with no attempt to disguise her obvious concern, Destiny returned the lump of luck to me. I retied the cord and placed it around my neck again, where it swung prettily and glinted menacingly in the light.

"One more thing, Destiny."

She focused her attention on me.

"As soon as the chaos is cut off, I want you to leave," I said. "Don't stay here. Don't try to find Life or me. And no matter what, don't try to stop me."

I broke into my incorporeal form and shot out of the building before Destiny or Justice could respond.

*Death may not create any more of those horrifying reapers as
they violate Rule 2. [Note from Justice: Since the reapers
directly borrow from Death's power, Rule 2 is upheld. Also, this
addendum would violate Rule 6 if passed.]*
-- rejected addendum to the Contract of Mortality
authored by Life, vetoed by Justice

- 28 -

rue to her promise, Destiny carved a hole
through the chaos straight to the rogue mortal.
I followed the path she left for me, chasing it all
the way to a suburban home too large for most to
consider a mere house. I knew from the rogue mortal's
file that this was not his home; possibly, he had rented
it when he came to the city to perform the soul jump.
More likely, he had taken the keys from the second
body he had absconded with. I had to hope that there
was no one else home, or he might try to jump again.

I shot down into the large house, diving through a
soot-crusted chimney and seeping into a spotless living
room. I returned to my corporeal form just as Destiny's
hold on the chaos slipped and it closed like a vice
around me.

Now that I knew what to expect from the chaos and
whose power had gone into fueling it, I was able to keep
my senses and center myself. Just as I had done back
home when I'd gone to visit the twins, I focused my
mind on the rules and choices that anchored my

existence as the chaos gnawed at me. I welcomed it, drawing it closer. I picked out the threads of luck, inspiration, hope, and pride that colored the chaos. One by one, I snapped them, until the fragments were nothing more than glittering ash fading around me. The chaos tried to tear at me as I broke the threads, but the more that I destroyed, the duller its teeth became, until its grip loosened and I could sense things beyond its cold embrace once more.

I felt the pulsing life of every insect in the walls, of the mice in the basement and the bird nesting on the roof, all oblivious to the chaos that swirled around them. And up on the second floor, still holding the blade that had leaked a flood of chaos across the city and almost broken the barrier of the mortal world, was a poisoned soul inside a stolen body.

There were times when I would creep up on the mortals and take them without warning. It was rare that they did not see me coming, but every so often, I needed to end a life when it was not expected. These tended to be fast deaths, painless when I could make them so, in concession to my own sense of unfairness that surrounded their circumstances.

I went stealthily through the house, but I had no intention of making this a quick or painless death.

I gently tapped my scythe along the hardwood floors and rich carpeting as I moved from room to room, heading for the staircase. I went as quickly as I dared with the chaos still swirling around me. I peered into each room I passed for some clue as to what, exactly, had been so worth living for that this mortal had sought to cheat me twice.

I passed neat, clean decorations and voluptuous furniture, a kitchen easily twice the size of the bedroom I had back in the apartment, and a room with what appeared to be a shrine to a massive television. In that last room, facedown on the off-white carpet, I found the body of a man. I recognized him immediately as the young man from the photos at the reaping site. I felt a twang of guilt as I studied his prone form.

The corpse was far more decayed than it should have been for the amount of time it had been lifeless, but I supposed hosting a chaos-tainted soul would have that effect. Black veins of the chaos taint spiderwebbed across his ashen skin, pooling in his eyes to turn them an unyielding black from corner to corner. He had been young and healthy before the soul jump; now, the chaos had devoured nearly all the fat off of his bones, and started in on the muscle. I could still see it pulsing as it gnawed at the corpse from the inside.

Strange, though. I had never seen chaos feed off on anything dead before, which also begged the question of where the extra soul was, now that a second jump had occurred.

And then I realized that the body on the floor was still breathing.

I have doled out gruesome ends in my time. I have taken souls from bodies that were crushed, bisected, disemboweled, burned, frozen, starved, diseased… any and everything horrible, I have touched.

I have never before nor ever since seen suffering so intense as that of a soul thrown into a body being devoured by chaos.

I cannot say that it sickened me to see a mortal in

such pain, but when I bent to cut the poor soul free, I found myself whispering, "I'm sorry."

The soul seemed to understand that I was taking it. I barely had to apply any pressure with my scythe before it jumped free of the body, and fell into my waiting hand. Even then, I did not pity the mortal who had lost this soul.

What did move me, what rekindled my anger all over again, was the bit of chaos that came with the soul. It wrapped itself around the severed soul, smothering the glow of life even as the soul fought to free itself. But in the end, the soul was too weak from its pain. It flickered to nothing as the chaos consumed it, and I was left holding a shifting, insatiable taint.

I threw it in the air, and swung my scythe around. The blade sliced through the chaos, which died with a piercing screech. The noise crashed through the silent house.

I maybe should have expected that a mortal wielding a chaos blade would have been able to hear the dying scream of chaos, but it was a surprise to me when footsteps raced across the upper level and came halfway down the stairs. I turned to see another mortal man staring at me, this one in considerably better condition than the one left to rot on the floor. He was pale, with fine features that I knew most humans would have considered generically handsome, but the chaos taint he carried was already wearing down this new body. I could see light moving slowly under the graying skin, riding in waves from the fingers and toes to the center of the chest before rippling back out in an anxious crisscross. It looked as though the edges of the body's torn mortality were trying to reconnect to their core. They kept coming up against the wrong soul with its poisonous tendrils, and in response, they retreated as far away as they could before ricocheting back. I followed one of the waves of light to his hands, and saw it clutching a black, serrated blade that dripped thick chaos on to the floor.

I took a step towards the mortal, and watched all of the blood drain from his stolen face.

Then he turned and ran.

He managed to get up the stairs and a few steps down the hallway before I felt that I had a firm enough grip on myself to dissolve and reform on the second floor, blocking his path. I failed to accurately judge what he would do with the chaos blade, however, and nearly had my bones ripped open by the serrated edge as the mortal sliced at me with all his strength. I fell back in surprise more than any sense of self-defense, and the blade snagged on my hood. It tore through the fabric and left ragged edges and spidery black smoke in its trail.

For a moment, all I could do was stare dumbfounded at my ruined hood, marveling at the audacity of a mere mortal to attack *me*. Then the chaos blade swung at me again, and I threw up my scythe to counter the blow.

"Enough!" I yelled as the blades rang together. There was a shuddering tension as the chaos blade struggled against my scythe, and then the resistance snapped as my scythe cut through. The chaos blade turned liquid as it was pulled into my scythe, and it spilled its own shape across the blade, overlapping the marbled pattern of the chaos I had pulled out of the ruined hopecloth.

I felt the weight of the new chaos as it settled into the blade, so heavy it nearly wrenched my scythe out of my grasp. I held tight. I would not let myself fall to chaos now, no matter how badly it wanted to be free. I knew that I needed to unleash the stored chaos soon, for it was nearly too strong for even me to contain, but I found myself very calm in the wake of the attack. I did, after all, have a prime target for all of that chaos right in front of me.

Hefting my scythe, I went after the mortal as he turned on his heel and tried to flee. I broke myself down and materialized in front of him again. The mortal skidded to a halt before I could strike, nearly colliding with my chest before he whipped around and tried to escape again. I lost my patience for the game, and shoved the handle of my scythe between his legs. He tripped and landed with a solid crash face-down on the carpet.

He lay motionless for so long that I wondered if I had accidentally killed him prematurely. Then he rolled over and looked up at me with a sluggish trickle of dark blood spilling out of his nose. And to my surprise, he looked angry.

With his voice thickened by his abrupt union with the floor, he snapped at me, "Who the hell do you think you are?"

I felt the answer to that particular question was fairly obvious, so I did not dignify it with a response.

The rogue mortal pushed himself to his knees. I watched with mild curiosity as he struggled to get the stolen body to cooperate. Now that he was not running for his very life, the limbs moved in a jerking, disjointed motion. I was surprised that he had been able to run at all, let alone take a swing at me.

I tilted my head as he finally sat up, and the ruined edge of my hood flicked across my gaze. It struck me that I was very fortunate he did not have better control over his motor functions. I closed one hand around the lump of luck hanging around my neck and silently vowed to indulge whatever questions the twins had for me the next time I saw them.

The mortal eventually came to rest on his hands and knees. He kept his gaze on the carpet as he fought to catch the breath that avoided him. "You're no one to me," he grumbled. "I got the better of you."

That was clearly a false statement, so once again, I chose to ignore what he said. I did have one question for the mortal, however, and I wanted the answer before I personally claimed his soul. "Why?"

He looked up at me, and his gaze was bitter.

I knew that Life had given him all that he needed to make the soul jumps, but I felt the itch to understand why this mortal had been so desperate to follow through with an idea that was not his own.

"Why would you so desperately try to evade me?" I asked. I crouched down next to the rogue mortal, bringing my fleshless face level with his. I took a small bit of pleasure in watching him shrink away from me. "Why did you so badly want to live?"

He did not answer me for a long time. When he did, it was with a slow, slimy smile that strongly reminded me of Shame when he was getting ready to feed. "I just wasn't ready to die."

"That's it?" I asked.

He sat back and looked at me with open disdain. "Yes, and why should the old Grim Reaper get to say otherwise?"

I held his gaze for a few silent beats of his stolen heart. "I am no reaper," I said. I stood up in a fluid motion and a soft whisper of my robes. "A reaper would have given you a much kinder end than I will."

The mortal scoffed at me. "You can't kill me. I got the better of you." With a grunt and a massive amount of effort, he pushed himself to his feet. "I beat Death, and you know what?" He smirked. "I think that qualifies me as a god. You watch." He jerked his arm around, turning the palm of the hand up. "I'll get another one of those knives, and I'll show the world how to be immortal, and then I'll pick the ones who deserve it and make them my disciples."

It amazed me how thick Pride's influence was on the mortal. I wondered if the Sin knew.

"Actually," the mortal said, eyeing my scythe, "how about I take that blade from you and we see about sending you into an early retirement? That pretty thing's probably a whole lot better than that little toy I was using."

He reached out, nearly brushing the handle of my scythe with his fingertips, but I closed my grip around his hand. His eyes widened in shock as the flesh died beneath my touch.

"A heart attack," I said as his fingers went stiff and cold in my hand. "A few moments of pain, and then it would have been over. Quick, clean, and so, so easy."

The mortal tugged his hand back, and I released him. He gasped in pain and looked at me with burning hatred.

Hatred, and the starting bud of fear.

"Now," I said, thrusting my face close to his again. The fear took root and blossomed. I grabbed ahold of his shirt and raised my scythe. "Since you're so eager to conquer death, I'll give you a gift: the deaths of every mortal dying in this moment."

I slammed my scythe down, and scattered us into fragments on the wind. With the destruction of the serrated blade, the chaos swirling in the air had already begun to dissipate, so I only lost a few fractions of the rogue mortal to its hungry reach. I felt no guilt at the loss. The rest of the mortal I carried with me as I followed the soft rustles of my reapers' wings. They flocked to me when I called, and led me to all the ends I demanded to see. I took the rogue mortal through the dying breath of sicknesses; deep inside the violent pain of terrible accidents and tragedies; under the burning agony of drowning, burning, freezing, starving; to the torture and executions that had no right to be, and yet the Contract demanded that I allow. And I made him feel all of them.

Every.

Last.

One.

When we returned, both a moment and an eternity later, myself whole and unscathed, him broken and weeping, I released my grip and let him fall. He crumpled in a heap on the floor.

"It seems you were not fit to overcome me after all,"

I told him as I idly examined the blade of my scythe. The chaos patterns shone dark against the natural bone white of the blade. "You should have let the reaper take you." I gently swung the blade down, letting it come to rest against the mortal's back. My touch was so light, the blade barely made a ripple in his clothing. The mortal felt it anyway, and he looked up at me with naked terror. "It's so much worse when I do it myself."

He opened his mouth to beg, and I pulled the scythe through him.

The blade passed through the mortal's hijacked flesh as though it were water, snagging momentarily on the poisoned mortality threads tying the soul to the body. I released the chaos inside the blade then, letting it burn the lingering threads to nothing. The body cried out as the soul came untethered, and I could feel the cries continue as the soul ripped free. It clung to my blade in a sticky, decaying mess, clogged with chaos tinted with pride so thick it had become pure arrogance.

I grimaced as I wiped my blade clean, gathering the rogue soul in my hand and shaking off the remains of the dying chaos. The soul struggled weakly, but had no chance of breaking free from me. Not anymore.

If I expected in that moment to be able to pause, to wonder what to do next, I would have been naïve. I was never allowed to rest on the mortal world.

At least I had not needed to break my promise to Justice.

No sooner had I collected the soul than there was suddenly another presence near me, warm and bright and achingly familiar. My grip on the rogue soul tightened, and I held it close as I turned to face Life.

We stared at each other for a long time as I waited for him to say something, anything, that would make me believe that he regretted even a fragment of what he had done to the mortal world, to our partnership, to *me*.

He said nothing. He just dropped his eyes to the soul in my hand, and he said nothing.

"I wonder what would happen," I hissed, "if you tried to reclaim *this* soul."

Life flinched, his gaze locked on what was in my hand.

I held it out to him. "Come claim your work, Life," I spat. "Truly, this is your greatest achievement yet: a soul that tried to defy and destroy me."

He shut his eyes and looked away and *he said nothing*.

"Fine." I pulled the soul back, my anger seething like molten venom at my core. "Then as always, I must clean up your mess."

Life must have realized what I was about to do then, for he lunged at me. It was surprising that he was able to guess, given that I didn't even know what I was intending until I had shoved the soul into my mouth. I swung my scythe to block him, and the blade caught on his arm, where it sparked and refused to cut.

Life held my gaze as I swallowed, his mouth working furiously, but I was deaf to anything he might have said in that moment.

I could only hear the rogue soul's scream as it went down.

No Force may push a mortal away from their designated fate, as crafted by Destiny. [Note from Justice: Even though Destiny has been granted co-creator status, Rule 6 clearly states that the influence of Life and Death ONLY cannot be overridden. (What is it with you all and Rule 6? It's there for a reason. Leave it alone!)]
-- rejected addendum to the Contract of Mortality authored by Destiny, countersigned by Death, vetoed by Justice

- 29 -

oldness radiated out from the rogue soul, running through me in waves as I absorbed it. Trace amounts of raw chaos tried to entrench themselves in my core, but I drew power from the untainted remains of the soul along with my own fury. I found the strength to kill the chaos inside of me. Once that was gone, all that was left was a thrilling rush of energy as the soul filled in parts of me that I had been carving away over the millennia to create the reapers and build the mortal world with Life. It was over too fast, the soul too feeble to fully restore me, but it took the edge off of a gnawing hunger I had learned to ignore. I felt more complete than I had in a long time.

More… *myself.*

In that wild moment—bracing my scythe blade against Life's arms as he gaped at me and I glared at him with my renewed strength—I felt a vicious desire to reap every last mortal's soul and swallow them all, the Contract be damned. There were so many out there, waiting, full of power and potential and strength…

I thrust the craving as far down and out of my reach as I could, just as I had always done. Life was addictive, and I knew that this was not the last time I would feel the itch to satiate the bottomless appetite that I had disciplined myself to ignore. I also knew that I could control myself far better than this.

When the moment of danger had passed and I trusted myself not to fly off on a ravenous rampage, I flexed my grip and twisted my scythe, throwing Life off balance and away from me. I had no desire to be anywhere near him in that moment, but I knew that I could not let him go unpunished. Justice would not have approved, but any thoughts of his opinions were far, far away from my mind as I swung my scythe at him again, whipping the blade in a glinting arc that would have bisected Life neatly across his hips. Life channeled his own power into a defensive block, catching the blade in his hands before it could rip into him. More sparks flew up from the contact points.

I wrenched my scythe free with a snarl. "Why did you do this?"

I readied myself for another swing as Life shifted into a fighting stance, bouncing lightly on his feet as he prepared to leap out of my reach.

"It was for you," Life said. He kept his eyes on my blade as he spoke. "Everything I did was for you."

"Lies!" I hissed and swung again.

He danced backwards, just edging out of the range of the blade.

"How could this have possibly been for me?" I growled as I followed Life down the hallway. "You violated the Contract." I swung again. "You cheated my reaper." And again. "You cheated *ME*." I hit him this time, and my scythe bit deep before he could focus his power on hardening his skin.

Life cried out in pain as he rushed power to the wound, stopping my scythe before it could cut to his core. The blade was ejected out of him with such force that we both stumbled. I recovered quickly. He hit the wall and flattened himself against it as the blade of my scythe came to rest under his jaw.

"You were going to leave me," he said, his voice high and tight, but he was looking at me, not at my scythe.

He wasn't lying now.

"I was your partner," I bit out. "I wasn't going to leave you."

If he noticed my use of the past tense, he did not acknowledge it. Instead, he tried to shift even further away, but the wall of the mortal dwelling held firm. "Yes, you were," he said quietly. "You finished the reapers. You didn't need me anymore."

I had just spent an entire day searching for answers to questions I never thought I had needed to ask. At the end of it, all I had really learned was that I was so tired of my partners not trusting me. And I was furious for it. "All I wanted," I said, "was to rest. Just a little time away after being chained to the mortal world for so long, after fixing all of your mistakes and returning all those souls to you so that you never had to compromise your own power."

Life's vibrant green eyes were wide with accusations.

"You were showing me that you were done with me. You made the reapers knowing that I could never make something without you, and you let them loose on the best thing I have ever created, and no matter what I did, I couldn't make anything without you." A spark flared against his neck when he turned his head to fully face me. "You were *done*, and you wouldn't have come back."

"Yes," I said, pulling my scythe away from his neck, "I would have!" I swung one last time, and felt a jarring force as the blade buried itself...

... in the wood of the wall.

Life had dissipated in time to avoid the strike, and he flashed against my ankles for a moment, his touch on my bones warm and unwelcome. I stepped out of his embrace with a disgusted grunt and tugged on my scythe. After two hard pulls, I ripped it out of the wall and whirled to see Life—still in his incorporeal form—rushing down the hallway and out a window. I flung myself after him, following his trail.

I chased Life across the winds and into the sky, not caring how many mortals might have seen thin flashes of green light pursued by a thick, roiling stream of black smoke. I chased him through clouds and around the moon, past a sunset and under the crust of the planet. He headed for the stars and I cut across his path, containing him to Earth. He tried to hide in the core, and I flushed him out. He had sacrificed far less of his power to create and maintain the mortal world than I had, but I had far more fueling me on that wild chase. He had only fear.

When I caught him, he rounded on me with all the

radiance and intensity of a newborn star, trusting his own strength and my exhaustion to save him. And yet, in spite of my sacrifices, I knew that Life was not stronger than me. I rose to meet him, throwing darkness and shadows into his light, matching blistering heat with aching cold. We whipped ourselves at each other, striking where we could and twisting and wrapping where we could not, always trying to gain the upper hand. Where our essences met, countless beings were created and destroyed before their hearts could beat. Not all of them left the world as painlessly as they came into it. We fought for an eternity. We fought for only a moment.

We fought until the color of infinity came between us, and cut us apart.

I fell back and gathered myself to charge again, but an echo of pain reverberated through me, and in my mind, all I could hear was, *Stop!*

I hesitated, not daring to take my attention off of Life, but he had fallen as still as I had. After a tense moment, he coalesced again, back into his corporeal form.

I did the same.

I found myself standing in a small clearing in an unknown forest, Life less than an arm's length away from me. There was soft grass under my feet, damp with dew or rain. The sky overhead was starting to lighten with the first touches of dawn, or maybe it was darkening in the wake of a sunset. I did not know. I did not care.

All I really cared about, all I really knew, was that Destiny was standing with one arm thrust between Life and me. She had recast her human glamour, and the face she wore was contorted into a frozen mask of agony. My gaze slowly moved down to her shoulder and then along the length of her arm. There was a tightness in my ribcage, but I forced myself to look at what I had done. What *we* had done.

Even though it had started out as just a glamour, Destiny's arm had become all too real. Blotches of necrosis bordered patches of healthy skin, but from those patches rose fresh growths that looked like partially-formed limbs and fingers. Her arm was heavy with them, and Destiny clutched at her shoulder, trying to hold herself up under the weight.

Shaking myself out of my horror and guilt, I reached for Destiny's arm and gently began touching the growths, killing and draining them until there was nothing but smooth skin left behind. Smooth skin, and patches of black death. Destiny whimpered while I worked, but she did not ask me to stop.

When I finished, I stepped back and looked at Life, waiting.

He did not move.

"Help her," I snarled.

That snapped Life out of his stupor, and he quickly set to work reviving and healing the pieces of skin that my power had killed. Destiny grit her teeth against the pain as Life tended to her arm, but her suffering eased with each passing moment, until finally, her arm was unmarred and she looked weak with relief.

None of us said a word as Destiny hugged herself, but I was beginning to sense something very wrong with her. It was as though I was somehow becoming more aware of her, or that she was becoming more real to me. That made no sense, but I knew that it could not be good.

Life shattered the grim silence by asking, "Why are you here?"

I looked at him sharply.

Destiny did not. She kept her eyes closed when she said, "I stabilized the last of the chaos ripples. Managed to contain them at safe levels within the free will clause. Thought you ought to know."

"But why are you *here*?" Life asked.

In that moment, I questioned how I had ever thought that there could be a viable partnership (let alone relationship) with him.

"Justice and I cleaned up the last of the chaos, and then he went out to find you. I was getting ready to leave when I saw you fly over the apartment," Destiny said, still not looking at either of us. "I didn't see Justice, so I followed you. Caught up when you started to fight." Her eyes opened and focused on me, and with a start, I realized that she was actually looking at me through those eyes. She had never done that before. Not intentionally. "I had to break you apart," she said, and her voice cracked.

I did not dare touch Destiny, but I motioned her aside and led her away from Life. He did not follow us.

"You just came between Life and Death," I murmured to her. "What's happening to you?"

She grimaced. "I don't know," she whispered, "but my arm. It feels… heavy."

My anger turned cold then, and self-reflective. I did not know what was happening to her, but whatever it was, I could not deny that it was partly my fault. "It's just a glamour, right? I could try to take it off?" Even to myself, the suggestion sounded like a horrible idea.

Destiny shook her head, swaying away from me a little. I was grateful that she did not take a step back from me, but I wisely kept my mouth shut and did not move.

"I don't think that would fix it," Destiny said. "It *feels* like a dead weight, but it's still me. And it's... pulling on me. Like it... wants to keep me." A shudder ran through her. "I'm scared," she whispered. "I wish I hadn't seen you and Life go by."

I wished the same. If she had not stopped us, Life and I may have destroyed each other, maybe taking part or all of the mortal world with us. Destiny had spared the world from our wrath, at the price of... I did not know. I was not certain of anything now. Except that Destiny had not deserved that. It had just been bad luck that had brought us to her attention.

Terrible luck, to balance out the good luck I had received earlier, when the mortal had failed to harm me with the chaos blade.

I felt for the cord around my neck. It had fallen inside my robes during my pursuit of Life and reassembly into my corporeal form, but the lump of mixed luck was still there. It shone gold and silver in the weak light and somehow felt heavier than it had before.

"I'm so sorry," I said to Destiny, knowing that the words could never make this better.

She was quiet for a long time before she said, "I need some time alone."

"Of course." I took a small step away to be polite and waited for her to shift into her incorporeal form.

She took a hard breath, then shut her eyes and stood still for a long moment. A very long moment. So long that she began to frown, and her face heated with the effort of her concentration.

That was when I realized exactly what price Destiny had paid for saving the world. At least a part of her—the part touched by Life and Death—was mortal now. That was why I was suddenly so aware of her. I knew her as something that could and would eventually die. I had never felt that from any other Force before, nor would I ever feel it again. I swore to myself it would not happen, that she would not die, even as I watched Destiny struggle before me, refusing to meet my gaze as tears spilled from her eyes as she tried and failed and tried again to take her incorporeal form.

Her true form.

Her non-mortal form.

I feared for the worst.

Then the color of Destiny's skin shifted, and her edges became fuzzy. She gasped with relief, but she never made it all the way to her true form. Instead, she retained a faintly human shape, and although she swirled with color again, there was a part of her that remained dull, muted where the rest of her was pearlescent. That was more than I had expected, and less than I had hoped for. I said nothing.

Destiny seemed disappointed with her incomplete shift, but she still managed to find the strength to rise up, and disappear into the sky. I stood gazing up at the burning clouds long after she was gone.

Of course, I was not alone, and so my attention was soon demanded elsewhere.

"Are you still going to leave?" Life asked from behind me. He had come up close again, now that Destiny was gone. Too close.

My grip on my scythe tightened, then slowly relaxed. I was so tired. I did not want to fight anymore. "Yes," I said, simply. This time, I knew I would not come back.

After everything, Life still did not want to let me go. "Please stay, Death." I heard him move into the space directly behind me, and I felt the air stir as he spread his arms wide, as though hoping I would turn and fall into them. "I know I made a terrible mistake, but you fixed it before it got out of hand. You always make it better. You make *me* better. Please, please don't leave."

I finally turned to face him, and the impassiveness of my expression hit Life harder than my scythe ever could, but he recovered and swayed even closer to me. Our faces were almost touching as I stared up at him.

"Look at everything we've made." He did not take his eyes off of me, but he gestured wildly with his hands, as though trying to encompass the entire universe with them. I followed the motion without smiling or frowning or betraying any emotion. "I know you don't need me, but we are good together," he said, his voice edged with desperation.

My gaze wandered past Life, alighting on a tree that, like Destiny, had been caught in our struggle. Parts of it were scarred with decay, accelerated into death before their time and marked by my own touch, but natural nonetheless. The other parts were so heavy with life, the branches creaked and groaned under the weight of giant leaves, thick moss, and vines twisting tight around every space they could reach. That included the dead patches, as though they could not stand to leave those bits of the tree in peace.

"No," I said, stepping around Life and heading for the poor tree, "we are not." I reached out and placed my hand against the bark, killing the overgrown patches and the strangling vines. The tree seemed to relax under my touch, until it groaned and fell, too rotted to sustain its own weight any longer.

*In the event of uncertainty around a contract breach that
cannot be rectified without sustained damage, Justice shall
serve as a binding arbiter and decide on the scope and severity
of the punishment. Justice may seek counsel from any other
Force on the matter, including those not involved in the breach,
but his verdict will be the ultimate authority.*
-- excerpt from the Contract of Mortality

- 30 -

I spent some time away after that. I did not go back
to Eternity as I wanted space to myself to think, and
I knew that if I left the mortal world, I would not
have the strength to come back. So I hid myself
somewhere among the stars where not even Life could
sense me. My solitude quickly turned into restlessness,
which became anxiety around what would happen
when I was forced to face the others again, Justice
included. That in turn eventually became a burning
desire to find such a perfect solution that Justice would
have no choice but to agree with it, and so I set myself
to work. I used that work to dull the pain that lingered
in the wake of what Life had done. I did not fully
understand all the things that I was feeling and wanted
after his betrayal, but having a solid trail of logic to
follow helped keep me calm, or at least distracted. So I
found something to occupy my time. When I was
finished, I reached out to Eternity, and let my presence
be known.

I knew that Justice was there. Even in my self-imposed isolation, I had sensed the moment when Justice had left the mortal world. Either he had something else that he needed to attend to, or he had grown tired of trying to find me when I did not want to be found. Whatever the reason, he was off the mortal world, but once I announced my presence, Justice came screaming across the realms, barely coalescing next to me before demanding to know what, exactly, I had been doing with my time while he had tried to figure out what to do about Life.

I read aloud to him the final addendum to the Contract, drafted in my time alone. Justice gave me his silence and his attention. Then he gave me his signature.

He was not happy that I had drafted the final addendum without him, but he had to admit that it was an appropriate punishment for Life, all things considered. He only picked at a few words, making the language more airtight, and then he let me be.

With Justice's approval and agreement that I could deliver the news alone, I carried the addendum with me back to the planet that had caused so much trouble, and flew as a black bird to the apartment I had sometimes thought of as home.

It was a little before dawn when I began my vigil at the windowsill in the kitchen, the very same one that one of my reapers had alighted on when it had brought me the wrong soul. I gripped the wood with my talons and watched to see who would come into the kitchen first. Before the soul jump disaster, I would have easily bet my powers on Destiny to be there before the sun was up, long before Life or I would have made our appearances. Now, with the first light of dawn warming the feathers on my back and an empty room before me, I realized how much everything had changed through the fallout of one selfish act. Although, thinking back on everything, it wasn't just one moment of selfishness, was it?

Destiny did eventually wander into the kitchen, killing any hope I'd harbored that she'd been able to leave the mortal world after all. She still wore the same human glamour I had last seen her in, along with a new, fluffy, mint green bathrobe and slippers, and she looked exhausted. Dark circles ringed her eyes, and she moved with a heavy, sluggish gait unfitting of a Force. She paused in the middle of the kitchen, and stared for a little while at the coffee maker on the counter before turning to the pantry and pulling out a box of cereal. I let her pour a bowl and replace the milk in the refrigerator before cawing softly. Destiny looked up at the sound. Her eyes widened when they found me. If I had not been watching her so closely, I might have missed the smile that started to form before she masked it with a frown. She pushed the window up and let me inside.

"What are you doing here?" she asked, but without malice.

I cawed again and twitched my head in a meaningful glance around the room.

"He's not here," Destiny said. She took a seat at the table and crossed her arms. "Just like you, he hasn't been back since the soul jump."

I hopped into the kitchen and shifted back to my

normal form in a quick roll of smoke and feathers. "He'll be back," I said. I withdrew a rolled piece of worn, fragile parchment from my sleeve. It was the same color as my bones and bore a black seal stamped with the print of my thumb. "He has nowhere else to go."

Destiny looked with interest at the addendum to the Contract, but made no move to take it. "Did you bind him here?"

"Yes." I set the parchment on the table and sat down across from Destiny. "As long as there is a mortal world, he cannot leave it. I've also restricted his power and made it impossible for another soul jump to ever occur."

Destiny frowned and reached for the document. She hesitated before touching the paper, as though reminding herself that it was just parchment, that it could not hurt her beyond a papercut. She finally pulled the amendment across the table, but made no move to break the seal. "How do you intend to balance all of that?"

I draped an arm over the back of my seat. "Simple. I leave and do not come back."

Destiny started and nearly knocked her cereal off the table. "What about all the souls and the ends that must come to them?"

"That brings me to the reapers." I glanced around the kitchen, wondering where the one I had left in the apartment had got to. I spied a new litter box in the corner, and shot Destiny a questioning look.

"The landlord thinks I have a cat now," she said. "The reaper hides under the bed if he comes to check something in the apartment, and I get to have a pet, so it all works out." She crossed her arms and frowned at me. "You're not taking it away, are you?"

"No, the reapers will still be here," I assured her. "I'm actually giving them the ability to distill and distribute the souls' power, just like I used to do. They'll also be able to help you more directly with your fates, but in return, *I* won't be able to influence the mortal world ever again." I hesitated for a moment before adding, "I will still be able to destroy it."

Destiny did not react the way I expected her to. She did not grow angry with me, she did not yell at me, cry, scream, laugh, do any of the things that I had imagined she would do. Instead, she simply nodded. "Wouldn't be much of a failsafe if you could not call a Ride," she said.

A small pause fell between us. Destiny stared into her cereal, and I stared at her, trying to memorize every detail of that moment.

"I do not know if I'll be able to bring myself to do it," I finally told her. "I know that if things somehow get out of hand again and they can't be contained, an Apocalypse Ride would solve all those problems." The light from the window caught on the blade of my scythe and bounced back, throwing a wicked arc of reflected brightness across the wall. "But you would not be able to leave this world, would you?"

A long moment of silence passed before Destiny shrugged and sat back again. "Eventually," she said, as though she were talking about the weather, "I'll make peace with what happened to me. I'll learn to accept my fate." She sighed and stretched her left arm. Her mortal arm. "If you can give me time, then maybe I can give you my forgiveness."

I nodded, not knowing what I could say in that moment, except: "I am truly, truly sorry."

"I know you are."

Another silence descended, and I felt the dire need to shatter it. "The seal will break when I leave," I told Destiny. "The addendum will go into effect as soon as—"

"I know how it works," Destiny said, but she was smiling. "You turned me part mortal, not part stupid, much as you think those are synonymous."

I curled my toes uncomfortably. "How is that going? Are your powers…?"

She grimaced. "It's hard. Some things still come easy, like knowing that I'm going to have a visitor not long after you and I say goodbye, and it's going to be difficult and wonderful."

"The goodbye or the visitor?"

"Don't interrupt," Destiny said. Then she looked off and tried to hide a small smile. "The visitor." She turned back to me, and I realized that her eyes were a swirl of color, not the usual soft brown she often used in her mortal glamours. "Other things sometimes feel like they're falling out of my reach," she continued. "This is the only glamour I've been able to cast. It's getting harder and harder to go without sleeping, and I suspect I'll need to start thinking about what I'm eating soon." She swirled her spoon around her bowl and poured more cereal. "Thankfully, not today." She took a large bite and contemplated her colorful breakfast. "Where did you go?" she suddenly asked. "Life and Justice both tried to find you, but you really shook them off your trail. How did you do that?"

I studied her sidelong. "Are you asking out of curiosity, or because you want to know if it's actually possible to get away from Life?"

"A little of both, I suppose."

I told Destiny about the patch of deep space where I had gone, so far from Earth that I had almost gotten myself lost out there. I saw no point in going into much detail, considering we both knew that there was no chance Destiny would ever be able to make it there herself. Not anymore.

"It must've been nice," she said wistfully. "You were lucky you found it."

I gave her a wry smile, and pulled the cord that held the lump of mixed luck out of my robes. "Lucky I found it, and then unlucky enough to almost get eaten by a black hole that drifted by."

Destiny snorted, sent a spray of milk and cereal across the table, tried to restrain herself, and then burst out laughing. "Serves you right if you didn't see it coming," she said once she had calmed down enough to breathe again.

"The black hole seemed to think so, too."

Destiny chuckled, then abruptly sobered. She tilted her head, as though listening to someone whispering in her ear. I knew that look well, and waited patiently for the premonition to finish.

"Life is going to come back here soon," she said when it was done. "He feels bad, but he won't apologize." She fixed an uncertain gaze on me. "Is there anything you want me to tell him after you're gone?"

I shook my head and stood up. "I've said it all in the

addendum. He'll understand that soon enough."

Destiny made a thoughtful noise before going quiet again.

I moved to the window and stood looking out at the view I would never see again. More details I wanted to memorize, but knew that I would eventually forget.

"Will you miss it here?" Destiny asked gently.

"Of course," I said, and I could not keep the regret out of my voice. "This place was supposed to be for all of us, something to help us grow and learn about ourselves and each other." Quietly, so Destiny could not hear me, I added, "It was supposed to be beautiful."

"But it was all of those things," Destiny said. "Just not the way you intended."

I did not know what to say to that.

Destiny spared us another awkward silence by bringing her bowl to the sink. She rinsed it, dried her hands, and then turned to face me. She gave me a smile coated in false cheer. "Well, I'd invite you to stay for coffee, but I don't think you want to risk running into the ex." She smirked more genuinely at me. "Plus, I threw that awful stuff out after you did this to me." She punched me lightly with her mortal hand.

"You monster," I muttered, rubbing the spot where she had hit me.

She held up a finger, then opened one of the kitchen drawers and withdrew a large package of coffee beans. She handed it to me. "Good luck brewing it."

I took the bag reverently. "It'll be the first thing I do."

Destiny shot a pointed look at the mixed luck hanging against my chest. "Better make it the second thing, after you give that back to the twins."

I flinched as all the terrible things that could happen to innocent coffee under the influence of bad luck flashed through my mind. "Excellent advice," I said, then carefully slipped the precious bag inside my robes. "Thank you."

And then, just like that, there was nothing more to say.

Awkwardly, I opened my arms a little, then snapped them closed, remembering that me embracing a mortal, even a part-mortal, was unlikely to end well.

Destiny rolled her eyes, then moved forward and gave me a quick kiss on the cheekbone. Her lips were dry and firm. "Don't let them forget me," she whispered.

"Never," I promised.

Destiny gave me a small, sad smile, then stepped back. I lifted my scythe, and brought it crashing down to shatter the world around me. The last thing I saw, fractured across the scattering pieces of the mortal world, was Destiny standing with her mortal hand raised in a final farewell.

Then she was gone, forever.

*In exchange for relinquishment of all statuses and privileges of
their co-creator status and bestowing all harvesting-related
duties and abilities upon the reapers, Death may permanently
leave the mortal world. Death may still destroy the mortal
world through an Apocalypse Ride, should the dire need arise,
or the Ride be summoned by Destiny, regardless of her status as
a Force, mortal, or anything in between. In exchange for Justice
waiving capital punishment, Life shall be locked to the mortal
world, unable to travel to Eternity or any other dimension,
until the complete and permanent destruction of the mortal
world. No Force, mortal, or any other shall be able to break this
binding. Life shall only be able to exert and/or grow his power
by creating souls for the mortal world. He may not use his
power in any other way, including establishing communication
with Forces other than Destiny and Justice. Life may not
directly or indirectly strike bargains or request favors from any
Force or other being while the Contract of Mortality is still in
effect. Should Life attempt to breach these rules, he will be
immediately removed from existence.*
-- excerpt from the Contract of Mortality, Final Addendum
authored by Death, countersigned by Justice

- 31 -

It turned out that brewing Destiny's gifted coffee
was far from the first thing I did after returning
home. Following her wise advice, I tracked down
the twins as soon as I was back. I handed them their
twice-cursed lump of mixed luck before it could get me
into any more trouble, then answered as many
questions as they could throw at me, just as I had

promised. It took some time to circle their attention to my experiences instead of focusing on whatever tangential wager they were entertaining, but once we began, I was surprised by how thorough and analytical they were. Chance and Fortune each took copious amounts of notes and had many in-depth discussions with each other regarding each of my experiences, the level of luckiness involved, and whether it had been pure luck or mixed luck acting upon me as I had finished my investigation and confronted Life.

Their enthusiasm dulled when they learned what had happened to Destiny. I told them about my theory that it had been a backlash of bad luck to counterbalance my earlier good luck in dodging the chaos blade. The twins exchanged a long look at this, then returned to their line of questions. None of us brought the theory up again. I thought about that silent glance for a long time after I left them, and wondered if they had not challenged me out of pity, or something else entirely. I did not press them for an answer.

After the twins, I went straight to the Riders' lair. Things were still tense between Famine and me, and while Pestilence was glad to see me back and I was thrilled to see her unharmed, her attitude was still frosty. I knew that I had a lot of work to do before we could return to our old footing, if that was even an option, but I took encouragement from the pale yellow burn of my relit torch, and the partially cleared pathway into my cave. I learned from War that Pestilence had done the majority of the work in moving the stones out of the way, although she had stopped once she realized that War and Famine were watching her. She'd said something cruel about me being able to fit now that I was so much smaller than the rest of them, but we all knew that she was hoping to cover her embarrassment and conflicted feelings. In private, I thanked her, and she did not snap at me. Our tension was not gone, but it had eased a bit. We could work with that.

I did eventually move back in with the Riders. All of us were very aware that I did not have anywhere else to go. I could have gone off to seek a new place somewhere else in Eternity, but I wasn't up for being by myself, and the Riders seemed to understand that. War kept up his teasing flirtations while Famine made a joke out of gnawing on my bones when I wasn't paying attention, which provided a great deal of amusement for everyone except me. I did chuckle about it in private some time later, however.

The best and worst part about living with the Riders again was being reunited with my beloved horse. Its firm but gentle gait, wispy mane and tale, supple pale hide, and milky eyes were exactly as I had remembered, and as I had begun to forget. I walked with my horse quite a bit after moving back in, taking it along the path and even into chaos fields whenever it grew restless. It wanted to start a Ride as much as War, Pestilence, and Famine did, but I could not bring myself to do it. Not yet. And especially not after I had promised Destiny that I would give her time.

For the first time, another Force would call forth the Apocalypse Riders. It somehow seemed fitting that the one who was part mortal would be the one to summon the end to the mortal world. I explained this to the others, and to my surprise, they agreed.

Once I was settled back in the Riders' lair, I enjoyed a good deal of quiet reflection and (much as I hated to admit it) peace. I had not heard from Life since the fight, which I knew was for the best. And which was why I had made it extremely difficult for him to contact me, thanks to the addendum I had left with Destiny. It was still technically possible, if he could find a willing and consenting messenger to carry his correspondence, but it needed to be a matter of importance. More so than "I miss you," or "I made one mistake, come back." Something more like, "Destiny says we need a heavy dose of hope and pride to counteract all the shame that's been washing over the mortal world or all of the humans are going to lie down and die."

I suspected Shame's amplified influence was also playing a part in Life's silence. The manmade Force had been doing irritatingly well as a Sin, sliding neatly into his role and causing enough trouble on the mortal world that Pride began seeking me out on a regular basis, begging me to just kill him and demote Shame back to his former status.

"Surely that would be a fair tradeoff?" he said to me on one such occasion.

I was lounging outside the lair, sharpening my scythe with a whetstone fashioned out of a loose order stone from the path. "No," I told him, "because who would counterbalance him if you were gone?"

Pride was on his knees, his eyes shining with unshed tears. "There has to be a way," he said.

I ran the whetstone along the blade one last time before testing the edge with my thumb. Satisfied with the small nick the blade left in the bone, I reminded Pride that I had already promised to diminish Shame once an appropriate amount of time had passed. Justice and I had already set a date, we were so sick of Shame's smug swagger around our realm, but suffering was part of Pride's punishment for his role in the soul jumps.

Pride, however, had not learned this lesson yet. "But when will that *be*, Death?" he needled. "How long do you expect us to wait?"

This stirred my ire, so I said, "I'll diminish Shame once I have forgiven Life."

Pride paled to an unpleasant hue. "Will that ever happen?" he asked.

I gave him a nasty smile and did not answer.

Outside of the Sins learning to adjust to their newest member, things returned to normal for the majority of the Forces. Many had not been impacted by the soul jumps, and so there were little to no disruptions for them to overcome. Others, like the twins and Hope, found themselves much more restrained and cautionary when it came to flexing their power and sharing their work.

The twins especially took the theft of their luck to heart, and began maintaining a strict catalogue of their excavations along with the raw, unharvested veins that ran through their mines. They rationalized this to anyone who asked by claiming that the new system would help them better understand (and, therefore, better bet on) how their luck would fall. I had the feeling that they were actually having a great deal of fun with the more methodical approach, but were not about to admit that to anyone.

Poor Hope became more reserved, however, and less willing to weave his cloths. This was a blow to us all, and while we struck a pact to never allow anyone, *anyone* to steal from him again, he was far from comforted. He spent more time with Justice and less at his loom, which at least helped him recover a little happiness.

As much as he loved his partner, it pained Justice to see Hope move away from weaving. He sought me out one day, and asked me what I intended to do about Hope's despair. I pointed out that, as we had already dealt with Pride and Life, there was nothing left that we could do. I, for one, had no intention of going beyond what Justice had already agreed to. Justice was not satisfied by this answer, and stormed off. I convinced my fellow Riders to keep a watch over him after that, fearing what form Justice's fury might eventually take. I think Hope talked him down from anything drastic, but there's always the risk that something may slip past my notice. It certainly wouldn't be the first time.

The hardest thing I did after returning to Eternity was go to Destiny's abandoned home. I could not bring myself to tear it down, and the Forces who knew what had happened to her and why she was never coming back all agreed that they did not want the last piece of her destroyed. So we turned that cave littered with pearlescent crystals and shining geodes into a monument to our fallen Force, and a warning of what could happen if we were not careful with ourselves and with each other.

Shortly after this, Inspiration disappeared.

This was not like her normal disappearances, when her sparks were still around and we could find traces of Inspiration if we looked hard enough, promising us that she would be back. No, this time, Inspiration took off and did not return. No one knew where she went, but I remembered Destiny's prophecy of a visitor after I left, and the way Inspiration had looked when she had talked about Destiny. I was fairly certain that I knew exactly where Inspiration was, but I did not want to interrupt. Especially since Inspiration had not returned nursing a romantic wound. I figured things were going as well as they could between the two of them, and they could use some time together, alone. It would not last forever, after all.

Eventually, I started thinking about creating a new world with the assistance of another Force, but in the wake of my break with Life, I could not imagine what that would look like. War, of course, eagerly tossed his helmet into the ring as a potential candidate, but I rejected this idea outright. Pestilence agreed with my decision.

I suppose that, after everything, I am simply not up to throwing myself into something new just yet. There will come the day when I will need to call upon my fellow Riders and destroy the mortal world, once it has fully run its course. But as I said before, that is Destiny's call now, for when I next ride, I'll be ending her as well.

I am Death, after all, and I come for everyone, in the end.

About the Author

K.N. Salustro is a science fiction and fantasy writer who loves outer space, dragons, and good stories. When not at her day job, she runs an Etsy shop as a plush artist and makes art for her Redbubble shop, both under DragonsByKris. She was serious about loving dragons.

For updates, new content, and other news, visit www.knsalustro.com.